ONCE A RANGER

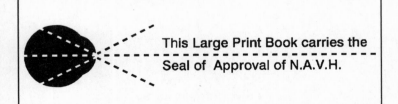

This Large Print Book carries the
Seal of Approval of N.A.V.H.

ONCE A RANGER

DUSTY RICHARDS

THORNDIKE PRESS

A part of Gale, Cengage Learning

GALE
CENGAGE Learning·

Farmington Hills, Mich • San Francisco • New York • Waterville, Maine
Meriden, Conn • Mason, Ohio • Chicago

GALE
CENGAGE Learning®

LIBRARY OF CONGRESS CATALOGING-IN-PUBLICATION DATA

Richards, Dusty.
    Once a ranger / by Dusty Richards.
        pages cm. — (Thorndike Press large print western)
    ISBN 978-1-4104-6597-9 (hardcover) — ISBN 1-4104-6597-7 (hardcover)
    1. Texas Rangers—Fiction. 2. Arizona—Fiction. 3. Western stories. 4. Large type books. I. Title.
PS3568.I31523O53 2014
813'.54—dc23   2014007237

Published in 2014 by arrangement with The Berkley Publishing Group, a member of Penguin Group (USA) LLC, a Penguin Random House Company

ONCE A RANGER

ONE

The pink-purple glow of predawn backlit the distant Chiricahua Mountains. Seated on his good saddle made by a famous San Antonio saddle maker, the new sheriff of Crook County, Arizona Territory, Phillip Guthrey, rubbed his shirtsleeves. The temperature had fallen to the depths of a desert night — to feeling downright cold. This would not last very long — the coming sun would soon raise the mercury to one hundred degrees or higher.

Beside him, deputy Noble McCoy, an older man with white whiskers bristling his firm chin, held a Winchester across his lap and sat on a stout bay gelding. He cleared his throat and hocked up some phlegm. He spat it aside.

"They're going to be surprised we got up this early," Noble said under his breath, sounding amused.

"Yeah, let's go arrest them. They may give

us a fight."

Noble nodded he'd heard the warning, then booted his horse forward. The loud sound of their horses' iron shoes crushing the gravel blended with the whit-woo crowing of the topknot quail scurrying nearby in the desert vegetation. A sharp smell of creosote from the greasewood brush was heavy on the soft breeze stirring the new day to life.

At her first sight of them coming, a woman screamed, and Guthrey charged his horse forward. "You all are under arrest. Throw down your guns or my posse surrounding you will shoot every one of you."

Two men, half-dressed, stumbled out of the palm-frond squaw shade and threw their hands in the air. The screamer was a Mexican teenage girl and, wide-eyed, she gave up too.

"Go around back," Guthrey said to Noble with a toss of his head. He kept his six-gun trained on them, watching carefully for any others as he stepped down.

"Who else is here?" Every nerve ending in his body tingled when his boot soles hit the gravelly surface, and he studied the three of them and the area around the ramada.

"Ain't no one else here but us," the heavier-set man said, holding his hands up as Guthrey circled the shade and went over to check them for weapons. They appeared to be weaponless.

"You can put them down." Guthrey holstered his six-gun.

"What the hell do you want from us?"

"Your name is Bergman?"

"Yes, Del Bergman. Why?"

"You sold a horse to Humbolt's Livery in Soda Springs that you stole from the Three Y Ranch at Sonoita."

"Not me."

His deputy went over and shoved the rifle in his scabbard. "There's four other horses in the corral out back."

Guthrey nodded. "What's your name?" he asked the younger man.

"Nelson Mercer."

Guthrey made a note of his name with a pencil in his tally book along with Bergman's name. "I need the information on the horses in the pen too."

"I'll get it," Noble took his book, and in a bobbled walk he left them.

Quickly Guthrey handcuffed the two men and told them to sit on the ground. He turned to the scared girl. "You the cook?"

"*Sí,* senor."

"Wash your hands and make us something to eat."

"I can heat frijoles and make some flour tortillas."

"That will do. What is your name?"

"Nannia."

"You live around here?"

"No, I live in a Sonora village, St. Joseph."

"Fix the food. We have a long day's ride to get back to Soda Springs."

"*Sí.*" She turned in her too-short dress and the garment showed too much of her shapely brown legs.

Guthrey had no interest in her, but he knew she was a teenage *puta* that Bergman had picked up on the border, probably near where he rustled the horses. Such a female had little future in such a small village but to become a wife and child bearer in poverty, so many of them passed up that opportunity and sought a dream.

Guthrey was satisfied they had arrested the real horse thieves. It was a very busy trade in the entire region of the Mexican border country. Most such animals went to Tombstone, where the market for any form of transportation was high. It was obvious no one in law enforcement there was doing much about horse stealing in their jurisdiction, but Guthrey promised the people of Crook County he'd do his best to make such horse thieves feel unwelcome in the legal confines of his district.

"Those three all belong to the same ranch," Noble said, indicating the other mounts.

Guthrey nodded and took back his book. The old man did a good job of putting the descriptions of the horses and their brands in his notes, facts Guthrey would need for the two new prosecutors sent down by the governor to clear up the mountain of cases, the ones that were brought on by his sweep of all the lawbreakers rounded up when he started his first day on the job less than a month earlier.

After eating the meal the girl prepared for them, Guthrey put the prisoners on horses and let the girl pick one of them to ride too. All the time he was eating the spicy burritos, he considered the squaw shelter on this abandoned camp. The structure probably needed to be destroyed so as not give shelter to any other trash like these two rustlers going through the country.

"Who owns this camp?" Guthrey asked Noble.

"I don't know. The spring dries up here by the middle of summer. Probably why folks abandoned this place."

"I think we should burn it. And have one less hideout setup."

"Good idea, Captain. No one will complain."

"I'll do that before we leave."

The housekeeping gear was stowed in two tow sacks and tied on the horse the girl rode bareback. Guthrey told her the gear and the horse were hers to keep.

She smiled and thanked him.

By eight A.M. on his pocket watch, they headed out for Soda Springs. En route, he sent the girl on her way. They arrived, alone, in midafternoon. The Crook County jail was inside a sprawling adobe building that was one story and served as the county offices. Cam Nichols, the big man who ran his jail, registered the prisoners on the jail log. A veteran jailer, he came looking for work when he heard Guthrey had taken over the office of sheriff. His past experience as a jailer made things run smoothly. With a cook and four other deputies on duty around the clock, the jail had a military air about it and smelled clean.

The territory prison wagons had kept the road to Yuma busy. And the last trials held there were sweltering hot in the improvised courtroom similar to the squaw shade of palm fronds he'd burned behind them earlier that morning. But the convicted felons would be a lot hotter in Yuma Prison.

He spoke to Tommy Glendon, the young man who operated the town's telegraph key in the county offices.

"You got another two rustlers?" the young man under the celluloid visor asked.

"Yes. We found two more. What's happening?" Guthrey asked.

"There is a New York news reporter here wants to talk to you. I knew you'd love that. Right now he's over at the trial being held against Curt Slegal. Three women are going to testify to the jury about him raping them."

Guthrey nodded. "That is serious in the case against him. I had a hard time getting those women to even talk about this matter, but it's very important. I'll go by and listen. What's the reporter's name?"

"Albert Gooding."

"Gooding. I'll try to avoid him."

Tommy nodded and Guthrey headed over to hear a portion of the case.

Two of his new deputies were there to keep order. Teddy Baker and Ramon Zamora stood at the back. Both were veterans of New Mexico law enforcement. They came with letters from their past employer, the sheriff at Socorro, as good men with a record of perfect conduct.

In a whisper, Guthrey asked Zamora, who

13

stood in the back, how the trial was going.

"This woman up there now is very forceful. Her name is Sally Landers."

Guthrey nodded. "I had a hard time getting them to file charges."

Zamora agreed. "I'd bet this jury finds him guilty."

"I hope so. Have the others testified?"

"Another woman did before lunch."

With a quick check over the crowd, Guthrey asked, "This crowd peaceful?"

"No trouble. They came to see these criminals get what they deserve. This place must have been hell before you took over. Night riders really scaring everyone or running them off."

"There was no law. Now there is. I need to go home. My wife may think I've died, I've been gone so long. But I'll be back. If anything goes wrong, send word. I can be back here in a hurry."

"Yes, sir."

He walked back to his horse, watered him at a public trough, then cinched him up to head for home. In the saddle, he reined his mount around and left the county seat in a long trot for the Bridges Ranch. Cally, his new wife of six weeks, would be looking for him.

He short loped the horse up the lane to

the ranch house in the last hour of daylight. A fiery sunset blazed in the west, burning out behind the last tall mountain range. He slid to a stop at the sight of Cally coming out of the log adobe house. Busy drying her hands, his redheaded wife burst into a run and tackled him.

They were both on the ground kissing and laughing like a pair of hound pups.

"I am so glad to see you," she declared.

"You could of got hurt doing that." He tousled her hair.

"No, never. I have been trying to keep busy with everything. How's Noble?"

"That old cuss is fine. We arrested two horse thieves early this morning who stole those horses at Sonoita and they're in jail now. The trial for Slegal is going on. Two or three women already testified about his raping them. He'll be put away for a long time. Another week of trials and then all of them will be behind bars in Yuma." He kissed his pretty young wife, now sitting on his lap. "Now I need to clean up."

"Just sit here and let me hold you. You had supper?"

"No."

"I'll get up and fix you some. Then you and me can both take a bath."

"Sounds wonderful."

"But you need to eat first."

"Yes, mother."

"Hey, I don't get to boss you around very much."

"Where's your brother?"

"Oh, in town. You didn't see him?"

"I was at Soda Springs, not Steward's Crossing. Was he back at that big house?" He called the house of ill repute in Steward's Crossing the big house.

"I guess he's just young and restless."

"Let's forget about everything but us."

"Good." She pulled him up by the hand.

"Are they going to settle with Killion returning twenty thousand dollars to the county for the charges of misdeeds when he was on duty?"

"I told the county council that was their decision to make and I'd honor it. With my payroll of deputies, they are going to have to raise some money. They really didn't save much by not having law in the county."

"That's been like a nose on your face," she said. "You ought to know sooner or later it would cost to have a peaceful place to live."

He agreed and she set in to fix his supper. Sitting at a chair at the table, Guthrey wrote in his log about his wants and needs for his job. He didn't realize where the time went

16

when she told him, "Food's ready."

She served him frijoles and fresh corn bread. Seated across from him at the table looking mischievous, she crossed and recrossed her legs several times. "I always wondered what was so great about being married. I am a believer now."

"This job will keep me away from you a lot."

"No, it will fulfill your life. You aren't a cowboy, you aren't a farmer; you worry about people and how they are being treated. Behind that badge you are where you need to be."

"I once was a cattle drive boss. My last trip up there, so many men died or were killed. That trip left me so upset I went into hiding. Then I took up the Ranger business and liked it, but they never paid us all our money. In the end I resigned a job I enjoyed but could not afford to keep."

"I'm just glad you came along here because I now have a husband I love. Let's go shower."

"You sure don't have much in me." He stood up and kissed her. Then, armed with towels, they headed for the sheepherder shower under the drum filled by the windmill and heated by the sun. Laughing and teasing, they managed to wash their bodies under the pull-down chain on the shower-head, and then they dried themselves as the sun set in the west.

He'd never had such a free relationship with any woman. Despite the age difference of more than a dozen years, Cally was so grown-up and such a good person at heart. He considered himself lucky to have found her. It all turned out so neat. He knew she loved her irrigated garden and all the things about the ranch, but maybe they should move to Soda Springs so he could be around her more. Time would tell.

Later in bed that night, they continued their honeymoon.

Two

He stood on the porch in the early morning light. A steaming cup of coffee and the freshness of the desert's pungent smell filled his nose. He heard a horse coming down the road.

A cowboy named Chuck Malloy who worked for Jim Duval at the Duval Ranch came by to try to catch him and said that some raiders had struck their place the night before. The raiders took more than two dozen ranch horses, and they were not Apaches. No one was hurt, but the raiders shot up the place and took the best horses with them.

"Who would you say they were?"

"Mexicans. They whooped a lot and rode around like they didn't give a damn. Maybe a half dozen of them. Drunk."

"I'm surprised they came this far up here. The army's down there on the border and there are lookouts up here at every spring trying to stop the Apache renegades' movements."

"These guys were a rowdy bunch last night. The boss and Randal, who's another hand, were already tracking them south when I came up to find you."

"I'll get a fresh horse, and then I need to pick up a deputy and ride down there to see if I can track them."

"Oh, I figure they're back in Mexico already. I just came to tell you for the boss."

Cally looked at Guthrey with a serious expression. "Isn't that dangerous, going out of the county?"

"Outlaws have no boundaries. I'm going to go check on it though."

She raised her gaze at the ceiling. "Just be careful."

"I will."

So one night spent sleeping in her sweet arms and he would be gone again. Noble would want to go along. Guthrey would get him in Soda Springs and then head south. Better take along a packhorse as well. They might be gone for several days.

The cowboy had some breakfast with them and left, thanking Cally for the meal. Then she packed Guthrey some extra clothes. She threw in some of her beef jerky along with a tin of her oatmeal raisin cookies. Then she added two towels, a bar of soap, and some hankies.

Guthrey tied on his bedroll, then put a coffeepot, a small sack of her ground roasted coffee, a pot, an iron skillet, and some frijoles in a cloth bag and loaded them in the pannier. Then he kissed her good-bye. Riding Lobo, his tough Roman-nosed horse, and leading a bay packhorse, he headed for Soda Springs. He was there by midmorning and checked with Deputy Zamora, who was at the desk.

"Back so soon, boss?" the man asked.

"Yes, someone stole several horses at the Duval Ranch last night. Duval figured they're headed for Mexico and they weren't Apaches."

"Bad deal, huh?"

"Yes. How did the trial go yesterday?"

"They found Slegal guilty on all three counts and the judge gave him ten years."

"Good. I don't know much about this rustling, but I'm going to look for this bunch. I'll get Noble and we'll ride that way."

"Will they try to sell them in Tombstone?"

"I don't know," Guthrey answered, though he agreed with his deputy's speculation. "Beyhan, the sheriff down there, won't do much. But I need to try and stop this bunch

21

from doing anything else."

"The Wells Fargo man dropped by and wants to meet you."

"You ever deal with them up in New Mexico?" Guthrey asked.

His man nodded. "They're a tough bunch. I think sometimes they shoot first, then ask questions."

"I dealt with some as a Texas Ranger and I drew the same conclusion. They don't bother to bring many outlaws in for trial when they do catch them."

"There's lots of agencies like that. I was pleased when you told us we were law enforcers, not judges and not juries."

Guthrey agreed. "We each need to remember that."

"I'm sure of the men here. They do remember that. They know your feelings. You still don't have many folks wanting to come tell us much like they did when I worked at Socorro, but you'll build their trust in time."

"They never had any law here, only a drunken deputy who tried to run over everyone. No one was ever in the office tending business, only Tommy out there to take messages. I never saw such a lack of officials in my life. They said they had no crime, but when Jim Burroughs shot my wife's father, no one went to the crime scene or even got the bullets or had a coroner's trial."

"I heard about that. You be careful. I don't have to tell you those Mexican bandits are ruthless."

Guthrey found Noble at the adobe jacal and corrals he kept for the two of them to stay in when they were in town. The old man was cleaning his rifle and finished up quickly at the sight of Guthrey.

"Saddle up. We need to go see about some more horse rustling last night at the Duval Ranch."

"Dad-blame bastards, who was it this time?"

"Duval's cowboy told me they were Mexican bandits."

"They're getting bold, huh?"

"I think the shortage of horses around here has made them most valuable."

"That could be. That sure could be it. How was Cally?"

"She misses you."

"Aw, she's a sweet lady. Made a fine woman for you."

"You up to going along?" he asked as he dismounted to wait for Noble to saddle his horse. Guthrey knew Noble was past seventy by several birthdays. But while he was a little slow getting around, he'd soon be ready to ride.

"By damn, if I can't go, I'll go in and sit at the old soldiers' home in Tucson on the porch."

"You an ex-soldier?"

"I don't recall, but they wouldn't know the difference."

"They might." Guthrey shook his head, amused at the old man's notions.

He slapped down the stirrup and nodded. "I'm ready."

They mounted up and rode for Duval's place near the south end of Crook County. They arrived past noontime, and Guthrey knew that Jim and one of his men had already ridden out to try to track down the rustlers. Gladys Duval, a large rawboned woman in a wash-worn dress, met them as she stood in the doorway, shading her eyes from the high sun with her hand. "I can fix you some beans?"

"No, we'll go on and try to catch them. My wife sent jerky."

"You tell that sweet girl hi for me and I'll see her at the dance if you ever get time to go now that you're the sheriff." She smiled and laughed freely. "Jim will be glad to see ya. Those bandits sounded tough last night when they took them horses. Shot the blazes out of this place taking them. Lucky none of us got hit. They done stole one of his favorite ones too."

Guthrey thanked her and they rode on in a long trot.

"She's a good woman, but I bet she could tail a big steer and throw him on his back." Noble laughed at his own joke as they went down the dusty road.

Smiling, Guthrey agreed. "She really wouldn't fit at a fancy social event, would she?"

"Naw, but she's big hearted as any female living."

Both nodding, they rode on. The mid-July day was heating up and some clouds were coming up from the Gulf of California — monsoon rains could start anytime and not a rancher between there and the Mogollon Rim would complain. Summertime in the chaparral country was always hot and this one had been no exception.

Most people tried to work in the early morning and get done by noon. Law enforcement knew no right time to get things done.

"This man Burroughs who killed Cally's daddy is going to be hung in September. Is it the sheriff's job to do that?" Noble asked.

"Yes. I told the county committee last week they had to build a scaffold. They grumbled about spending the money, but that was the judge's order."

"You have to handle that?"

"It says the sheriff will on that day provide for a scaffold and the things necessary for a proper execution."

"Does that bother you?"

"No. I never knew the father, but it's part of the job and should be a deterrent to others planning to kill someone."

Noble jabbed his horse with his right spur to pick up speed to match Guthrey's mount. "That will be a big day in Soda Springs."

"Yes, lots will be there and that's morbid, but that's part of the way folks get to see justice."

"I bet that warden down at Yuma Prison hates you by now too."

"I don't imagine we're very popular with him, all the felons we've sent him."

"Hell, I bet you don't lose any sleep about that."

"No, I'm glad they're gone."

"You didn't miss many. You ever hear anything from those Ranger friends who came to help us?"

"They don't write long-winded letters, but they're doing fine."

"You reckon they'll ever need you to go help them sometime?"

"If I have the crew I have now, I'd go in a minute."

"Why not count me in to go along and watch?"

"You'd like doing that?" Guthrey reined up his horse on a rise to let him breathe.

"I damn sure would. You could tell how they had been Rangers. It was like a good ranch hand in a branding pen. They did everything with authority."

"Let's get going. We're still tracking this bunch. Maybe by tomorrow we can catch Jim and his man."

"Sure enough. Hell, he may have them caught by now."

"Right." Guthrey took off his hat, wiped his wet forehead on his sleeve, and nodded. "We get much farther south we need to take off these badges. Our authority runs out."

"You planning on crossing the border if we need to?"

He nodded. Those horses needed to be returned, and he wasn't against bringing the rustlers back for their trial belly down either. When they crossed the south line of Crook County, they would simply be two men looking for stolen property. That didn't bother him — doing things right was all that was important.

Aiming for Nogales on the border, at

sundown they camped on the Santa Cruz River and gnawed on jerky for supper and then washed it down with riverbank coffee, which had a fishy flavor. Up before dawn, they headed on. The horse thieves' tracks had skirted the border town and gone south into Mexico. Guthrey removed his badge when they went past the post. No need in wearing it down here. He was just another horse hunter.

By evening, they joined Jim Duval and his cowboy Randal Stevens in their small camp. They had coffee made and shook hands. No doubt in Guthrey's mind that Duval and his man were grateful to see them both.

"What do we know about the rustlers?" Guthrey asked.

"I think they're holed up just over the hill," said the rancher, who was in his forties. "We studied them through my field glasses before sundown. The horses, theirs and mine, are in a bunch up here on the flats, herded by two young boys." Then he smiled. "Way I figure, they're going to have a fiesta tonight and get drunk to celebrate their big steal. Do you think when they do that we can take the ponies and make a run for the border?"

In his mind, Guthrey went over the terrain and the distance between them and the border — thirty-five to forty miles. The moon would be up early; the country went from flat desert to rolling country. In a twenty-four-hour push they'd be across the border and beyond the arm of the Mexican law if it rose up to stop them. If they also had all the outlaws' horses as well, the outlaws couldn't give chase. The plan should work if they didn't ride off into a hole at night. A good-size moon brought those thieves this far, so the moon would take them home as well.

"Let's get those boys that are herding them and their mounts, tie them up, and throw their horses in with the herd."

"I'm ready," Duval said.

"Randal, you and I need to find the herders." He took the young cowboy as the quickest of the three men. "We'll catch them, then tie them up and gag them. You two bring our horses and we'll give it a try. If anything happens and we get too much hell, we can quit the horses and run for the border."

Everyone agreed.

Guthrey and Randal started out on foot in the twilight, dodging cactus and mesquite until they drew close to the two horse silhouettes circling the herd in the growing darkness. The boys were well apart on their horses, keeping the settled ponies in a loose bunch. Guthrey and the young cowboy knelt in the grass to plan how to get their prey. The first boy came close by. They jerked him off his horse and, his mouth clamped shut by Guthrey's hand, smothered a short yell. Randal quickly tied his arms and legs with heavy twine. Then Guthrey gagged him. Satisfied they had that one, Guthrey moved low toward the other herder.

"Sanchez! Where are you?" the boy cried out in Spanish.

"Right here," Guthrey said and pulled him off the horse. Quickly he covered the boy's mouth. "No yelling or I'll cut your throat. Whose horses are these?" he demanded in Spanish.

"Montoya's."

"Who is he?"

The frightened boy did not answer.

Guthrey shook him. "What is his first name?"

"Royal."

"Bueno." He spoke to the boy in Spanish. "If you and your herder friend get untied before sunup and run to Royal, I will come back and cut your throats from ear to ear. You savvy?"

"Sí."

30

They tied him up and gagged him. Then Guthrey and Randal took the bridles off the boys' horses and turned them to the bunch. Duval and Noble joined them in the starlight. In another hour Guthrey knew the moon would rise to help light their way northward.

"Let's push them slow-like at first," Guthrey said. "Duval, you take the lead of the bunch with my packhorse, they should follow you. Me, Randal, and Noble will bring up the rear. When I whistle loud, set us a pace in a good trot. But we better walk them a ways, so those others don't hear us. And till we get more light."

Thunder rolled and the horses threw their heads up, clearly spooked. Guthrey waved at his men. "Fireworks is all that is. Lead out. We'll bring up the rear."

Those rustlers had some more powerful-sounding rockets that exploded over the hill. But to Guthrey's relief, the horses moved in a long succession about two horses at a time on the oxen-wagon tracks and headed north. They choused a few head by slapping their chaps with a rope tail — these were the slow starters. A few miles down the road, the rising silver moonlight on the chaparral began to make things clearer — it was time to move on faster. Guthrey whistled loud and more firecrackers broke the near silence behind them. The herd was on the move, smoothly making some dust, but it wasn't too bad for him and the others in back. The animals were tired enough from the drive down to be docile.

They took the smugglers' path to cross the border east of Nogales so as not to bother with border guards and explain where they were headed. Past midnight they were well beyond the international line and swung west to water the horses in the Santa Cruz River and get a few hours' rest. Guthrey never slept; he stayed on guard with his rifle on a rise. The horses were tired enough from the drive after a good drink to stand around hipshot and sleep. He couldn't see or hear any sign of pursuit, only the grunts of sleeping horses and every once in a while a complaint when one kicked another.

In two hours, they were on the road again, which swung east and eventually came around the east side of the Whetstone Mountains, and they made it up to Duval's place by dark. Tired as he could be, Jim had offered Guthrey any one of the Mexican horses that he wanted. Guthrey declined. Duval's wife, Gladys, wanted to feed them, but he and Noble pushed on to Steward's

Crossing, eating in the Home Café, then in a near groggy condition rode out to the Bridges Ranch.

Dan came on the run to meet them. "Where have you two been?"

"Some Mexicans stole Duval's horses. We went to Mexico and got them back." Guthrey, bone weary from all their riding, wanted to make his story easy to tell. "No shots fired, all Duval's horses and a few more are at his ranch in the pens."

Dan frowned at them. "Mexico? You got any authority down there?"

"No, we were simply returning my neighbor's horses."

"They didn't try to stop you?"

Noble laughed. "Naw, but we never gave them a chance."

"Good night," Guthrey said in his face, shooed Noble off to the bunkhouse, and halfway stiff, he hobbled off to the house. Dan had taken over unsaddling their horses for them.

"Did you get any sleep?" asked Cally, dressed in a robe, slipping in beside him and hooking his arm.

"None."

"Oh my gosh! You and Noble must be close to dead."

"I don't know about him but I'm going to

bed — somewhere."

Once inside the house, she tossed an old spread on the bed. "Lie down. Where did the old man go?"

"Bunkhouse. He'll get some sleep," he said. "Up there."

Numb-minded even in her company, Guthrey dropped onto the bed, then unbuckled his gun belt and had to get it disengaged to place it on the floor. Cally pulled off his boots and he was near asleep before his head hit the pillow.

Her voice was an echo he recalled later. "Sleep easy, my love."

THREE

Rested some after sleeping in his own bed but still half-asleep, Guthrey got up and took a shower in the coolness of the early morning. Back at the house, shivering, Cally met him with a cup of hot coffee. "You didn't sleep for very long. How was your journey?"

"Oh, it wasn't so bad. It turned out we brought back Duval's horses and even some of the thieves'. I bet if those Mexicans ever try to steal his horses again he'll meet them head on."

"I'm glad you all came back all right. Mexico is another country."

"Those rustlers probably woke up with no horses and bad headaches. For miles coming back, we could hear all the fireworks over the hill from them celebrating."

"Really?"

"Miles north they still boomed behind us." He poured some hot water in the wash pan. Then Cally took over and lathered his face with a hog hair brush and shaved his face with the straight edge while he sat in a chair. After she finished, she used hot water and a towel to wipe his face of any residue and then she kissed him. "You need a haircut whenever you find some time."

"I'll let you do that. I better eat some breakfast, then go over to town and see what fell in while I was gone. I plan to go to the dance Saturday night with my wife."

"Good. I bet she'd go with you."

He spanked her friendly-like from behind. "I'll go saddle my horse while breakfast is being made. All right?"

"Sure. I'll have some eggs, bacon, and biscuits ready by then. The biscuits are in the oven now."

He winked and kissed her. "I could smell them."

"You know I do like having you around."

"Me too." Then he went to saddle up.

Dan came sleepy eyed from the bunkhouse. "I let the old man sleep in."

"He needs to. We about wore each other out bringing those horses home."

"He'll raise hell about me doing that." Dan smiled, amused. "But I thought so too."

"How is the ranch operation going?"

"Okay. I finally found that calf we've been

looking for forever — the one they branded as theirs that was one of our cows. I used a bar to blank out their brand and put ours on him. He weighed about three hundred pounds when I caught him this time and he about got me down."

Guthrey frowned at him. "You be careful up there working cattle by yourself. You can get hurt easy."

"I know. I'm still not over the last horse wreck."

"How is the mine coming along?"

"It isn't a big operation, but we've sold lots of gold. Sis has the books on it. We discussed doing more drilling work up there, but we're waiting to see how far this vein goes."

"Good. I need to go and be sure that things are all right at the office, and then I'll be back to go to the dance. You going to join us?"

"I doubt it, but thanks. I have some other plans."

"Just wanted you to know you were invited." Raising hell with the ladies of the night was no way for that boy to ever find a wife and settle down. He didn't need to get married, but he did need to become part of the mainstream community. This gold business would provide the opportunity for their

37

family ranch to expand, and it would require more applied management. Oh well, maybe he'd grow up in time.

Made Guthrey think about his own vices growing up. Damn, he was glad he'd found Cally. He led his saddled horse to the hitch rail and washed his hands at the porch dry sink in the enamel basin, dried them, and went inside. "Am I too late to get food?"

His wife shook her head in an amused way. "No, no, you're right on time."

"Good. Hear that, Dan?" Guthrey elbowed his brother-in-law for an answer.

"I won't get on her bad side. No way."

"Oh yes, I am way too easy on both of you. I should be tougher than I am."

"Please don't do that." Then Guthrey broke into laughter. "We love you, Cally. Keep feeding us. How is the garden doing?"

"I'm canning something every day. I will have a couple of years' worth of food in the cellar soon. But the hotter weather is taking a toll on my plants. I'll back off until it gets cooler, then add more new varieties in the garden."

"Hey, we only tease you. I'm proud you work so hard on this garden." He clapped his hand on top of hers on the table. "I will try to be back tonight. If not, I will be back in time tomorrow to go to the dance with you."

She smiled. "I understand, and both of you are a mess. What about Noble?"

"We let him sleep in. Tell him I'll be back if I need him, otherwise he can go to the dance with us tomorrow."

"I can do that. I know he wants you to think he's as tough as a twenty-year-old. Unfortunately he is probably closer to eighty. But I know he has lots of knowledge about people and places, and he's got good sense too."

"Right." Guthrey wiped his face on the napkin. "I sure like your food. I'm headed for the office." Standing up, he kissed her, and she jumped up to walk with him to his horse.

"I'll be here when you get back."

"I count on that." He untied the reins. Parting with her was hard for him every time. They kissed and he mounted the bay horse they called Bill and reined him around. With a salute, he rode off down the lane for the road to Steward's Crossing and then west on the stagecoach road to the county seat at Soda Springs.

Guthrey had learned a lot about the territory since he came here from Texas. From Soda Springs it was forty-some miles to

Tucson, the main city in southern Arizona Territory. Actually, Tombstone, thirty miles south of Steward's Crossing, was the larger city due to all the mining activity going on down there. The amount of dollars it generated along with the support of that industry made gambling, saloons, and flesh palaces readily available to keep the workers broke and on the job. Nothing illegal, but it was a wild, sin-filled place not for the faint of heart.

Tucson started out as an old Spanish fort and actually, to Guthrey, it still seemed like a run-down adobe village with dead animal carcasses in the streets and not much sanitation. Cally told him they would wrestle each legislative session for the state capital-ship after Lincoln had chosen the capital to be Prescott — pronounced Preskit by the citizens who lived there.

At this time the governor was at the cooler place in the north until the next meeting of the territorial legislation voted to move the seat back to Tucson. Political leaders in the south were deeply involved in keeping all the soldiers they could in southern Arizona so as to hold down the Apache renegades. In addition, a ring of those men held all the cards when it came to supplying those military outposts with everything they needed — the Tucson Ring was no fable. They controlled it all and openly made enormous profits.

Old man Clanton held the beef supply contracts for both the military and Indian reservation needs. This old border bandit stole about half the cattle he used to supply them. Only thing worse was the combine who also, no doubt, fortified the renegades with arms and firewater to keep the war alive. Guthrey had heard of many deals being made in these situations, but he didn't have enough hard evidence to close those operations down. It wasn't because he didn't have his ear to the ground on all these matters though. If he found the evidence, he'd stamp them out of business. But proof wasn't always easy for him to harvest and without it he had no case despite all the hearsay about this corruption.

His responsibility to enforce the law rode on his mind all the way to Soda Springs. After checking with his deskman, he took a late lunch at the café and then put his horse in the corrals at his jacal. He walked back to the office in the hot afternoon. The clouds gathering in the south looked like thunderstorms. He hoped they arrived that afternoon.

In his office he went over some reports filed about a stolen milk cow. *Who stole a milk cow?* He laughed. The deputy who answered the complaint looked the situation over. The cow was there one day, gone the next. It was a brindle Jersey cow and the farmer had searched the area with no answer for where it went.

Next was a complaint that someone stole a woman's chickens. The deputy decided the poultry thief was a masked bandit called a coatimundi. The lady agreed and in the traps set by the investigating officer, they caught him. Another crime solved in the county seat.

There was a note about the theft of silverware from a lady he did not know. Miss Janice Gardiner, who lived in the Silver Canyon District, had mysteriously lost her valuable forks, spoons, and knives while she was gone on a picnic. The deputy who investigated suggested it might have been a hobo who broke into her house, found them, and carried them off. No sign of such a transient was reported.

Three horses were missing from the Two Bell Ranch. Tracks pointed to Apaches stealing them. Four young bucks had left the San Carlos Apache Reservation for Mexico four days earlier. The deputy on the

case agreed with the ranch foreman —
Apaches stole them. They filed their horse
losses with the federal government for
repayment with the deputy's opinion.

Things looked quiet, and Guthrey decided
to ride back home and share his wife's bed
and attend the dance. But first he had to
discuss with his main deputies, Baker and
Zamora, the matter of the way Guthrey and
his crew had brought back the stolen horses.
They agreed that what he did was the best
way to handle the international business.

"Had you ever heard of the man those
boys called Royal Montoya before?" Zamora
asked.

"No, but he may be the next big outlaw to
come from down there. Who knows, but we
better mark him down as our enemy up
here," Guthrey said. "Sounds like if he ever
goes back to Duval's, he may not return to
Mexico alive. If we'd been in the U.S., I'd
have gone down and arrested him and his
boys even if they were beyond my Arizona
Territory boundaries. But we were deep in
Mexico and there was the chance we might
get mixed up with international legal issues,
so we simply brought the ponies back."

Zamora nodded. "We'll be more careful
trying to watch for them coming up here."

Guthrey shook his head. "It'll be a hard

thing to do."

His deputy made a face, then nodded. "I may try for some contacts in Mexico who could wire us when they leave down there."

"Sounds wonderful. I'm heading home. I won't be back till Monday unless you need me."

"Have fun."

"I hope to." He chuckled. *Cally, here I come.*

He arrived at the ranch and his wife rushed out to hug him. Damn, she was a neat lady and her happy spirits rejuvenated him.

"I have some supper I kept warm."

"I'll put the horse up. Where's Noble?"

"I think he went to see a woman." Smirking, Cally glanced up at him to see if he knew anything.

"Oh, we're all looking for a woman. Dan's gone too?"

She looked at the sky for help. "I think she works in the big house."

"He's lost. He'll find himself."

He kissed her on the forehead and went to put the horse up. In the corral the pony rolled in the dust and grunted in gratitude at being back home. Guthrey was looking forward to being in the comfort of his wife's company for the next few days and away from the pressure and problems of his office. They'd only been married six weeks and so far all his time had been taken up by his efforts to get the county back under the protection of a strong law enforcement unit. He'd hired a few men as tax assessors to count cattle and evaluate property for the taxes due. He expected them to produce the county revenues in a fair manner.

He and Cally had a leisurely supper together and soon the honeymooners went to bed — early. For a man who'd resisted marriage for so long, he found the rewards sure exceeded any of the pitfalls. But Cally had no big agenda for them, and she was there for him — as well as enjoying the entire process of man and wife. The situation left him as relaxed as he'd ever been and he looked forward to their trysts.

At dawn he milked her cow while she made coffee and breakfast for the two of them. Then she started cooking for the potluck supper that night.

"What will you do about the cow tonight?" he asked, putting the milk pail on the floor near her.

"Noble said not to worry. He's staying here, and he said he'd milk her tonight and in the morning for me."

"That was nice."

"Or I'd stick her calf in the pen with her." She smiled at him. "I wanted us to have another night together and not have to drive home after the dance."

He hugged her and kissed her cheek. "Sweet idea."

"Where will you have to go next?"

"Oh, I suppose sometime soon we might borrow that cabin up on Mount Graham where we honeymooned for a few days and escape the heat."

"That would be nice. I bet we can arrange that."

"If you get a chance to speak to those folks, ask them about it."

"We will tonight. Are all your deputies working out?"

"Yes, I have a good staff. We may get a contact on the border to warn us about any approaching gang headed north. Zamora knows some people down there. I hope we can get that notification system in place."

"How would it work?"

"Oh, say a spy knew that they were leaving Mexico for Soda Springs. The telegram would come. 'I will see you in Soda Springs in a day,' signed José."

"No one would suspect that, would they?" she asked.

"Right. It could tell us in time to fortify

our guard if they're coming."

She nodded. "First it was Whitmore wanting to control the entire range. Next some Mexican bandits ride up here like they own us."

"There's always criminals like that around. A sheriff needs to be aware of all law breakers."

"Was it like this as a Ranger?"

"Oh, we had gangs to be rounded up. People who tried to run over others to crowd them off a range or run them away. Bullies. They exist all over. Men who have no respect for their fellow man's property, his family, or their assets."

She leaned against him. "I love being married to you. If I don't please you, tell me, and I'll try to do better. I don't have any experience except what I've learned in the past six weeks with you."

He hugged her head to his chest and closed his eyes. "You are wonderfully honest. I am so proud of our relationship. You and I learn more and more about ourselves, about what we like and what we enjoy. I *am* pleased — more pleased than I guess I can tell you."

"I was afraid you would think me wanton if I said it's wonderful — to be in bed with you."

"No, no, that's our part of this deal."

"Thanks."

He squeezed her hard. "We have a great, powerful marriage."

"Good. Sit down and we'll eat lunch. Then — we're alone so we can do what we want to do."

He chuckled. "And we will."

"Good."

He clasped his hand on top of hers. "You are a real winner."

They didn't get much of a nap that afternoon, but they damn sure learned lots about the power of love between them. He couldn't believe what all they did and his back ached along with his brains — whew!

FOUR

They got a late start for the schoolhouse but made it before everything really began. Cally gathered some women to help her get the food she'd fixed on the serving table. Guthrey put up a wall tent and several teenage boys came to his aid.

Cally came back out of breath and put her butt against the wagon wheel to catch up. "We made it."

He laughed, then whispered in her ear, "It was worth coming late for both of us."

She smiled, proud as a kitten, and they went inside arm in arm. They ate off their own tin plates piled high with food, sitting over in a corner of the schoolhouse among other ranch folks they knew. Everyone was in a good mood. They bragged on Guthrey's fast enforcement of the law since his election and how many were going or had gone to prison.

Mike Newton, a rancher, said, "The judge

gave Slegal ten years for his rapes and for night-raiding ranches to make people run away. He won't ever live for that long in Yuma Prison. He can sure rot there for my money."

Heads bobbed. The worst one of the lot was going to sweat out his life in that hell. Guthrey picked through all the food on his plate; he'd taken more than he could eat. Oh well, it wasn't the first time in his life he'd done that. He'd do the best he could.

Cally must have noticed. "Did you save a place for some desert?"

"Lord, Cally, I can't eat any more," he whispered.

"No problem. Give me your plate. There's strawberry pie and pecan."

"Cut me a sliver of each."

She shared a smile and took off with both plates. In a few minutes she was back with both kinds of pie on a clean plate for him.

He shook his head at her delivery. But he enjoyed it, like he did her.

She asked Thomas and Ruth Nelson, who owned the Mount Graham cabin, about that property while Guthrey was outside talking to other folks, and they told her that anytime she and Guthrey wanted to use it, just give them the word. Cally told Guthrey this while they waltzed to a fiddle song across the floor.

"Wonderful." He gave her a tight hug and then whirled her around. She laughed and they were off again.

They went to their tent around midnight. On the cot, they took another turn at wife and husband activity and fell asleep in each other's arms. He awoke a few hours before dawn. Someone was calling his name.

"Sheriff Guthrey. Sheriff Guthrey?"

He stepped into his pants as Cally got up, wrapped herself in a blanket to hide her nakedness, and swept up his pistol. "Here, take this. You don't know, it might be a trick."

"Thanks." He kissed her quickly and stuck it in his waistband. Then, bareheaded, he ducked outside in the predawn buttoning his shirt.

"Who's calling my name?"

"Me," a woman said, coming back. Tears wet her face under the starlight. "They've murdered the Carlson family. I have been riding for hours to find you. They said you'd be here."

She fell into his arms, and he dropped to his knees to set her on the ground.

"Anyone know these folks?" he asked as other half-dressed men and women poured out of tents to see what was going on.

51

"Who is it, Guthrey?"

The woman was huddled and crying her eyes out.

Dressed, Cally joined them, sat down beside the woman, and forced her to sit up with her. "Where is their place?"

"In Gregory Canyon. I hadn't seen them in two days so I went up there after dark — they're all dead. Murdered —" She broke down and cried some more.

"I want someone to loan me a horse and someone to show me their place." Guthrey rose and looked over the crowd in the starlight for a volunteer.

"What should I do to help you?" his wife asked him privately.

"Cally, they'll help you take down the tent. I'll be back to the ranch when I solve this matter."

She nodded her head. "Be careful. I'll be fine."

He went to the tent and dressed. He strapped on his gun belt and holstered his six-gun and, with his hat on, he went outside to put a saddle on the big horse that rancher Ervin Ralston had brought up for him to ride.

"Your wife'll be fine," Ralston said to him. "My teenage boys will take her home. That place is north and it will take a few hours for us to get up there."

"You know them?" Guthrey asked, trying to think who the victims were. He didn't recall meeting them.

"I've been there before," the man said.

"What did they do?"

"George worked for people, did odd jobs. They were pretty poor, and folks around there fed them for him doing some work when they were out of money. That's being too poor to move on, but they never hurt anyone. It could be Apaches done it."

"Before we get everyone in a lynching mood, let's not share any ideas like that. I'm not holding up for them, but so far as we know, they've only stolen horses going back and forth to Mexico. There were some killings a few years ago south of this county, and the Apaches were blamed. But I don't want an uncalled-for war started."

"I savvy and you're right. We're all too vulnerable to attacks by them if we stir them up."

"We need the killers, and I want to see the murder area as undisturbed as I can. Maybe they left some sign for us, Erv."

The big rancher agreed.

"Who is the lady came to tell me?"

"Claudia Haynes. Her husband is Ralph Haynes. They're good folks, have a spread up there close by to the Carlsons."

"I will stop by their place and explain what we find when we get through."

Erv agreed.

They pushed on hard northward in the night under a thousand stars. Their saddle leather complained and horseshoes struck rocks exposed on the road surface as they kept their course. Desert owls hooted in the night, bats swooped in the sky, and coyotes lent their voices to the sounds of the night.

The trip proved long and dawn was pinking the New Mexico horizon far in the east. They entered a deep chasm and the dry wash was the only way up the deep, shadowy gorge. Erv led the way in on his good horse, and up on a small shelf, a dark hovel sat backed to a huge sandstone bluff wall behind it.

"I want this area as untouched as can be so we can search it in the daylight. Criminals drop things. Once, we found an old letter from his girlfriend that a killer dropped at the scene. He denied doing the murder. But we had the letter with his name on it that could not have gotten up there except it fell out of his pocket."

Erv looked serious enough peering inside the house in the dim light. He nodded. "I never thought about that but I do see what you mean."

"Since we have no suspects so far, any evidence we can find will help us arrest the guilty ones."

"I guess being a lawman all your life makes that job easier."

Guthrey shook his head. "You need to be lucky too."

Erv agreed and they both squatted down on their heels at the open doorway.

"Is there any other way in or out of this canyon?" Guthrey looked around at the still-dark surrounding bluffs.

"You could, if you were part goat, go out over that back range. Some men and kids have done it just to say they had."

"It gets to be daylight, you search that dry wash we rode in on. See if we and the nice lady who came to get us did not wipe out their tracks and try to learn which way they went when they came out of the canyon, if you can."

"Oh yes. That might be hard."

"Look close where they went out at the opening."

Erv said, "I can do that. Are the bodies inside?"

"Let's go peek." Guthrey had a knot behind his tongue to swallow. He'd seen lots of dead folks. None were ever pretty to look at. With just enough light to see by, they peered in from the doorway. A naked body, perhaps that of a teenager, was on the bed.

"That was their daughter, Casey. My God, she never harmed anyone. She's tied there, ain't she?"

"Looks that way. Don't step in the dirt inside the door. Move to the left so we can see if there are any footprints."

"There's George's body." Erv pointed to the corpse of a man in old overalls lying on his back on the floor beside the back door, increasingly visible as more of the morning light gained access.

Guthrey nodded. He was more shaken by the sight of the naked teenage girl's corpse tied by the wrists and ankles to the bed. The only reason for that was to rape or torture her. He'd never seen such a sight, but had been at trials where men were tried for doing such crimes and the judge excused all the women in the courtroom when the prosecution got set to produce a drawing of what that looked like.

"I see a perfect boot print right there."

"Find some newspaper. We need a tracing of that boot. It's a large one."

"The old man don't own any boots like that either."

They found George's wife facedown on

the ground outside. Her head was bloody black from being beaten to death.

Finding no other good footprints inside the doorway, Guthrey went back in the room and looked at the dead girl. From the look of her bluish face he felt certain they had smothered her to death, perhaps with an old pillow. He searched around the bed. Carefully he shook out each blanket that had been tossed on the floor. He watched a wadded up goatskin roping glove fall out of the last blanket he had shaken and he carefully picked it up. The room had the real bad odor of an unemptied nightjar or unwashed bodies — he didn't dare swallow much of the foul air.

Why was this glove in these blankets that were tossed aside? He pocketed it in his vest to examine later. The murderers must have raped her. But why? Lots of ladies of the night in town to use — the murderers must be some crazy, wicked animals. Normal folks would have no stomach for all this horrible violence.

Candles were melted to hard puddles of hard wax. He had no idea what time of day all this had happened. But it was a recent crime, happened maybe on Friday or even Saturday.

Guthrey found some butts of roll-your-own cigarettes outside the house. Also the large boot print they'd seen inside the house was there again near the woman's corpse. Some other ranchers came in about then and tethered their horses a ways from the house. Guthrey went to join them. He told them what they'd found.

"Have you found anything to use in court?" Hal Jones asked him, shaken by his description of the corpses.

Guthrey shook his head. "Nothing to point a finger. I would say more than one person did this. One was a large man; we have his boot print, not many features except being huge. But to run down three people and murder them like this took some help."

Then recalling the glove, he removed it from his pocket and opened it up. "I found this in the blankets that were tossed off the bed." It was an expensive handmade goat-skin glove used by many for roping and thin enough a man could fire a six-gun wearing it. On the cuff there was a very accurate drawing of a star made by an indelible pencil.

"Anyone seen one of these?" he asked, handing the evidence around to the four grim-faced men standing outside, who were obviously shocked by the violence that had occurred there.

"This is an expensive glove," one rancher said, handing it on.

"Anyone seen this star before?" another asked.

Heads shook in the circle. Erv told Guthrey that he had sent one of the men to go get some more horses to transport the corpses to Soda Springs.

"Guthrey, how will we ever catch these killers?" Joe Butler asked.

"Good question. But someone will slip up. Someone will have passed by the killers on the road. They may be transients, just going through the country, or people that they knew. I'll get the word out and offer a reward for information. This horrendous crime was not thought up and managed by normal people. They were crazy, wolflike animals. Let's not get people too upset; it could lead to innocent people being the subject of a lynch mob. I worry about that. We need a clear-cut trial for the ones who did this, despite the human emotions that will arise. Am I clear?"

The sober-faced men in the group were, all of them, community leaders — they all nodded. In another hour the bodies were wrapped and bound in blankets and the horses arrived. Two of the men agreed to deliver them to the undertaker in Soda Springs. Guthrey told them he needed to hold a justice of the peace hearing on these deaths — something that hadn't been done when Cally's father was shot in the canyon. Guthrey had found that killer; he hoped he could get these killers as well.

A quiet, somber party started out to leave the canyon with three corpses. Guthrey studied the towering walls. Erv told him he thought the killers had ridden out and headed north, but the tracks were ordinary enough it was hard to tell which ones belonged to who.

Guthrey and Erv stopped by to thank Mrs. Haynes. Red-eyed, she came out to greet them.

"I am sorry you had to discover them. It was a horrific scene. Did they have any enemies you know about?"

"No." She wearily shook her head. "They were such gentle people. Always kind."

"Mrs. Haynes, was the scene fresh when you found them?"

"Oh, it must have happened on Friday. They'd been dead awhile when I found 'em."

"I think so too. Thanks. We will do all we can to find the killers. I'll put out a reward for information. You have any ideas?"

"Was it Apaches?" she whispered.

"No. It was someone else."

"Thank God."

"I've sent the bodies to Soda Springs. We'll hold an inquest. Can you come testify?"

"Yes."

"I know this has been hard on you. I appreciate your concern. Thanks."

"Tell your lovely wife, Cally, thanks. She was so kind to me."

"Cally is a good woman, well beyond her years in her ability to help people."

"Yes she is. I hope you find these vile people."

"I'll try."

"God bless you, sheriff."

He replaced his hat and nodded to her. Then he remounted and headed home. He was going by to check on his wife. His belly growling at his backbone, he short loped the borrowed horse to their place. Erv had said one of his boys would ride over and get the pony. The sheriff had enough to do.

Skirt in hand, Cally rushed out to hug him as he hitched the horse. "You have any food?"

"No, I waited for you to feed me." He kissed her and then she shook her head.

"You must be starved to death."

He slapped his muscle-corded belly and laughed. "I'm starved to see and hold you."

"Come in, I'll fix you food." She swung on his arm. Her enthusiasm for him always boosted his deep feeling for her even more.

The smell of cooking soon began to fill his nose as Cally worked over the wood range and he filled her in on the murders while sitting at the table.

She soon brought him a stack of hot pancakes, butter, and her syrup. He thanked her and started to fill his plate.

"I can make some more," she offered.

"No. I'll take a shower and sleep a few hours."

"Nice to have you home." She reached over and squeezed his hand.

"Nice to be here." He shook his head to try to clear the whole scene away. "Where's Noble?"

"Looking for a horse rustler. A man named Darrel Thayer came by looking for you. Noble and Dan went to see what they could figure out about who took Thayer's horses."

"Where does this man live?"

"South and east of Stewart's Crossing."

"Did you think I needed to back them?"

"Not until you take a bath and sleep a few hours. They can handle the matter, I am certain."

He chewed on his lower lip. "I hope you're right."

"I am. I'm your wife." Then she laughed and he reached out, hugged her narrow waist, and shook his head. "Bath comes next."

"I'll go along so you don't fall asleep taking it." She tousled his hair.

"Thanks." With resolve he got up and went with her.

The bath went fine. Cold but at least he felt clean. Then he dropped into bed and slept, but not without some bad dreams about the murder scene. He woke in a cold sweat, sat up in bed in the darkness of night. Both dread and the dead were on his mind.

Cally woke up too. "Are you all right?" Her voice was a soft whisper that brought a smile to his face, realizing how close his bride's warm body was to his.

He settled down and took her in his arms. "I'm fine. Now I have you."

"Good," she said and snuggled into him. It was still honeymoon time for both of them in the coolness of the desert night.

FIVE

The sunrise outlined the distant Chiricahua Mountains, which were stretched out like a huge body sleeping on its side. The flavor of smoked bacon and breakfast on his tongue, Guthrey rode for town on a solid roan gelding that Monday morning. His horse's running walk was fast and carried him down the dry road that needed rain to settle the dust, but moisture in this climate was always scarce.

He stopped in Steward's Crossing to see his deputy Ike Sweeney, and he found the man on his porch drinking coffee. He didn't know a thing about any stolen horse deal. The rancher never stopped by to tell him anything. Sweeney knew Thayer, but neither the rancher nor Noble nor Dan had stopped by before going to investigate the crime.

Guthrey made up his mind then to go assist them, or try to.

Sweeney, a big man with a white mustache, offered to join him, but Guthrey told him no, he'd handle it and try to establish some better rules about how to report crimes. He set out for Thayer's and reached another man's place by midmorning. A woman in her thirties came to the door with a broom.

"Morning, sheriff," she said and under her breath told her children to stay inside. She looked well along to having another one, but she smiled. "I'm Gert Cassidy. My husband, Bob, went to St. David today. He'll be sad he didn't meet you."

"Tell him I said hi. Have my men been by here?" He'd removed his hat for her, and he took the opportunity to wipe his forehead on his sleeve.

"Yes, sir, I'm sure they're all right. They were going up in the Dragoons to Thayer's place to see if they could find any trace of the rustlers."

"I understand. I guess I'll have to track them, then."

"Mark Peters has a place on the west side of the mountains. Go by there; he may know more than I do."

"Thanks, ma'am." His Stetson back on his head, Guthrey sent the roan horse northeastward in a lope. He knew about the Peters Ranch and the location she meant.

An hour later, he found Peters in his small shop repairing a buckboard wheel.

The man looked up at his approach and Guthrey swung down.

"Morning, sheriff. What brings you up here?"

"Did two deputies and Darrel Thayer come by here looking for some stolen horses?"

"They came by here yesterday. Must of been noontime, like now. Olive has some lunch ready. Stop and eat with us."

"I need to —"

"Everyone needs to eat. She's a good hand at cooking, if I may say so myself."

"Can't refuse that."

"Come on and wash up."

They washed their hands on the back porch, dried them on a sack towel, and hung it up. When Peters's wife turned around, Guthrey blinked. He knew her from somewhere else — some place.

"Olive, this is Sheriff Guthrey."

Hat off, he nodded. "Nice to meet you."

"Yes."

Her name wasn't Olive before — where had he met her back then? His mind like a file searched for the time and place of that first introduction. She was close to thirty by his estimate. Nice-looking face, a medium

66

body size, well distributed, her dark brown hair shoulder length with a slight curl. Dressed more than plain but respectable. He wondered where their paths had crossed.

"Olive and I've been married two years. I lost my first wife five years ago. She lost her mate two years before. We met in Tucson at a church function and I've been so blessed to have her as my wife."

"Oh, Mark, I'm sure the sheriff has a good wife too."

Guthrey nodded. "Do you know my wife, Cally?"

"No, but I hope to."

"She's active with the group that has the potluck suppers and dances at the schoolhouse up there north of Steward's Crossing. You two need to come some Saturday night and join us."

"We'll try to do that," Mark said and smiled at his wife. She agreed and put the bowls of food on the table, asking Guthrey if he drank coffee.

"Yes, ma'am."

The noon meal was fried ham, sweet potatoes and fresh green beans from Olive's garden, and soda biscuits. Her coffee was rich tasting and Guthrey enjoyed the dinner with them. He still did not know where he had first met Olive. Obviously the Peterses were not Mormons. Those folks never drank coffee because of their religion.

Guthrey rode on in the direction that Noble, Dan, and Thayer had taken into the Dragoon Mountains. The mountains rose off the desert floor with a reddish rock surface. Soon juniper clad the slopes, and in places on top, ponderosa pines supplemented them. This was once Apache country, and somewhere on the west end of the Dragoon range the legendary Cochise signed a peace treaty with the one-armed General Howard that disgusted General Crook, the Apache chaser. Of course, later the entire treaty was thrown out and the Chiricahua people were moved to the San Carlos Apache Reservation with tribes they hated, and that eventually caused the Apache war to continue. Cally was his expert on history and she had told him to watch out. Reports of renegades hiding in these mountains were told at various functions like the potluck supper and dance.

Guthrey carried his Colt .45 on his hip and a .44/40 Winchester in his scabbard. The roan horse was sure-footed and scaled the dim mountain road easily, but still in the heat the horse's shoulders were shiny with sweat. At a spring, Guthrey stopped and watered himself and the gelding. He hoped he had taken the main route that led into the mountains and his men had not turned off on a lesser way.

Off a mountaintop he crossed he could see wood smoke, and he dropped into a basin that held a ranch house, sheds, corrals, and some fenced pastures. When he rode up, a woman in a wash-worn dress came out on the porch.

"Good day, ma'am. I'm Sheriff Guthrey."

She nodded. "I am Darrel Thayer's wife, Nell. They left this morning going east to look for those horses." She looked like a white woman, but there was something Apache about her speech.

He searched around still in the saddle. "You two live up here alone?"

She nodded. "Five years ago, my family was massacred on the east side of the Chiricahuas. An Apache took me for his wife. When my husband was killed by Mexican soldiers, I did not wish to stay down there any longer and walked out. Darrel did not shun me when I met him and he made me his wife. I am very fortunate."

Her back straight and ramrod stiff, she dropped her gaze to her apron. Guthrey realized there was still in her some of the Apache woman who once had shared a

69

wickiup with an Apache in the Sierra Madres.

He looked around at the valley. "I see why you live in these lovely mountains."

Her smile was slight but she appeared pleased that he spoke of their homestead. "I have a very good man in him as well."

"Nell, I'm a former Texas Ranger. I took this badge to make Crook County a better place to live. My wife, Cally, and I live north of Steward's Crossing. Dan is her brother. I know you've met him."

She smiled more widely. "He already told us to come to the dance on Saturday night. Darrel says we will. That means we will one day. I will look forward to doing that. Do you need anything to eat?"

"No, I have some jerky. Thanks. I will waltz with you if you come to the dance. You'll like my wife, Cally."

She almost smiled at his invitation. "I will hold you to that promise. They were headed east."

"Nice to have met you, Nell. I'll catch up with them."

She nodded. "I can see what she saw in you, sheriff."

He laughed. "Thanks, she didn't get much."

He short loped the roan and felt pleased

to have met a woman whose life had sure been one of turmoil. Thayer must be a powerfully confident man to have accepted her. Three different women in a row he'd met on this trip, living on an outlying ranch like his own wife did, efficient and proud.

He spooked up three mule deer in the next mile. They bobbed away through the thin timber and he rode on. By late afternoon he could see the playa lakes in the Sulphur Springs Valley. The water was only inches deep, and he thought about people fooled by real estate scoundrels who sold them ranches on those lakeshores. So shallow a killdeer could wade across most of them.

He watered his horse at a windmill tank and spoke to a Mormon woman who came from a squaw shade to talk to him. Tall and raw-boned with a ruddy complexion, she had hair that looked sun bleached like stiff wheat straw. The small children stayed at a bashful distance. No beauty there, no smile, a suspicious set to her face, and she wore men's old brogan shoes. On his day of meeting wives, her harsh looks made him grateful for his own.

His two deputies and Thayer had passed there a few hours earlier and they had told her they planned to go by Fort Bowie, then to Portal on the east side of the Chiricahua range. He thanked her and rode on. He realized next time he should carry hard candy in his saddle bags for the women and their children — this was a political job he held, and it was important he acted friendly to everyone.

By late in the second day, he caught up with the three men before they reached Apache Pass at the stage station. Two familiar horses were standing hipshot at the hitch rail in front of the building that housed the stage stop. They'd no doubt stopped there for supper.

"There he is, Dan," Noble said when Guthrey came through the open door. "A man can't hide, can he?"

The three rose and Guthrey shook their hands. The Mexican woman asked if Guthrey wanted to eat. He told her yes in her language and took a seat.

"How long have you been coming?" Noble asked.

He shook his head. "Awhile. I met your fine wife, Nell," he said to Thayer.

"She feed you?"

"No, I was trying to catch up with you all."

"She don't get much company at my place. She usually tries to stall folks to hear what's happening outside her small world."

"She did tell me her story. She's a fine lady. I was impressed."

Thayer shook his head. "Her father must have been a fool. He tried to come across the Cherrycows in a covered wagon with his wife and two teenage girls. Of course, her father was killed and her mother too in the raid. Nell said her younger sister was more abused than she was, and the girl died in Mexico. I don't know all her story. No one will ever know all the hell that she went through down there. But I think the man she married considered her his and may have protected her from the others' abuse and wanted her for himself. She said she was happy as his wife every day and never considered leaving him. He provided food and must have been tender with her.

"But when he was killed fighting some Mexican soldiers, she had no one to turn to. So one day she put some dried fruit in a cloth and filled an army canteen with water. Then she set out with that and a blanket to find her own people. She was on the way, walking, she thought, for over a month. Someone brought her from the Peralta Springs to Tombstone. I was down there in all the celebration and hell-raising that her return caused. Those people just like to party. But there were lots of suitors wanted her that day — she was nice-looking even when she got there.

"I never felt I'd have a chance to impress her. The Dixie Mine superintendent's wife, Emma Neal, took her in and she did the housework for her board. I was back in Tombstone a month later and asked about her. They told me she was still up there. I asked was anyone courting her and they shook their heads — who wanted something the Apaches had had?"

Thayer picked up his coffee cup in both hands. "She was too pretty a woman. Too nice and polite speaking a woman for my money to not want to know her, at least.

"So I took her a box of candy. Mrs. Neal called her to meet me. She came to the door, accepted the box, thanked me, and bowed out. Mrs. Neal told me she wasn't ready to be courted. I felt lower than a snake's belly. But I guess when I got on my horse she peeked at me from behind a curtain."

Guthrey looked across at him sipping his coffee. "Did that help you?"

"It sure did. So I kept coming by and taking her candy every week or ten days. Then I started bringing an extra horse to hitch there with mine outside the white picket fence."

"She came out one day and blushed. 'You must quit bringing me candy. People are teasing me. I can't eat all of it you have brought so much.'

"But I was not going to give up. 'Could I take you to supper tonight?' I asked her.

"Her face turned white. 'What would people say about you? I have been an Apache's squaw.'

" 'No, you are a nice-looking woman who's been through a ton of hell.'

"She straightened her spine. 'What time will you come for me?'

" 'Six o'clock,' I said.

"Still uncertain, she shook her head. 'I fear for your future. No one will ever trust you for doing this.'

"I told her, 'Nell, I am a rancher. I have a pretty place in the Dragoons. I have a house and cattle and horses. My house has a cooking range. Well, it might need a dusting. It is peaceful and quiet up there and cooler than down here as well.'

"She nodded that she'd heard me. I had all day to rent a buckboard to take her out, buy a new starched white shirt, silk scarf, and vest. I drove over and walked up to the door, knocked, and the missus told me to come inside. Standing there was the prettiest girl I'd ever seen. The missus had Nell's hair fixed and had bought her a new dress. We went to supper at Nellie Cashman's famous restaurant, and I figure I was one leg up on convincing her I was damn serious."

"Tell him about the wedding," Dan said, grinning at Noble, who agreed. They'd heard the story already.

"I had been bringing the extra horse along for her to ride if she'd go back with me after we were married, of course."

Guthrey smiled. "You were ready."

"Damn right. And in six weeks she agreed for us to be married. I asked her if I needed a buckboard to take her home after we were married. She scoffed at the notion. Said she could ride a horse. She had so few things of her own that we didn't need a wagon."

"Guess you were about like I was last June — a little anxious." Guthrey shook his head, recalling those days.

"Yes, sir. But the preacher married us and we came out and I was going to boost her on her horse.

"Now, she had on a pretty wedding dress that Mrs. Neal and her husband had bought for her. She grasped the horn and flipped into the saddle. Perfect deal, but I guess the horse saw this flying white thing land on his back and he went to bucking. My heart stopped, and she flew off. We rushed down there to help her up and she was laughing.

" 'What's so funny?' I asked.

" 'I have never been thrown off a horse in my entire life. You go catch him.'

"And she did ride him that next time. I blamed the dress for not being the proper attire. But she sure got mad about being bucked off. We both laugh about it today."

"I can tell she's a great lady. You're a lucky man to have her."

Thayer agreed.

"Why are we going to Portal?"

"An Apache buck that Thayer knows, who we met on the trail, told him that the horses we were after had been over there. Thayer knows all them Apaches," Noble said.

Thayer agreed. "They all know Nell. They stop by for food and she feeds them. They have never taken a thing and I think I live in a safe place up there with them being around there like the wind. They come and go."

Guthrey smiled at him. "I don't know if anyone told you, Thayer, but you're one of the good guys."

"Aw, hell, I never figured I'd ever have a real wife. Nell is a wonderful woman and she fits in my life. You know what I mean."

"Yes, I do. I have one of my own at home."

Dan smiled and said, "Thayer, she about ran him off the day of my gun-fighting experience I told you about."

They all laughed and drank more coffee. Finally Guthrey paid for their meal and they found a place in the dry wash to spread out their blankets, and they hitched their horses, which had been grained and watered. There was no feed in the brush-choked canyon, so they tied the horses up. Then they slept till before sunup. Maria, the lady at the stage stop, had breakfast ready for them before they rode on.

When they headed east on Wednesday, they took off their badges and pocketed them, now being simply citizens looking for stolen horses. Everyone agreed. Activity at Fort Bowie was minimal and they hardly stopped except to water their horses at the fort's spring. By midday they were close to their goal. The Apache didn't know the names of the property owners near Portal, but he did make a map in the dirt that Dan copied. There were many small places in that country and they rode right up to the adobe house and corrals where the Apache had seen the horses. Dogs barked. A man came out, putting up his suspenders and unarmed.

"What'cha need?"

"Four stolen horses," Guthrey said. "Mind if we look?"

"They ain't here."

"Where did they go? They were here two days ago."

"Listen, I ain't no damn horse thief."

"Did I say that? We've rode several days and an eyewitness told us they were here."

"Who told you that?" The man scowled, looking them over.

"A reliable witness. Now where are they?"

"I ain't —"

Guthrey spurred the roan up against the man and he staggered back.

"What the hell are you doing?"

"I want an answer. Those horses were here. Who moved them?"

"You ain't the damn law. I don't have to tell you nothing."

"Do you like your teeth?"

"Sure, why?"

"How would you like them in your hand?"

"All right. All right. There were some horses — here earlier this week. How would I know they were stolen?"

"Who brought them here?"

"Two guys."

"What were their names?" Guthrey forced

the roan with his reins to confront the man.

"Wyllis Saddler and Guy Quinn."

"Where did they go?"

"New Mexico, I reckon."

"Where over there?"

"Lordsburg, hell, I don't know."

Guthrey reined the roan away from him. "You put up any more stolen horses and you will find yourself busting rocks in Yuma. You hear me?"

"Yeah." The man swallowed hard. "Who in the hell are you anyway?"

"My name's Phillip Guthrey. What's yours?"

"Norm Logan."

"Just remember, Norm Logan, where you'll be if you hide outlaws and stolen property."

"Yeah."

"Let's ride," Guthrey said to the others.

When they were headed back east, Dan rode in close to him, being certain they were out of the man's hearing. "We going to Lordsburg?"

Guthrey shook his head. "Too far and by now they ain't there either." He twisted in the saddle. "I'm sorry, Thayer, we tried."

"I understand. You've done all you could do. I sure appreciate you two as well."

"No." Guthrey shook his head disappointed. "But it will have to do."

They headed back toward home. Late the next day they parted with Thayer, rode the stagecoach road to Steward's Crossing, and got home past midnight.

Sleepy eyed and swinging a candle lantern, Cally welcomed them and said she had food if they wanted some. They gratefully accepted her offer. Guthrey hugged and kissed her as they went inside.

"I'd drop dead right here," he told her.

"I know you three must have gone to the ends of the earth. Did you get them?"

"No, they were gone to New Mexico."

The men ate cold brown beans and leftover corn bread, then Dan and Noble staggered off to the bunkhouse. Guthrey took a towel and soap to the shower. The water and air was cool by then and his shower was brief, but afterward he felt clean enough to share the bed with his lovely wife.

In their bed, he hugged and kissed her and then fell asleep.

She let him sleep in the next morning while she did her chores. About ten she made breakfast and rang the triangle. Dan and the old man stumbled in from the bunkhouse and Guthrey put on fresh clothes to join them.

"What next?" Dan asked.

"You two better check stock. I'm headed for the office and will try to be back here tonight."

With her slender butt against the dry sink, Cally went to pouring coffee. "You boys have some good meals on the road?"

"No," Dan said and they laughed.

Dan shook his head. "We never had time for anything but to ride and search. We invited people we met to come to the dance and so did your husband."

"We invited all of them to come up for the dance," Guthrey said. "Thayer's wife, Nell, was kidnapped in an Apache raid, married one, and when he got killed, she left them and walked back up here from way down in Mexico. He has a dandy story about courting her."

"You'd like her," Dan said. "I bet they come to the dance one Saturday night."

Guthrey and Noble agreed.

"That sounds neat," Cally said.

Guthrey said, "She's some gal. He said she got bucked off a horse in her wedding dress and was mad because she'd never been thrown before." He turned to Noble. "Do you know Mark Peters's wife?"

"Naw, I never knew her. They haven't been married for long. Why?"

"Well, she looks like someone I once met

or knew. I can't recall the meeting except she looked real familiar. Some people have mirror images. Maybe she does."

"He met her in Tucson, didn't he?" Cally said. "I'd heard of her."

"Yes, she said she was a widow. I never heard anyone say where she came from."

Noble shook his head. "I hadn't either."

"She may come to the dance too, you said," Dan put in.

"They all said they might. Now you have all the gossip we learned," Guthrey teased her and smiled.

"Will we go to the dance this week?" she asked.

"Certainly. I am going to check on things at Soda Springs and come right back."

"Good." She hugged his shoulder. "Nice to have you all back. I'll get busy and bake some pies."

"Whew, we sure saw lots of country not to have gotten them horses back. Those two that stole them went over into New Mexico and we quit. I don't like it one bit."

She nodded, understanding his concern. "Maybe they won't be back."

Guthrey stopped. "No. They got by with it once. I'd say they'll do it again."

After breakfast, he saddled a big bay ranch horse called Jim Green. He'd chuckled several times at what cowboys named horses in their remuda. Many times he'd picked a different name for the one he rode, but to the rest this horse would still be Jim Green. As Shorty Harris told him one time when he was Rangering down in the Waco area, "The damn horse won't come when you call it by it anyway."

Jim Green had a running walk he could hold all day. And he always shortened the ride over to town and back. So Guthrey set out and arrived in midafternoon.

Things must be quiet. Teddy Baker was behind the desk and reading wanted posters. He stood up and shook Guthrey's hand. "How are you doing? We had word you'd gone fishing."

"I wish." Guthrey laughed. "Thayer, a rancher in the Dragoons, had four horses stolen. Dan, Noble, and I rode our butts off over to a place the other side of the Chiricahuas called Portal. They'd gone on to New Mexico. So we came back."

"He's the man that married the woman that was an Apache hostage and she walked, I heard, on foot all the way back from the Sierra Madres."

"Yes. Nice lady. What's happening around here?"

"Some big outfit bought the Whitmore

84

Ranch, or they said they did. The ramrod is pretty much a big mouth. His name is Walter Pierson. He came in here demanding to see you and said the small ranchers were eating his beef and he wanted it stopped. I asked him if he had any proof and he simply went on talking about what he was going to do to them, spouting off about running the other ranchers out or shutting them down. I simply told him there was law here and he was not the judge or jury. I don't think he liked it, but I think we have more trouble — like you had before."

"Should have put him in a box and shipped him back to where he came from."

"I damn sure wanted to. I have the funeral home report on the Carlson bodies."

Guthrey took it from him and read the report. The missus died from being beaten over the head with a club. George Carlson died from two .44 bullets in his chest. The girl had been raped and smothered to death. The paper had been signed by the doctor and funeral man. They'd done a thorough job.

He put the paper down. "I have a boot print of a large boot. It's a real big one. And a goatskin glove with a star on it drawn with indelible ink."

The glove, retrieved from Guthrey's vest

pocket, he handed to Baker, who examined it. "Nice job of sewing it. The woman who made that was a real craftsman. You know anyone makes them like that?"

"No, but we need to find her if she's in the area. You think a woman made it?"

Baker nodded. "Those small stitches took lots of care and time. We'll find the maker if she's around here, plus she hand worked lots of sheep fat in that leather to ever get it that soft."

"She's probably made hundreds and she won't recall him, but the star may be a lead. Put it in the file as evidence in those murder cases. We don't have much to go on, but killers slip up. I sure want them in jail before they kill any more."

"The county board finally hired a man to build the scaffold."

"Good. You and Zamora be sure it's solid. I knew a Texas sheriff had one built and when all of them got up there to hang a man, the damn thing collapsed. The sheriff broke his leg and the prisoner got away. Don't ask me how; I wasn't there. But it was supposed to have happened."

"It will be secure."

"Keep an eye and ear on this Walter Pierson. He starts running over small ranchers, I'll run him out on a rail."

Baker agreed.

"I'm going to the dance tomorrow night with my wife, and plan to have a leisurely day Sunday at the ranch with her, but don't hesitate to send word if you need me."

Guthrey rode back to the ranch and arrived before sundown. His wife rushed out and tackled him. A long ways from the straight-backed young lady he'd met here months ago. Short of flattening him, she let go, rose up, and kissed him, as excited as a yearling filly colt. Whew, he never expected his married life to be such fun. Noble took the horse and the infatuated newlyweds went to the porch, both ignoring the rest, they were so concentrated on each other.

"Tell me about what you found," she said.

He put his hat on her head, rolled up his sleeves, and washed his hands in the enamel washbasin. Then he took a towel down and mopped his face and dried his hands.

"Let's see. Someone stole Mrs. Gunzo's best fighting rooster."

Cally laughed. "Did your deputies apprehend him?"

"I don't think so but they are hot on his trail."

"Good."

"On the other side, between Doc and the funeral director, they issued a report on the

87

murders. And some company must have bought the Whitmore Ranch. Their supervisor came in raising hell, saying that folks were eating his beef. His name is Walter Pierson. Teddy Baker wished he'd stayed in hell."

"Will he be like Whitmore?"

"Not for very long. I won't put up with him."

She hugged his arm when he hung the towel on the nail. He raised the hat brim on her head and kissed her. "Good to see you. Maybe we can have some peace this weekend."

She smiled. "I hope so."

She put food out for him and apologized for it being cold. Then she hung his hat on the rack and joined him. "Our guys thought everything was fine up range. They're going west tomorrow to check, then ride up to the dance, and Noble's coming back to milk the cow in the morning. He has a tent for us in the buckboard if that's okay?"

"Okay? That sounds wonderful to me."

"You sure are easy to please, Phil."

"Why not? I have a wonderful, hardworking wife. I simply appreciate you. I have been at so many houses in my life where the woman whines at her husband about the damnedest things. Maybe that's why I never married until I got you."

"Aw, I'm just proud we have each other."

"Let me sneak out and shower and shave, and then we can go to bed."

She winkled her nose. "I am so anxious for you I don't know if I can wait."

"Lordy, girl, then let's go to bed."

She laughed. "Wonderful."

He wiped his mouth, closed his eyes. He needed to write his sister in Texas. Bonny would never believe he'd found a wife. He swept Cally up and kissed her, then they ran off to the bedroom for more honeymoon time.

Six

They drove the buckboard leisurely over to the schoolhouse. Guthrey tied his Roman-nosed horse on behind, just in case. At the schoolyard he helped Cally down and then up set the tent. She carried her food dishes up to the table inside and covered them with cheesecloth. He unsaddled his horse and studied the clouds building in the south. By the time he had the three animals on the hitch line, he could feel and smell the rain coming in.

When Cally came out to check on him, she frowned at the approaching storm. "It may rain here."

"I think it will. We should go inside the schoolhouse. Folks are coming in and some will drink coffee if you make it."

"Sounds good. It's thundering hard down there."

"It sure is. I'll get our slickers in case we need to go outside."

"Good idea." She took her ground coffee, a can of milk, and some sugar, and they went inside the building.

"Heck, it's going to rain here in a short while," a large woman named Beulah said, joining them. "Sure enough I do believe it will storm here in a little bit." She took some things from Cally to help her. "That will be a great thing to have some coffee. You sure came prepared."

Guthrey hung their slickers on the wall pegs as others hurried inside and the blowing dust swept in. It would rain mud first, and the hope was that the rain following would wash it off again. Lightning cracked close by and more folks burst through the doors to escape the strikes.

Heavy rain and some small hail plinked on the shake roof, then the storm opened up in full force. The heavy downpour would make many usual dry wash crossings dangerously flooded.

"I hope this doesn't keep too many away," Cally said over the roar. She and the other women were putting out empty open tin cans under where the roof leaked. Nothing severe for all the force of the rain, but several cans soon plinked with water falling in them. Guthrey recalled enduring such storms in the Indian Territory and Kansas when he used to drive cattle north. They were sure hard on exposed cowboys trying to hold herds or make them move in formation to keep down any chance of a stampede. Another lightning blast shook the building. They could always use rain but he preferred gentler forms. He hugged Cally's shoulders.

"It will be over soon and wrung out. But this is a tough one."

With a smile for him, she said, "We needed it."

"I could have taken it in smaller doses."

They both laughed. In another half hour the storm moved away and the wet attendees arrived. They included Dan and Noble under slickers, but their felt hats weighed a ton.

Folks talked about how much rain fell. One man had two inches in a pail.

Dan said they had lots of rain at the ranch. That relieved Guthrey. Many such showers passed over a limited area and left many without any moisture.

Good, the monsoons have started. Guthrey just hoped they didn't end too quickly so the six-week grasses would pop up and there'd be a carpet of wildflowers. Those were the good summers in the desert. He visited with some ranchers in a corner of the big room.

"I heard Whitmore's bunch sold out and some big company bought the ranch."

Guthrey nodded. "The new superintendent is Walter Pierson. He's been to the county seat and complained to my deputy Teddy Baker that small ranchers were eating his beef."

"Maybe his cattle are eating their grass," one man suggested.

Guthrey nodded. "My man told him that we would not accept any harassment of ranchers. Enforcing the law is our job."

Heads nodded.

"I hope he listens," one rancher said.

"We won't allow him not to." Guthrey's eyes narrowed. "Anyone tries to cause trouble I'll meet them head on. That's my job."

One man spoke up, saying, "Thanks. We count on you."

"Hey, we've had a good rain. Let's have fun tonight. This new bunch will obey the law or rot in jail."

They dispersed and Guthrey went to join Cally.

"Problems?" she asked.

"They're upset about the new company moving in."

She frowned at him. "You can't stop that?"

"No, but I will watch them close."

Satisfied, she nodded and took his arm. "We'll have a nice crowd despite the rain."

"I think you will have when they all get here."

"I do too." Then she went to oversee more table settings for the dishes of food coming in.

Guthrey shook some hands and whiled away the afternoon talking to new people and old about things happening in the area. The atmosphere in the county sounded much calmer than it had been when Guthrey took over as sheriff, but he knew that was because his men answered requests and investigated all reported crimes.

Stage robberies had moved over into the adjoining county. Pima County was headquartered at Tucson, and Guthrey had talked to both the U.S. marshal and the sheriff about the men responsible for the robberies. Personally, he suspected it was a secret band of outlaws. But most holdups occurred on that side of the county line. At the U.S. marshal's suggestion, Guthrey had his men and even the tax auditors keeping an eye out to see if the outlaws were hiding in Crook County. They had to have a hideout to operate so successfully.

Wells Fargo had as many as three armed

men on the stages to discourage the outlaws. But that also was a flag pointing out the value of the strongboxes on board. Guthrey had no idea who the robbers were or where they hid, but he and his men had an ear to the ground. Someone would give them a lead.

The evening meal went well and more people arrived, celebrating the rain event. The instrument players began with a waltz, and Guthrey took his wife floating across the floor. His chest swelled with pride when he danced with her. Crook County had served him well, with a wife and a job in law enforcement in the place where he wanted to be and felt the most satisfied. He needed to face the fact that leaving the Texas Rangers did not diminish his desire to be sure things were fair and legal.

When the dance was over, they retired to their tent. They basked in their lovemaking on the narrow cot and finally fell asleep. When Guthrey awoke and went outside, the cool predawn swept his face. Folks were beginning to stir. They needed to get back home. There'd been no drunken altercations the night before, which made him feel even better. He didn't know how long it would last, but it sure had been peaceful.

They arrived home midmorning on Sunday. He unloaded their gear and cleaned his guns after lunch. Things were almost too quiet. Dan rode off to see someone female and Noble caught up on his sleep in the bunkhouse. In the afternoon it showered more over by the Chiricahuas. But the storm swung northeast and Guthrey watched the tall thunderheads sail away in the distance.

"Noble, can you think of a hideout or old ranch where those stage robbers might be located?"

"There are some places scattered west of us that are like where we burned that ramada. Several folks gave up on ranching or their wells went dry and they just moved away, abandoning them. That country is harsher than this area. Gets less rain too."

"You think the Pima County bunch looked at all of them?"

"No. They do more tax work than being lawmen, to my notion. Oh, they do some police work but that isn't their main goal."

"Why don't you and I swing up through there and see what we can find on our side of the line this coming week?"

"Good idea."

"There's a reason they aren't robbing stages on our side of the line. I think we may be able to stop it."

"No telling. What's the plan?"

"In the morning we'll go over to Soda Springs and check with my bunch, then we can ride around and see these old ranches. Maybe take a packhorse and swing back on Wednesday and come home Thursday. Would that be all right, Cally?"

"I guess. If you two can root out one more bunch of outlaws it will be a safer place to live. Both of you be careful. I am counting on you."

"Yes, ma'am."

Their plans made, they left before dawn to check things out. Guthrey found Soda Springs quiet and Zamora told him they'd had no big crimes. He'd inquired with several folks about a good glove maker and had no answer. Maybe she was down at Nogales or Tucson. Baker planned to write the sheriff in Tucson and ask if he knew of anyone. Wherever she was, she would be sought after, as good as that glove was made.

After lunch, they headed into the mountains north for a place called the Devil's Ranch and found it deep in a canyon. They approached it with care, but anyone could have heard the ring of their horseshoes on the rock-floored canyon. The steep mountainsides above them were covered in talus rock — flat loose rocks all over the slopes to the peaks.

Some cottonwoods and a few palm trees marked the setting. A palm frond–covered ramada had once served as the house. There were no horses or signs of human inhabitance as they searched the place. Guthrey was ready to scratch it off his list.

Noble came riding back. "There's a grave beyond the corral. It looks fresh. You think we should check it out? I think whoever was here didn't use the corral so no one would know they'd been here."

"You're thinking they never used the corrals or the shade?"

"Yeah," Noble said. "They tied their horses up way over there where the horse apples are fresher."

When Guthrey saw the fresh dirt mound, he wondered who was planted there. "I hate to dig up a body that's been dead awhile, but I guess we better to try and identify it."

The dirt was loose and they used their short camp shovel. But finally they needed their bandana face masks as the copper and sour stink of the decomposing body became evident. Taking turns with the short-handled shovel, they soon unearthed a man, and when Guthrey saw the size of his boots, he knew they had come from the murder scene. The dead man's face had been obliterated by several shots of a large-caliber pistol at close range. At the sight of him, Guthrey knew the unknown corpse was one of the Carlson killers.

They bound his remains in a blanket of the least value they had and tied him on the unloaded packhorse. Guthrey said he'd take him back to Soda Springs and return here in the morning. Noble never argued when they parted and Guthrey headed for the county seat.

Past sundown, he arrived at the Combs Funeral Home and woke the attendant, who was already asleep. The two carried the smelly corpse inside and the young man promised to get Guthrey an autopsy report. Guthrey left him, went to the office, and wrote a note instructing the day deputies to try to learn the dead man's identity, since he could be one of the Carlsons' murderers.

Hard to escape the smell of death; the odor had saturated him and his clothing. He arrived past midnight back at the Devil's Ranch.

Noble woke up and greeted him. "You eat anything?"

"No, I'll have some jerky. I haven't wanted to eat much, as bad as I stink."

"It sure ain't a pleasant odor." Noble

shook his head.

"How far are we from any other old ranch? I wonder why they chose to shoot him here, or bury him here anyway."

"They stayed away from the ramada and pens. But I almost forgot, I found a note up there near that grave. I jammed it in my pocket at the time but you need to read it."

Guthrey frowned. "What does it say?"

"It's a receipt for some goatskin gloves. They cost twelve dollars a pair and Ramona Garcia made them. The man bought them in June. No address. But we know a helluva lot more than we did."

"That's great. This man's big feet and the glove are about all I have. Does Ramona Garcia sound familiar to you?" Guthrey lit a stub of a candle to read the note and then agreed it was more evidence.

"Only the Ramona part sounds familiar to me," Noble said. "I once knew a Mexican woman by that name who treated horny cowboys."

They both laughed.

"She was married to a man who repaired saddles in his shop. But she earned her money repairing ranch hands." Noble slapped his knees and laughed. "I'm certain the glove maker and her are not the same one."

"But we have a name, and someone will know of her."

A coyote yapped on the mountainside. Another answered and the cricket chorus chirped away in the star-filled night. Guthrey went to sleep pleased that they had more evidence on the grim murders. His hope was restored; someday they'd solve the case and arrest the killer or killers. Then he slept, missing his wife's warmness to cuddle with.

Seven

Another isolated ranch they rode up to at midday hosted a Mexican man and his family. His name was Guermo Diaz, and his very pregnant wife was named Deloris. They had three small children and had carefully raised a small garden with limited spring-water.

"Is this your ranchero?" Guermo asked him.

"No." Guthrey shook his head at the man.

"Can I stay here? I have no work. I have no place. When I found this place I tell Deloris it will feed us."

"I'm Sheriff Guthrey. As I said, no, I don't own it. But I can see you two have worked hard here. I see the garden is doing well. My wife at our ranch could use you, and then you'd have a job and we could find you a house, I am certain." He drew them a map in the dirt of how to get there. Guermo nodded that he could find the place.

"Don't try to go until the baby is born. The job will be open for you."

"*Muchas gracias,* Senor Guthrey." His dark-faced wife hugged his arm and acted excited standing beside him as he shook Guthrey's hand.

"Have you seen any strange men around here lately?"

Guermo's face had a look like he was considering something. "Three men came by here last week. They asked me lots of questions like they owned this place."

"What did they look like?"

"One was a giant of a man. He was like a big bear. The redheaded guy was the boss and he kept looking at my wife. He worried me."

"Were there more?"

"A Mexican boy was their slave. I only know they called him bad names."

"This redheaded man was how tall?" Guthrey's mind sharpened at the challenge.

"Taller than you, senor."

"He was an *hombre muy malo,*" his wife said and shook her head as if she was still wary of him.

"Had he ever been by here before?"

"No and I hope he never comes back."

"Be careful. Those men are killers of innocent people."

"*Sí*, we will. *Muchas gracias,* we will be anxious to work for you, senor."

Guthrey almost hated to leave them, but he wanted to go cross-country and get home. His clothes still stunk of the dead man. At last they had a suspect — a red-headed man and his slave.

He told them, "We're going home. You be careful getting to my place."

"Ah, *sí,* senor, we will work hard for you."

Guthrey and Noble arrived back at the Bridges Ranch after sundown. Cally must have hurried and dressed, 'cause she came hard on the run to hug him.

"Maybe not," he cautioned her when she was within six feet of him.

"Oh, you do smell bad but I have missed you." She snuggled up and hugged him anyway. "What is that terrible odor?"

"We had to dig up a man's corpse and take it back to town."

"Oh, that sounds horrible. Have you eaten?"

"No, ma'am. I'm sure glad you asked," Noble said.

"I will get you two some soap and clean clothes. Then I'll fix you some food, all right?"

"Fine," Guthrey said. "Oh, I hired you a

nice man and his wife. They'll come when she has her baby. His name is Guermo Diaz and her name's Deloris. They've been subsisting on an old abandoned ranch but they will work."

Noble agreed. "They really are hard workers."

"I don't need any help," Cally said, sticking her heels in the ground at the notion.

"Yes, you do. And we can afford it."

"Well, sheriff, I'll go get your clothes and soap."

Noble said softly, "I figured she'd be happy about them coming to help her."

"I knew she'd rebel. She wants to do it all herself." They both laughed.

"Yeah, you can't never tell about a woman, kin ya?"

"In all your years on this earth you finally figured that out?" Guthrey asked as they headed for the house.

Noble was laughing too hard to answer him. He simply nodded.

After his shower, Guthrey joined Cally at the house and Noble came in a short while later.

She made them pancakes and fried up some ham. After pouring them coffee, she swept her dress under and sat down. "Now tell me about the dead man."

"We found a fresh grave on this abandoned ranch and wondered who was in it. We dug up a big man who we figure was one of those on the scene of the murders. I knew it would be bad, but Noble will tell you it was even worse. His body is at the funeral home now and I hope to get it identified."

"This is one of the men who killed those poor Carlsons?"

"Yes, I had his boot print. We have a description of the gang leader too."

Cally shook her head at them. "You two are regular detectives."

"We also found the name of a woman who may have made that glove I found on the scene."

"So watch out for any redheaded stranger. He may be the killer," Noble said.

"Do you think he might come here?" She frowned at them.

"Darling, I hope not. But he slips around, Noble will tell you. The only people who have seen him that we know about are that Mexican couple. Just be aware."

She agreed. "Any more word on that new superintendent at the former Whitmore Ranch?"

"We've been in the talus looking for those

killers, so we haven't heard anything. If there has been no word from my deputies, I guess Pierson thought better than to tell them what he'd do again."

She scowled. "I bet he tries to push people out like Whitmore did."

"They still have rooms available at Yuma."

She laughed and clapped his shoulder. "My husband has hotel rooms down there, doesn't he?"

Noble looked up and smiled. "He made sure near all of that bunch was sent down there. Those law clerks told me he had a record number of convictions on that roundup of criminals in this county."

"I didn't do too bad, then, marrying him?" Cally shook her head and smiled.

"You did terrible," Guthrey teased and squeezed her arm.

Frowning, she shook her head. "You are the best, and I am proud to be your wife."

He leaned over and kissed her. "As long as you are."

"I'm going to bed," Noble said. "What are we doing tomorrow?"

"Is Dan here?" Guthrey asked Cally.

She shook her head. "He's supposed to be back early."

Guthrey nodded. "If he's still alive then, why don't you two take the north range and check stock."

"I'll do that even if he can't."

Guthrey nodded again. "In the morning I'll go make certain things at the office are all right, and try to be back for supper."

"Do we need to move down there?" Cally asked.

"Not yet. This is your home and Dan needs you."

"Not much." She made a face. "I hate all the traveling you have to do."

"I always have you when I get back."

Dawn came early. Guthrey set out for Steward's Crossing first to check with his deputy Ike Sweeney and be sure he didn't need any help. The man was a solid veteran of law enforcement, but one never knew what could spring up in this job.

In the cool morning air, Guthrey found Sweeney in his usual spot, on his porch in a rocker, drinking coffee. His pleasant wife, Myrna, who came to the door, went after a cup of coffee for him.

"How are things going?"

"Peaceful. I've arrested a drunk or two when they get too wild. The justice of the peace fines them or makes them work around town and they soon settle down. What do you have?"

"There's a murderer on the loose. Killed a family up north a week ago. The suspect has red hair, medium build, and has a Mexican boy who they say is his slave."

"I got a report from Baker about that crime and read the newspaper. How did you find this suspect?"

"We dug up a dead man over at an abandoned ranch up north of Soda Springs. I think he was at the murder scene. Bad deal, but his boots fit our prints from the scene."

Sweeney frowned. "Dug him up?"

"Yes, a real bad deal, but we wondered who was buried in that grave and we found him. I can still smell it."

"Anyone know who he was?"

"I'm headed over to Soda Springs to see if anyone recognized him."

"This redhead didn't have a name either?"

"No. I suspect the killer was a fringe rider."

"He shows up, I'll send word."

"Good. But remember he's a killer, so don't risk your life. I never saw the like of the scene we found up there. I won't ever forget it."

"I'll poke around. See if someone's seen him or knows where he's sleeping."

"Don't try to take him by yourself. Wire for help if you get a lead."

Sweeney agreed and Guthrey rode on after thanking the deputy's wife, who asked to feed him.

At the sheriff's office, Zamora was behind the desk, sorting wanted posters that came in the mail.

"How are things going?" Guthrey asked him.

"Oh, fine. Pretty damn quiet. Do you know Sammy Enrico in Tucson?"

"No, who is he?"

"I think he's with that Tucson Ring you told us about when we first came over here."

"What's he doing?"

"I don't know, but he was in town for two days this week holding meetings with some suspicious people."

"Who were they?"

"A guy named Ryles was one of them."

"What does Ryles do?"

"I think he's a lookout. He gambles some. Close-chested kind of guy, but he knows lots about what's going on. He may work for the ring as a front man."

"Maybe we need to run him out of town as undesirable."

Zamora nodded. "Baker and I will look for an excuse. How's that?"

Guthrey was pleased. "Good idea. In

Tombstone they may have to put up with them. We don't answer to mine companies here. We answer to citizens. Any identification on the corpse we brought in?"

Zamora handed Guthrey a page of paper. It was from the funeral man Combs.

The victim had been shot twice in the face with .45-caliber bullets at close range. He had been dead for some time before being dug up. I wired ahead to Tucson, and Sheriff Ramos reported by wire to me that he thought the corpse belonged to a Johnny Cord. He was a small-time thief and was wanted for various crimes in his district. Associated with known criminals, like Clell House and Knute Yarman.

Zamora pulled out all the wanted posters for those two and spread them on the desk. House's and Yarman's descriptions — no red hair — made Guthrey shake his head.

"That rules those two out."

"We'll start checking for a guy with red hair."

"Good. Warn everyone that he's dangerous and not to try to arrest him by themselves. Right now he's only a suspect for us. But there are enough charges that we can arrest him and hold him for Sheriff Ramos."

"We'll watch for him."

"I'm making rounds. Things are quiet, so that's good. I may slip off for a few days with my wife to Mount Graham. Noble will know where I'm at."

"Escape the heat, huh?"

"It's cool up there, that's for sure. Did you have any luck on a spy system to warn us if a Mexican gang is coming out of there?"

"No, but I wrote to a man I know who is on the Santa Cruz County Sheriff's staff down there at Nogales. He may have an answer."

"Good idea. I'll head back home. Can Baker hold the justice of the peace inquest on both the murders and this other guy — Johnny Cord?"

"Baker's preparing it and told me he figured he'd get the job."

"Tell him thanks. We've covered lots of ground here in a short time. I think people are pleased, but only if we can hold our place."

"We will."

"I'm counting on everyone."

He rode back to the ranch and his bright-faced wife met him at the corral while he unsaddled.

"Good to have you back so soon. All is well?"

"Fine. Maybe we can go up on the mountain this week."

"Good. We can go over and talk to the Nelsons about it and see if the cabin is available."

"I'll hitch the team."

"No, let's eat supper. We can check in the morning."

"Fine." He hugged her. "Tomorrow is fine."

To sleep with his wife in his own bed was relaxing and he was up at dawn. He walked around the house and saw a saddled horse in the dim light and a figure lying on the ground.

He squatted down beside the body under the starlight and could see it was Dan. He was breathing but his breath smelled like whiskey. Guthrey rubbed his own shirtsleeves in the cool predawn. He shook Dan's shoulder.

"Huh? What'cha want?"

"I think you better get up and go sleep in the bunkhouse."

"I'm fine here. Leave me alone."

Guthrey got under his arm and hauled him to his feet. Then he half carried him to the bunkhouse, with a staggering Dan complaining all the way. The door was open and, once inside, Guthrey propelled him facedown on top of the cot.

"Where did you find him?" Noble asked, sitting up in bed.

"Sleeping out in the yard."

"Aw, hell, that boy has lost it."

"I better tell Cally."

"Might break her heart."

Guthrey agreed but didn't see a way around it. He went and caught Dan's horse, unsaddled him, and put him in the corral. Then he went back to the house and washed his hands on the porch.

"Anything wrong?" Cally asked.

"Dan made it home."

She frowned at him. "What?"

"He made it back and was sleeping on the ground out there."

"Oh my, Phil, whatever is wrong with him?"

"He must be on a drinking deal."

"Why? Dad's death has been resolved. Whitmore is in prison. We have a good future."

"Cally, why most people drink is never simple, but mostly they do it to escape reality."

"Reality. We aren't filthy rich but we do have money. We have no obvious enemies

114

trying to run us off our land. I wish Dad was here to see all this."

"Morning, Cally," Noble said, coming in and putting his hat on the wall.

"Good morning. Is Dan all right?"

"Snoring when I left him."

"Thanks."

"Noble, do you know of anything wrong in his life?"

He shook his head, taking his place at the table. "Except he's not happy."

"What could change that?" she asked.

"Oh, Cally, I don't know. Things like that are like worms inside a person. You can't see them but they roll around inside of them."

"Phil, what's your best idea?"

"Keep him busy. He acted pleased with things when we were with Thayer looking for the horse thieves."

"But we don't have jobs like that all the time," Noble said.

"You're saying we need to keep him occupied?" Cally asked, filling coffee cups while the rich aroma of her breakfast cooking filled the house.

"I'm afraid it's more complicated than that," Guthrey said. "I'll talk to him."

"Good." Cally went to setting plates of food before them. "You two eat. Biscuits are coming next."

After breakfast, they drove over to the Nelsons' ranch to see about the cabin. Thomas's wife, Ruth, welcomed them. Thomas was out working cattle, and Guthrey and Cally spoke to her about using the cabin.

"Lord yes, Cally. We can't go up there anytime soon. We're too shorthanded right now. Our best ranch hand broke his leg and is laid up. Thomas won't leave the place till he's able to get around."

"We better go home and pack," Cally said. "Before he changes his mind."

Loaded up after breakfast the next morning, Guthrey and Cally left the ranch to Noble and Dan. The drive was a hot one until they were halfway up Mount Graham. Cooler winds felt good on Guthrey's face as he reined the team around curves and the altitude increased. By late afternoon they were at the snug cabin. He unloaded Cally and kissed her hard. Then they took the food and supplies inside. Enjoying the late afternoon wind in each other's arms, they were content in their own company. Two hearts beating that close together and enjoying the intimate pleasures of marriage were their rewards.

"Should we go to bed?" he asked.

"I am so glad you asked me." Then she laughed, trying to tickle him. He was complete with this young woman nestled in his life.

EIGHT

Vacations always end. When the weekend was over, Guthrey and Cally drove back down to the desert heat that hit them in face with oven-hot winds. She kissed him on the cheek when they reached the bottom and hung on to her straw hat when a small dust devil passed close by.

"I guess that was the chaparral welcoming committee." She laughed. "Hard to believe a few hours ago it was so cool up there. The Apaches used to live up on those mountains and the others when it got hot in the summertime."

He'd heard and understood that was their way of life, interrupted by the white man's push to the Pacific Ocean. And the Apaches were in that path. The white man called it progress; the red man called it intrusion. That war was still going on. With so many soldiers stationed on the border, the Apaches did not even consider going back and forth from here to the Sierra Madres down in Mexico. They still posed a danger to white people, but so far incidents had been minimal, except for the theft of horses. But that was an ongoing problem with white men and Mexicans as well.

Guthrey's return meant he needed to check on things across the district in the morning. Time to get back to work, and he wanted be sure everything was secure in Crook County. They arrived in mid-afternoon at the ranch. Cally opened all the windows and mentioned it would be nice to have a squaw shade someday to live under in the hot weather and give them more airing out, plus the thick shade would stop some of the sun's intensity on the hottest days.

"That's all some folks have for a house," he said, hauling inside the things they brought back.

"I don't think I'd want to winter in one," she said. "I'd be under the covers all the time."

"That would be where I'd find you, huh?"

"Oh, Phil, that sounds bad."

"Where's my wife? Oh, I know, under the snow-covered blankets in the squaw shade."

"That's right. Was that thunder?"

"Yes, I think so. We may have a good rain

coming. I watched those clouds gathering all day coming home."

"We can use it for sure."

"I'll unhitch the team and put off going into Steward's Crossing if we're going to have some rain."

"Probably two inches," she said, busy getting ready to cook supper. "Two drops apart, huh?"

"Oh, one can be hopeful. Could we hire someone to build the shade? We can afford to hire a builder."

She agreed. "I'm certain I could find someone. If you want one, we can get one built by fall anyway."

"Good," he said.

"You spoil me. I can recall counting my money just to buy groceries when Dad was alive. Between the gold and your cattle sale, we can do what we want."

"We're past that."

"Worked out well. That is a big concern, making enough income to survive. Have you ever thought about another ranch? I think in time my brother will settle down and he can expand this one. I'd hate to move anywhere, but I know when you marry a man, you belong where he belongs. I worry about you making so many trips to be certain that things are being handled right over west in Soda Springs."

"I stay over there in that place I bought for me and Noble. That's all we need for now."

"When you get time, tell me the plans you have for us in the future."

"Aw, Cally, I share my life with you."

She fell in his arms and he knew she was crying. Things one minute were fine, then sad thoughts must have swept her. He'd never hoarded any secrets from her. Holding her weight in his arms, he realized some of her efforts to please him left him seeming outside her reach. He'd have to do better whenever the hell he figured out what was really upsetting his wife.

"I'm sorry, Phil. I guess things must be balled up inside me. I missed my monthly session this week. It may be late or going to happen, but I . . . well, I may be pregnant. Too early to tell but —" She chewed on her lower lip. "That's what we wanted, wasn't it?"

"Oh yes. Has that been bothering you? That I wouldn't accept a child?"

She crushed his head to her chest. "No, no, I just didn't know how to tell you we might have one."

"My lord, I am excited. You need to see a doctor?"

"No. Not yet anyway."

"Wow."

"I may only be late. But I can count and it may be or may not."

Thunder sounded like artillery. It even shook the dishes in the cabinets on the wall, and the smell of rain swept over them, followed by the pounding of hard drops of rain on the shake roof.

He hugged and kissed Cally, rocking her back and forth and feeling more happy than he could ever recall. The sound of the storm grew greater, like an angry woman fighting a swarm of hornets with a broom.

She peeked out at him. "I wonder where Dan and Noble are at."

"Probably heading in and looking like drowned rats or maybe holed up under some roof someplace watching the water flood off eaves." There was more roaring outside and strikes of lightning. Cally managed to close two windows where the rain was blowing inside.

Then she got busy making coffee and lighting a lamp before she filled two cups on the table. Looking recovered, she took the pot back to her stove. The rain-cooled air made her scrub at her arms. "Cold feels good anyway."

Guthrey agreed, blowing on the surface to

cool the coffee enough to sip on. Still too hot. The rain continued. The clouds must have parked over their ranch. Good, it would refill the tanks and bring on some quick forage. And they might be parents next spring — it was bound to happen with a man and woman. And the notion pleased him.

Next morning he headed for Steward's Crossing before the purple-pink outline of the sun came up from behind the Chiricahuas. The air felt cool and the rain had settled the dust. In places it was even muddy. Neither Dan nor Noble had come into the house that evening on their return, and Guthrey and Cally discovered, before dark, the cow wasn't bawling because the men had turned her calf in with her. But they never left a note. It was too late then to know where they'd gone, but Guthrey expected to find them in town or at the county seat. Something had to have come up to draw them away like that. Guthrey simply didn't know what.

In Steward's Crossing, he found his deputy Sweeney again on his front porch drinking coffee in the big rocker. Guthrey dismounted, and Sweeney's wife must have heard him talking to her man because she brought him some coffee.

"Noble and Dan are gone. You know where they went?"

"There was a stage robbery yesterday on this side of the Pima County line in that dry wash. They shot the guard, and Baker sent me word to send you word. I went up there and told them two. They said not to bother you, that you were up on the mountain with your wife, resting."

Guthrey narrowed his eyes, listening to his man. "They went off to see about it?"

"I couldn't stop them —"

"Here, take my coffee. I better go see where they went." He also thanked Myrna as he was leaving.

He unhitched his horse, swung into the saddle with a hold on the horn, then sent him off in a lope for Soda Springs, shouting thanks to the two openmouthed people on the porch.

No telling what those two were up to. Chasing outlaws and him not there. Noble was an old veteran, but Dan was the one who couldn't keep the gun in his holster seven months ago. Maybe longer than that, there was no telling. Anyone desperate enough to hold up a stagecoach and shoot a guard was liable to be too tough for those boys to handle.

He reached Soda Springs and rushed into the courthouse. Zamora was already there behind the desk.

"Where are the boys? Noble and Dan."

"They're after those bandits. Baker went with them. They thought they might catch them."

"Where were they headed?"

"I think north."

There wasn't much north Guthrey could think of except the Apaches. Zamora shook his head. "That's all we know. Of course, they could have circled back. This time the robbers got lots of money and gold coins, I understand. I thought you might be with the Wells Fargo men. They always rush in and out. Did you have a nice break on the mountain?"

"It was cool and peaceful. Not one horse was stolen up there while I was on the mountain."

"Great. I can't say that about down here."

They both laughed.

"So how will I find their trail?"

"Ask Tom Aiken at the livery. He rode some of the way with them yesterday and came back late last night."

"I'll check with him. Take care of things here. I'm going to try to catch them. Send word to my wife I am going after them. I'll be home when I find them or they come back."

"I can do that. I'm sorry, someone needed to stay here."

"You did the right thing. I'm glad Baker is with them. We need to maintain this office. Having a sheriff means we have a place people can go to report crimes to the legal arm of this county."

"Baker and I had talked about that too."

"I'm headed for the livery and will ride on. Thanks."

He spoke briefly to Tommy Glendon at the telegraph key. There were no messages concerning the holdup. He left the county building to find Aiken in his livery office. The man was going over his books at a desk.

"Oh, sheriff, have you heard from your deputies?"

"No, where did you leave them yesterday?"

"Almost San Carlos. They had the robbers' trail and those outlaws had a pack train to haul the gold coins. That slowed them down some. But it was no small deal. They had military-like precision. They sure knew what the hell they were doing."

He heard the man's words. Obviously Aiken had seen enough to be impressed by what he saw. *No simple bank robbers.* That made him shiver despite the one-hundred-plus degree heat. If they were ex-military men, they knew how to ambush anyone trailing them.

Where in hell could they go in that direction? Word would get out. They were too obvious. He'd have to trade this horse for another en route — he must push hard to catch his men and hope he reached them in time.

NINE

As day faded into night, Guthrey crossed into the San Carlos drainage. The bay had weakened by morning, when Guthrey saw a ranch in the early light. He headed for the headquarters, and a woman outside the house shouted. Soon a man with a rifle appeared.

He reined up the bay and shouted, "I'm the sheriff."

"Come on in. We're just jumpy." The man set aside his rifle. "I'm Tad Bowlin. My wife, Esther. What are you doing out here?"

"Two days ago, there was a stage robbery, and three of my men are trailing the outlaws." Riding up, he'd looked over the man's horse stock and they looked as weary as his horse was. There were none in his corral worth considering a trade.

"Yeah, they came by here. Name of Baker, an old man called Noble, and a boy named Dan."

"When were they here?"

"Yesterday. They're about a day behind the robbers they want was how I figured it."

Guthrey frowned at the man. "You saw the gang too?"

He nodded. "Oh yeah. They're a tough bunch. I thought they were an army unit when they rode up and helped themselves to watering their stock. But I went into the house with Esther and barred the doors when I figured out they weren't that. My old rock house has held off Apaches. I was concerned that they might blow us up, but after they watered their stock and fed them out of my grain bin, they simply rode off instead. My woman and me were ready to blow them up. I have explosives planted all over the place, and in a case like that I could of blown them up."

"Shame you didn't," Guthrey said. "Get any names?"

"One's called Clancy."

"Anyone else?" he asked the man's silent wife with the gray-streaked hair.

A drab-looking woman in her thirties wearing a wash-worn dress, she said, "Lane was another name. I was so scared. My hands on that rifle were wet from fear. You know what I mean?"

"Yes, I do. But they didn't take any stock?"

129

He shook his head. "No, they didn't. You sure look beat, man. Stop and rest here."

"No, I need to catch up to them boys. I doubt any of them have been up against this hard a bunch of men. Thanks. Nice to meet you two. If I can ever help you, call on me."

"Nice to have a sheriff who cares. Damn sure was no law before you. Visit us anytime."

"Keep your guard up." He reined the weary horse around. Then he rode out the gate headed northwest for the San Carlos Apache Reservation headquarters.

The couple were tough people who'd somehow cut out a ranch in the chaparral and existed under fear of Apaches and outlaws on the fringe of things. Strong individuals. Guthrey could appreciate them and their efforts, but one steel-tipped arrow in the back from a short bow out of nowhere could close down their lives.

Guthrey rode on. Clouds were coming north. He doubted that it had rained any in this basin. Noble told him the climate at San Carlos and the surrounding country didn't even grow saguaro cactus. A tough enough place located on the Gila River.

By early afternoon he reached San Carlos. Two blue uniformed Apache police guarded the porch as he dismounted.

"Halt," one commanded. "What is your business here? This is the agency of the Apache. Only people on official business may enter."

"My name's Phillip Guthrey. I am the sheriff of Crook County, and I am here to see the agent in charge."

"Let him by, Lone Wolf. He's official enough." The man on the stairs wore an old shapeless suit and no tie. He was nearly bald, and what was left of his curly gray-black hair ringed the open top of his head. He extended his hand to Guthrey. "My name is Woodrow Styles, sheriff. I am second in command here. Unfortunately my superior, Sam Butts, is in Prescott on business, where it is a damn sight cooler than here. How can I help you?"

"Three of my men passed through here in the last twenty-four hours."

"Yes, they did. They said they were pursuing some bandits. But I never saw those men they described. Later some Apaches told me they thought those men they were after had been with the army, who have no jurisdiction on this agency any longer, and rode on."

"Were my men all right?"

"Seemed to be in good spirits and determined."

"Good. I need a tough fresh horse. Mine's about done in. I'd rent one or buy one but I want a good one, not some bangtail."

"Corporal Wolf, this man needs a good horse. Would you trade him one of yours?" He turned back to Guthrey. "He owns a couple of damn good horses."

"I would take sixty dollars and your horse."

"He a stout horse?" Guthrey asked.

"Plenty. You want him?"

"I'll sure look at him."

"Go get him. This man needs to catch up to his posse," Styles said, and the policeman ran off in a stiff, head-high gait to get the horse.

When the man returned, Guthrey's heart about quit. He led a big, powerful stallion painted in splashes of white, brown, and black. That would never do, but Guthrey might have to buy him — whether he liked the coloration or not. The horse flared his nostrils, and Guthrey could see the muscles and power in his hind legs, no doubt from breeding mares. He was an Apache's dream and a Ranger's laughable stock. But he had little choice at this point. His ranch horse was done in.

But a damn stallion — why hadn't they cut him? Not a typical Indian horse. He

132

checked him over some more and decided he was stout enough. He looked at the policeman. "What side do you get on him from?"

The man pointed to the right side. Guthrey nodded. He had no time to retrain a horse. He could do that later. Then he about laughed recalling the girl whose mother introduced her to him months ago as a future bride prospect for him and who had wanted a painted horse as her bride gift. Amused about that, he stripped his saddle and blankets off the bay and went to the right side to put them on his new mount. The big horse was sure anxious, but Guthrey had enough riding to do to take that edge off him. Whoaing to him, Guthrey set the saddle and cinched it down. He exchanged the bridle for his new one and then paid the man.

Before he mounted up, he thanked the guards and Styles as well. He swung on the horse from off the right-hand side and made the seat, found his stirrups, and christened him as Cochise, who immediately put his head down and went to bucking. Pretty much straight-line crow hops, but he had a helluva hump in his back, and the Indians were shouting and waving their hats to encourage him. At last Guthrey set him off in a hard run and decided he'd take some more edge off him for a few miles. He stopped at the ferry landing and waited for its return from across the Gila River. Cochise was a little less snorty at that point, but one thing Guthrey knew, he wouldn't ride down the horse's power for several days.

He passed through Florence, a sleepy adobe village, stopping only to get a bite to eat and to check if someone had seen the outlaws and his men trailing them. The liveryman nodded. He'd seen both parties passing by his location about a half day apart. At first he'd thought the lead outfit was an army deal until he spoke to the second group and learned they were the three lawmen in pursuit. They only stopped to rest their horses and grain them before they struck out on the outlaws' trail.

"I was damn sure fooled by them outlaws. I wondered where they put the flag, then I thought they might be on a secret mission."

"I think everyone else had been fooled too."

The liveryman standing in his outside door asked, "Where did you get that big stallion?"

"Mine about caved in. Bought him off a policeman named Wolf down there at San Carlos."

With some effort, the older man pushed out in the sunshine and checked his teeth. "Five years old?"

"My guess."

"I never saw as big and powerful a paint horse before. Where in hell did he come from?"

"I never asked. I needed a horse to go on with."

"Mind if I ask what he cost?"

"My worn-out gelding and sixty dollars."

"I'd give you two horses and a hundred dollars for him."

"No, I've rode him a couple of hours and despite his hide, I like him."

"Some horse, huh?"

"He's a little broncy, but I don't think anyone rode him much lately."

The liveryman was still circling and admiring his horse. He took off his weather-beaten Western hat and scratched the thatch of gray hair on the top his head. "I sure never saw one like him before."

Guthrey ignored his interest in the horse. "Did my men chasing those outlaws look haggard?"

"No. Determined as all get-out, but they looked all right. Guess you're worried about them?"

"I need to catch them. Is that vendor

across the street clean enough to cook me some food?"

The man nodded.

Guthrey hitched his horse. "I'll get me something to eat."

"I'll watch him."

"Thanks."

The Mexican woman made him a large flour tortilla and wrapped some mashed bean mix inside it for ten cents. It was large and he paid her two dimes, drawing a smile on her wrinkled face as she accepted his money.

The liveryman filled his canteen at the pump while Guthrey ate the hot, spicy burrito, and then the man hung the canteen on the saddle. "I've heard about you. You won a special election over there in Crook County, didn't you?"

"Yes. My name's Guthrey."

"You and your men are tough and damned determined, crossing county lines to get outlaws. My name's Earl Stone. I'm proud to have met you."

Guthrey agreed with a nod and shook his hand. Some other curious men came across the street from the saloon.

"Who's he?" one asked, inspecting Cochise.

"New sheriff in Crook County, after some

stage robbers," Earl said.

"Why, you ain't got no authority up here," the man scoffed.

"Don't worry about it. Unless you break the law in my county. Then there ain't no imaginary lines going to stop me from arresting you." His meal devoured, Guthrey wiped his mouth, then he led his mount to the water trough for another drink.

"He's after them six in uniforms rode through here," an onlooker said to the others.

"I hope you catch and hang them kind."

"I'll try to arrest them and let the judge hang them." He went to the right side and mounted his horse. Cochise skidded sideways out on the street until Guthrey got him under control with the bit.

"Thanks, Earl." He let the big horse single-foot out of town.

By nightfall he reached Florence Junction, a stage stop, and was reunited with his men, who he found eating supper.

"It's the boss," Noble said, and the three rose to invite him to join them.

"Sit down. You guys are hard to catch."

"We shut down," Baker said. "They sent four men out to meet us a couple miles west of here. I figured they were ready to fight

137

and they had the advantage of cover. So we decided rather than tangle with them, we'd come back here, eat, and consider a plan."

"Sounds like a good decision," Guthrey said. Then he told the short Mexican lady who came out to wait on him that he wanted the same meal and coffee that his companions had.

She agreed and shuffled off to get it for him.

Seated on the bench beside Dan, Guthrey clapped him on the shoulder. "You three making it all right?"

"Sure. Our asses are getting raw, but we're all right," Noble said. "They tried this business of sending back those four men to stop us. But we saw it, and Teddy knew it was a move to cover their ass like for a retreating army."

"Lucky you figured it out. Where in hell are they heading?"

While waiting to bring his food, the Mexican woman lit a few lamps. The sun was going down.

Baker shook his head. "They asked about the distance to Camp McDowell when they rode through here. That big mountain out there is called Superstition. The army outpost and reservation is about thirty miles north of here. Two rivers converge there, the Verde from the north and Salado from the east."

"Why did they want to go there, I wonder."

"Ain't no telling, but they've got a plan. We've been learning bits and pieces about them along the way. Two of them are ex-sergeants. Two are just plain soldiers and two are former officers. One was a colonel. Word is they were all court-martialed for raping Indian women captives and then selling them in Mexico for whores in the slave trade. Their trial was held at the army post outside El Paso. They were thrown out of the army and each one sentenced to prison for ten years, but they all escaped."

"Nice guys," Guthrey said as the woman delivered his bowl of chili and beans with some flour tortillas on a plate.

"Gracias," he said, and she nodded.

"Where else did they try to meet you head-on?"

"I guess it was before we got to San Carlos," Baker said. "Dan noticed them and we held up. I shot at them with my Sharps rifle, and since we weren't in their rifle range, when the lead reached close enough to them, they left in a hurry."

"You know they aren't through trying everything to stop you?"

"Yeah," Noble said. "They know now we're determined. I'm sure they'll try to stop us."

Baker set down his large spoon. "They are like a machine when they set up. One man moves and another covers him and they come on like hornets. I never was in the army but they're more like that than ordinary men."

"They sound efficient enough. We need to be damn careful from here on."

"Could one or two of us sneak up on them tonight?" Baker asked.

Noble shook his head. "Let them head for McDowell in the morning. Get a good night's sleep here and rest our horses. They can't get too far away from us without remounts."

"Tell me about it," Guthrey said. "My ranch horse was done in at San Carlos and I'm riding a big, stout paint stallion."

"Really?" Dan smiled at him.

"He's tough but he's also a loud color."

Baker smiled. "Just what you need. An outlaw that knew you had him could sure be warned you were coming."

They all laughed.

Then Cochise gave a loud whistle outside about something, and they scrambled for their guns getting up. Guthrey pointed for

Baker to take the back way out while he headed for the front door. Noble blew out the lights.

Guthrey could hear the beat of horse hooves, and three riders came by slinging lead at the stage depot. But their aim was wild and Guthrey got one shot at them before they were gone. More shots out back, and he sent Noble to go check on Baker.

"Will they come back?" Dan asked.

"I doubt it. It was hit-and-run, and had the stallion not whistled, we'd'a been sitting ducks. What have you got?" he asked Noble, who came in from the kitchen.

"Baker shot one of them. Bring a light."

"Dan, keep an eye out here. Be ready; they may try to come back."

He agreed and Guthrey took a candle lamp from the woman. On the back steps he saw Baker squatted down by a body on the ground.

"He still alive?'

Baker nodded.

Guthrey, after checking the night around them, knelt down beside the man. In the lamplight the man made a pained face.

"Who are you?"

"None of your damn business."

"You've been shot, huh?"

"Yeah. Hurts like hell." He gritted his teeth.

"You don't start answering questions, you're going to die right here. I'm going to let your life drain out of you right here in this gravel."

"All right. All right. My name's Bob Denton."

"You were court-martialed in Texas for selling Indian women as slaves."

"Yeah."

"You held up the stage with all the money. Now, why in the hell didn't you go to Mexico?"

"The colonel has a plan."

"You know that plan?"

He shook his head.

Guthrey rose and looked around. "Can we hire someone to take him to a doctor and then to jail in Florence?"

The man who managed the stage stop said, "One of my men can take him to Florence and do that."

"I can pay him twenty dollars. I'll write out the instruction for his arrest."

"We'll get a buckboard around here and some blankets."

Guthrey thanked him. Then he turned to Baker. "What happened?"

"He shot at me when I got to the back

door. I returned fire and shot him."

Guthrey asked, "Someone see his horse? We may need it."

Dan spoke up. "He's over by the corral. I'll get him."

Guthrey held up the light to examine the horse. He was a well-muscled Morgan-bred horse under an army McClellan saddle. Impressive. They obviously were well mounted, which explained why they'd made such good distances.

"Where were you going, Denton?" he asked the wounded outlaw.

"Damn if I know. I just follow orders."

"I don't believe you, and I'm tempted to kick you in that wounded leg."

"I swear I don't know. They never said."

Back inside, Guthrey wrote a note on the back of a wanted poster the stage stop man gave him:

To whom it may concern
This man is wanted by the U.S. Army. You are entitled to the reward they offer for him. If you can't do that I will have him picked up and we will try him for shooting a stagecoach guard and robbery.

Sheriff Phillip Guthrey
Crook County Sheriff, Soda Springs,
Arizona Territory

"Give that to the law officials down there."

"He will do that."

Guthrey turned to his men. "We'll take that horse with us. Let's get some sleep and ask this lady to have breakfast ready for us at sunup, and then we'll follow them some more. An opportunity will open for us to get them."

Everyone agreed.

TEN

At dawn, they finished their meal and the horses were saddled. On the back of another wanted poster, the stage man drew them the stage route around the great wall formed by Superstition Mountain. He pointed to the forks of the roads where the stages went to Mesa and on to the Hayden Flour Mill, then Phoenix, and the other road went to Fort McDowell from the north side of the mountain's base. His map also showed the way north to Rye and another site above there called Payson. Then the trails split to go to Fort Apache or north to the settlements on the northern east-to-west stage route.

They rode out and Guthrey's men teased him some about his paint horse, but it was his horse's whistle that had signaled the raid. Overnight, the wounded bandit had been taken to Florence and handled by the law down there, the stage man reported.

The day's heat began to rise and they reached the next stage stop at Apache Junction by midafternoon. They learned the outlaws had not stopped there, but rode by in a long trot. Five men instead of six now, which encouraged Guthrey to decide a few more needed to be separated from the outfit and they'd be vulnerable to him and his men. They never sighted them that day as they made camp across the Salt River on the north bank and ate dry crackers and jerky for supper.

After all their hot, sweaty days in the saddle, the men bathed in the sunset-bloodied Salado, or Salt River. But they were on the gang's trail and the horse apples were fresh on the rough wagon tracks that led northward.

Guthrey felt an opportunity to overtake them would soon appear. He was ready, as they drew for night guard shifts, to end this pursuit. Up before dawn, they made coffee and gnawed on beef jerky, saddled their horses, and headed for the reservation and the camp of soldiers stationed there.

An officer at Fort McDowell told him they had not noticed the outlaws passing, so they must have avoided the fort on purpose.

"Thank you, Lieutenant Moss. These men were court-martialed for selling Indian women into slavery."

"I know about that case. If I can be of service, tell me how I can help."

"I realize that rules now keep you from offering me men. We'll get them."

"Sounds unreasonable, but those are my orders."

"Thanks." He reined Cochise for the road to Rye and rallied his men.

Both Noble and Baker felt sure they were on the track of the outlaws. They knew the hoof prints well and moved northward in a trot. The wagon road wound higher into the boulder-strewn mountains, and they were forced to climb the steep grades at a walk to save their horses. Late in the day they reached a flatter surface. Guthrey went higher up and used his field glasses to study the road. He spotted the five-man formation and pack animals in a tight group, trotting no more than a quarter mile ahead.

He bailed on his horse and rushed off the mountain. The big horse half slid and half scrambled, but, sure-footed, he landed at the bottom and surged for the others.

"Let's take them. Time to shock them with a charge."

The others rushed after him with their guns drawn.

The outlaws looked back, shocked at first,

and waited for orders. The posse closed in and soon began shooting at them. Two men in green went down and another dove off his horse to save the packhorses' leads. One of the officers was spurring his horse to escape. Guthrey set Cochise after him. Like a rocket, the big horse charged into a furious race after the man and his mount. Cochise closed the distance on the flat road, and Guthrey holstered his .45, then undid the lariat on his saddle as he charged on.

He made a loop, swung it wide. It settled over the man's shoulders, and before he could free himself, Guthrey jerked his slack and turned the big horse aside. The man screamed but was unhorsed and disappeared in the cloud of dust when Guthrey stopped his horse. He whirled Cochise around and rode to face the man as he wound up his rope.

"My arm is broken."

"You had a chance to surrender. That's your fault. Get on your feet and don't try anything."

"Who are you?"

"I'm sheriff of Crook County, where you held up the stage."

"You can't arrest me up here." Holding his hurt arm and grumbling, he started back for the others, walking in front of Guthrey.

"I can arrest you in Mexico City or Paris. It might not stick there, but it will here. My men have been in pursuit of you since the robbery."

"We should have eliminated them when we discovered them."

Guthrey shook his head, reloading his Colt .45 and keeping his eye on the man walking ahead of his horse. "I would have tracked you down anyway."

"That's your thoughts."

"Pretty damn good ones, weren't they?" Guthrey saw the others were either hand-cuffed or lying prone on the ground.

Baker met him. "One man is dead. One wounded and the other two are all right. What's wrong with him?"

"Broke his arm when I jerked him off his horse. He says he should have killed the three of you."

"Yeah, he damn sure should have." Baker checked the man for weapons and then shoved him roughly toward the others.

"Hey," Dan said over his discovery of the loot in the panniers. "We have a fortune here in these packs, Guthrey. Let's go to Mexico and celebrate."

"Let's go home. Cally's worried about us. Right, Noble?"

"Yes, I bet she is. That little lady is plumb

worried by now."

There was some gathering of the stock. The prisoners were chained to their horses. Dan led them. The other wounded man had a small injury, and the dead man was wrapped in a blanket and tied over a horse. Even the broken-armed colonel rode in that line. Noble led their pack animals, and Baker rode guard, cradling a rifle in his arms like Guthrey did.

They put them in the brig at Fort McDowell overnight. They buried the dead outlaw, whose name was T. J. Goings, in the cemetery. The lieutenant had the army camp cooks really feed them, and everyone enjoyed it. His telegraph man sent a message to Soda Springs telling Guthrey's office and all the families, like Cally and Baker's wife, that they were all right and bringing back the prisoners and loot.

"You got anyone needs to be let known?" Guthrey asked Dan.

He shook his head. "The news will beat us home."

Guthrey gave him a shake of his shoulders. "Tough job, wasn't it?"

"Boy, yes. I may sleep for a week when we get back."

"We'll be there in a while. We get back to Florence we'll pick up the other one of the

150

gang, if he's alive, and then in three days after that we should be home."

"Please don't have another crisis for a few days. All right?"

Guthrey chuckled. "I'll try to space them out."

Guthrey had never met Baker's wife, but he figured she'd be glad when he got back. He would make it a point to meet her the first chance he got. His main crew would split any reward they received for the return of the wanted men. The three men plus Zamora, who stayed home and did all that work in their absence, would get the money. It could easily be a thousand dollars or more to split. That would help all of them.

They picked up Denton in Florence and thanked the sheriff. Guthrey offered to pay the man for his keep but the heavy, mustached man shook his head. "That's on me. Good luck to you. You're a tough force to have gotten them."

Three days later, they were in Soda Springs. Guthrey wired the fort at El Paso and told them to bring the reward money for the six escapees. He explained that one was dead and buried at Camp McDowell and he had a death certificate for him. The rest would be here when they sent their men to take them back. Save the county the cost of a trial. They also had the Wells Fargo money and would get a reward for that too.

Guthrey's four men, in the end, earned eight hundred seventy-five dollars each from the federal and Wells Fargo rewards. The express company sent an armed force on horseback with a wagon to pick up the loot.

Very grateful for his share, Baker bought a small house for his wife, Donna, and their three kids. Zamora planned on having a small house built on his place so his mother-in-law could move over there from Socorro. His wife, Candy, hugged Guthrey and kissed his face. The deputies cheered, "Grandma is coming."

Noble shoved his reward in his pocket for a rainy day and so did Dan. Both thanked him.

Back at the ranch, he found Cally disappointed. While he was gone, she'd found out she wasn't with child, but she was happy to have her man back. He was glad to be back too. She'd been there for the rewards payoff and thought he was good to do that for his men, and told him so as they went home in the buckboard.

"Can we go to the dance Saturday?"

"I hope so." He hugged her shoulder. "I think we have things settled down."

"I hope so too." She kissed him on the

cheek. "I sure miss you when you're gone."

"That makes two of us." He felt lots of pride in his woman as he drove the dusty road, ranch bound.

The next few days were nice and calm, and Guthrey and Cally went to the dance on Saturday, and then to church on Sunday. The next week, Guthrey sent Noble with a wagon over to get the Mexican couple, Guermo and Deloris Diaz, for Cally. The sooner the couple got here the sooner she'd have some help. And they might cheer her up — not being pregnant like she expected disappointed her, but he privately teased her that they could sure work on it some more.

He went to make his rounds while Noble went to get the Diazes. There had not been much going wrong in his absence. He wasn't mad that things were quiet, but they were too quiet to suit him. Arizona Territory was right on the trail of many bad guys, pickpockets, sham artists, and wanted killers who used this route to escape being arrested, moving like a wave into the areas with the least effective forms of law. It was a wonder they didn't set up headquarters in either town in the county since they both sat right on the main highway from Texas to

California.

Guthrey rode over to the house of ill repute in Steward's Crossing to see if Ellen Foster, the lady of the house, knew anything he didn't about what might be going on.

He hitched his horse at the fifty feet of hitch rail fronting her white picket fence, which shielded the two-story house's fine yard full of roses. The black girl he had once saved from being raped took his hat and told him she was sure glad to see him again. He agreed and asked where the boss was at.

"I goes get her. You's goes in de kitchen. They got plenty of food in thar and she be right along."

"Thank you, my dear," he said and went down the front hall into the kitchen.

A tall blonde jumped up from table at the sight of him. "Why, Sheriff Guthrey. What brings you out so early?"

Three other girls sat around the table smiling for him.

"It's not early for me. You girls don't have to get up with the chickens."

She laughed. "No, we stay up with old hoot owls half the night."

They all laughed.

"I'd sure be honored if you'd sit by me," Blondie said, holding the chair out for him.

He smiled. "I'd hate to disappoint a pretty

girl. How are the rest of you?"

Blondie rounded him up a cup of hot coffee, canned milk, and sugar. Then real intimately she asked him how he liked his eggs.

"Scrambled's fine."

"An omelet?"

"Fine."

"We heard you arrested a whole army a week or so ago."

"They were really prisoners that were supposed to be in jail."

"Those army men who come after them from El Paso spent the night here when they came over. They wanted to know all about you."

"Yeah, one said those prisoners were tough sumbitches. But we told them we had an ex–Texas Ranger captain that was our new sheriff." She stood up and clapped, and the others joined in.

"Damn right we do." Blondie kissed him on the cheek like she had rights to him. Thank God Cally would never know. He told them that the law was working fine, and if they needed any help, to call on him.

One of the thicker-set girls wearing a billowing one-piece sack dress and holding a coffee cup in both of her chubby small hands nodded. "We damn sure will. In most places the law and houses are at odds or be-ing shaken down by the police. Thank God for you, sir."

"Well, I see we're feeding you anyway." Shorter than most of her girls, Ellen Foster, with her large breasts on a shelf under the expensive velvet dress, stood with her hands on her hips. "To what do we owe the honor of your presence?"

"Just checking. We get lots of folks passing through this town. Some of them are out-laws. I can't be here, but you send word and one of my men will come to your aid."

"We knew that. What else?"

"I simply came by to break bread with you."

"Very kind. Blondie had a friend come by a few days ago. He's wanted in New Mexico. But he just came by for a short visit."

Blondie nodded. "You know of Bill Bon-ney?"

"He's Billy the Kid, right?"

"Yes, sir."

"Unless he makes trouble for himself in this territory, he's a free man."

"He's nice to girls," Blondie said. "And he has lots of them. To me he never grew up and that's the fun side of him. I never saw that killer side of the man."

"Lots of outlaws are like that. They say

156

Jesse James never forgot a lesson his momma taught him."

"Some of us knew Pete Crawford from El Paso. Most generous man in Texas," Ellen said. "And he gunned down two Rangers and two town marshals one night in Haileyville over just nothing."

Guthrey knew that bloody story too. "If you don't know any more, then thanks for the free breakfast, it was damn good. I'll mosey along."

Blondie caught his sleeve when he was getting up. "I serve breakfast in bed upstairs. Same price."

"Much obliged." Then Ellen went with him to the front door. "She don't recognize you're a real happy married man."

"No problem. You know anything I need to look out for?" Guthrey asked her.

"The man runs the old Whitmore Ranch. His neighbors should watch their backs."

"Walter's his first name. He met my best man over at Soda Springs. I'll watch him. Liquor makes men talk, don't it?"

"Damn right, and there'd be a lot more men hung if the law knew what we know."

"Just keep me in mind."

Ellen glared at him. "I had no association with the Kid."

"I understand. He was simply seeing an

old friend."

"Sorry. I am used to being accused by men in your place."

"When I accuse you, you'll know it. That other is behind us."

"Thank you. And you hurt my business some." She chuckled. "They won't stay around long enough for me to make real money because they fear you so much."

"Good."

She shook her head ruefully. "We will watch out for your troubles."

He left her on the porch and went to ride his paint horse on to Soda Springs. He put him in the corral at the jacal he kept in town. There were too many horses in town to bother a stud horse at a hitch rail while he had business to handle. Then he walked up the hill to the courthouse and entered the sheriff's office after speaking to the telegrapher at his counter.

"How's that Apache horse today?" Baker asked when Guthrey entered their office.

"Tough. I put him in the pen down at my jacal. No need to have him squealing at every mare comes through town."

"Hey, he's powerful."

"He's a great horse. Anything going wrong around here?"

"One of our cow counters said he'd seen

158

some suspicious-looking range riders down in the south. They avoided him and his helper, but he thought they were up to no good."

"They get any names or descriptions?"

"No, not much."

"I'll swing down there. I have some supporters in that area. Maybe they've seen something."

"Good. Those guys are keeping us up on what they see. They found two stolen horses abandoned in a valley last week. They'd been rode to death and the thieves must of left their own horses there to ride off on."

"I wonder what they got into?" Guthrey shook his head. "Thank them for helping us. Any word on the redheaded killer?"

"Nothing. The earth must have swallowed him."

Guthrey agreed. "I'm going to bear down on finding him before he does it again."

He decided as slow as things were going he'd ride home, spend the night with his wife, and in the morning go south and look at things down there. He'd check with the Mormon Bishop Brown and see if he knew of anything wrong.

The ride home went fast. The stallion was excited and flew across the chaparral-covered desert for the ranch. It was near sundown and Cally ran out to catch him. She swung on his neck, pleased to see him. He felt glad he'd come back and kissed her hard. Both of them laughing, they put his stallion up and went to the house.

"Noble and those folks you hired didn't make it back here today."

"It's far enough to over there to take a couple of days to get back here, and she has a new baby — or may be busy having it."

"All right. I have some supper I can fix for you."

"I'll eat."

"Good."

"I'm going south to check on things to-morrow."

"All right." She hugged his waist. They eased inside and she led him to the table. "I just love having you home with me."

"I love to be here, trust me. That's why I rode back. It was quiet."

"Oh, Phil, I hate to be a pest, I simply appreciate your spending time with me."

He hugged and kissed her.

In the morning, he milked their cow, they had breakfast, and he put his bedroll on his saddle in case he needed to go on after something. He left Cochise in the pen and chose a long-legged bay horse they called Tom.

"You need to throw hay to my paint horse. He can get water but he's by himself. I shouldn't be gone over there too long, and I'll do my best to be back for the dance."

"I know you will. You try hard."

"Thanks. Noble can figure out how to house the Diazes. They are gentle, hard-working people."

"I will be polite to them."

"You weren't hardly friendly to me when I came here."

"Oh, I'm more grown-up than that now."

"I know. Just be yourself."

They kissed good-bye and she smiled at him. "I will."

He mounted up and rode south. He went by Steward's Crossing — nothing happening. Next he rode over to see Bishop Brown, but one of his wives said he was gone to Salt Lake. No conflict happened there, according to her. He swung east and went to the Peters Ranch to check with Mark. Maybe he'd seen the strangers skirting around through there. Mark's wife met Guthrey at the door.

"Mark is out checking cattle. Come in. I'll make us some coffee, and I have few stale Danishes you might choke down. I know he'd like to talk to you."

Guthrey followed Olive into the kitchen. She lit the range and set the coffeepot on the iron stove top. She waited for the fire to start, then with a big breath, she blew out the match, which was about to burn her finger.

Head down, she didn't look at him when she started to speak, "I guess I owe you a big favor."

Seated at the table with the chair turned out to watch her, he frowned.

"You knew who I was?" The hard look in her clear blue eyes questioned him.

"You looked familiar from someplace. I'm sorry, but I knew I had seen you before."

She lowered her head to look out the windswept windows that fluttered the curtains. Satisfied no one was coming, she said, "It was in Texas years ago."

What did they call that town? A sleepy cow town, and he'd been stationed there once before the war. Her name then was not Olive. She was a teenage girl he'd kissed hard outside the dance hall in the dark — "Florence was your name then."

She nodded. "When you wouldn't marry me, I ran off like a fool with a worthless guy named Clay Freedle. Dumb girl, but I finally left Clay and started calling myself

Olive. I married Hemp Carter not long after. He was older but he treated me nice. I've been a respectable woman ever since. We were in several Texas towns but he ended up with a good freight business in Tucson. One day he had a heart attack and died. I met Mark in Tucson at my church. So I sold the freight business and came up here with him. He's a good man, but I felt like I'd faint when you came up here that day."

"I wouldn't ever have said anything."

She ran over and hugged his head. "God bless you, Phil Guthrey."

"Olive, I am pleased you have Mark and a real fine life here."

She backed to the kitchen range. The fire was blazing and she replaced the stove-top lid. "Oh, I have not slept for nights. Why did I think you would do that to me?"

"I have no idea. I almost married several women since that time. My sister about gave up on me ever getting married, and then I met Cally, and she was the one for me."

"You are a very lucky man. Where are you going today?"

"There were reports of some men slipping around the countryside looking like they were casing things for what they could get into."

"Have you seen them?" she asked.

He shook his head. "All I have is rumors about them."

She shook her head. "I have not seen any strange men, but we aren't on the main road."

"That's the road they'd need to take: your back road, so they could stay out of sight."

Her water boiling, she added ground coffee to the pot. "I have not seen them."

"I hope they went on their way. I'm also looking for a man with red hair who has a Mexican boy with him."

"What did he do?"

"Murdered some folks."

She shook her head. "I haven't seen him either."

"Good thing. He's dangerous and not many have lived to tell folks about him."

"I'll be on the watch for him. And now that my concern is over about you giving me away, I'll have Mark take me to that dance some Saturday so we can meet your wife."

"You bet. She's a neat young lady, she gardens and cans; we could eat for two years on her supplies in the cellar."

She laughed.

"She, her brother, and their father, who was shot before I joined them, lived on the income of a small beef herd. So saving food and having it was important. They do okay. Not rich but comfortable."

"Mark and I make it fine too."

He agreed, finished his coffee, and thanked her. "I'll get on. Headed towards the Thayers' next. See if they saw something."

"Tell Nell hi. She's a good neighbor. You learned her story, didn't you?"

"Yes, she told me. It is almost unbelievable."

"Brave, determined woman. I don't know if I could have stood all that she went through."

"Thanks, Olive. And you know your secret is safe with me."

She dropped her chin. "Thanks, my friend."

He rode out and headed east on the wagon road. En route to the Thayers' ranch, he stopped and spoke to several ranch people and a freighter coming out who'd delivered some timbers to a mine development. No one had seen any suspicious men roaming around. He felt better reaching Thayer's place, and the rancher came out of the house with his wife, Nell, to greet him.

"You two getting along all right?"

They nodded and smiled. Thayer said,

"No problems here. What brings you out this way?"

"Looking for some drifters. And a killer. Have you two seen any drifters?"

"Not lately," Thayer said and his wife shook her head.

"How about a redheaded man and a Mexican boy?"

"No. Is he dangerous?"

"Deadly. Keep your guard up for him."

Nell took his arm. "Come inside. I'll make us something to eat. My husband can put up your horse. Up here visitors are scarce so we hold them hostage. How is your wife?"

"Good. You met Noble. He's moving a family over to help her. They're a nice young couple to work on the place. She works too hard."

"I wish we had someone like Noble to help us."

"They come pretty scarce. I don't know how old he is."

"What's scarce?" Thayer asked, coming into join them.

"Good old men like Noble for ranch help are hard to find."

"He's a dandy. When I rode with them boys I couldn't believe how great a hand he was."

They discussed Guthrey's search for

166

troublemakers and resolved there weren't many of them hiding in the Dragoons. After eating the meal Nell served, they relaxed and talked about ranching and cattle. Thayer had bought three new shorthorn bulls and he wanted some more.

They talked about markets and, of course, old man Clanton, who held the reins on the beef market in the territory.

Guthrey told him, "I sold a small lot of fat steers about three months ago to butchers in Tucson — we rented some fenced pasture so they could butcher them as they needed them. It worked and we only made one drive over there, which saved us money and time."

"Maybe we need to form a ranchers group to do that."

"It might work, but the Tucson Ring would figure out how to beat you out of it. They have a strong force in deciding what happens in the territory."

Thayer agreed. "I guess we will have to take the old man's prices."

"Those Ring people are beyond my reach, but if I ever can get to them," Guthrey said, "I'll have them all on trial."

"I believe you will." The three laughed.

"Your food was delicious, Nell. Thanks."

"You will stay the night, won't you?" she

asked. "Neither of us get much company up here and talking with you is great."

"I bet that she'd bake a cake or pie if you would."

Guthrey chuckled. "I will."

"There, he's going to stay, Nell. What will it be?"

"Pie. I have some raisins and dry apples."

"Sounds wonderful," Guthrey said. "I'll definitely stay."

He left them after Nell's big breakfast spread and rode on the north trail to the main road and turned west to head for Steward's Crossing. He rode though the rock pile called Texas Canyon. A favorite place where they used to hold up stages before he moved into the sheriff's office.

So those reported shifty strangers must have, like Billy the Kid, simply ridden on. He could find no trace of them and figured it wasn't worth more of his time trying. It was the Carlsons' killer that he needed to find.

Eleven

Guthrey was back at the ranch by noontime. The wagon was there so he knew Cally had her help.

"Wash up, our guests are here," she shouted to him from the open door.

"I'm coming."

He hitched his weary horse, loosened the cinch, and hurried across the yard. On the porch he used the warm water she'd poured out for him to wash his hands and face.

"They have a new baby boy." She was breathlessly excited beside him. "He's so sweet. They call him Manuel."

"I told you they were nice people. They made it all right?"

"Oh yes, and we emptied the shed for them until we can get them a house built."

He kissed her. She smiled and hugged him. "Find anything?"

"No. Your brother here?" he asked under his breath.

"No. I haven't seen him since before you left."

He glanced around. Dan needed a good kick in the ass. The cattle were his job to take care of — checking for screwworm control was his job. Guthrey swept off his hat and spoke to the family, who were gathered in the room. Guermo rose and came to shake his hand.

"So nice of you to send Noble to get us. I was coming but I would have been much slower." Their younger ones were seated on the floor and all grinned when Guthrey passed out hard candy.

"How are you, Deloris?" Guthrey asked.

"Fine, senor." She showed him the new baby wrapped in a flannel blanket.

"Aren't little children sweet?" Cally asked.

"Yes. How are you, Noble?"

"Mighty fine. You find anything?"

Guthrey shook his head. "No sign of anything."

"I better check the cattle tomorrow, huh?" Noble asked.

"Someone needs to do that."

"No problem."

Guthrey spoke up, "You find any need to be roped, you leave them and get me. We can talk tomorrow."

"Sure."

"I can ride and rope, senor. I was raised on a large hacienda in Mexico."

"There, you have your helper."

Noble bobbed his head and smiled.

"Will you have to leave tomorrow?" Cally asked quietly.

"I need to find that killer before he repeats the crime. I may be in the saddle most of the time until I do."

She nodded and squeezed his hand. "I understand, Phil."

"I will try to be back for the dance. I spoke to Mark's wife, Olive. He was gone, and then I went on to the Thayers'. They told me to tell Noble hi. They like visitors and they don't get many. But no one down there has seen any strangers."

"Those two never came back to the old ranch where we were at," Guermo said.

Guthrey chuckled. "Maybe the earth swallowed them." Hell, he didn't know where they went.

His wife's food tasted good to him and he mentioned it to her. She nodded, pleased that he said that.

There was no sign of Dan when Guthrey watched the sky turn from faint pink to purple rising over the distant tall ranges north of the Chiricahuas. For two bits he'd go find him and sober him up with a swift kick in his ass, maybe punish him all over town. What in the Sam Hill was wrong with that boy? He and his family had worked hard to build a small ranch against all odds. They made it and he dropped off into self-pity, or was drowning himself in whiskey, which was just as bad.

Noble came up out onto the porch in the cool air to where Guthrey was holding up a porch post. "Where is he?" he softly asked the old man.

"Steward's Crossing. Some gal named Effie. I think he's got a jacal off south of town."

"I'll find him." Guthrey blew his breath out of his nose. *Damn.* He'd do it before he went to the county seat that morning.

"Breakfast is ready," Cally said from the doorway.

"If I can get this old codger inside, we'll eat," Guthrey teased.

"I'm following ya," Noble said.

"Good. Your new ranch hand is waiting for us."

"Ah, Guermo, *buenos días,* senor," Noble said, as though he hadn't just seen him that morning, and rambled off in Spanish at the new man.

Cally laughed. "Don't let them tease you, Guermo. They do that to new ones."

"Oh, senora, I am so glad to be here and have a job, they can tease me all the time."

"I understand that," she said and shook her head at her two men.

Breakfast passed and Guthrey saddled his restless paint stallion. His wife was standing on the corral rails and smiling as she watched him saddle up. "Will he buck you off today?"

"I hope not."

"Oh, that would be embarrassing with two hired hands watching it happen," she said, tossing her head at the other two getting Guermo fixed up with a horse.

Guthrey caught the cheek strap and drew Cochise's head to his left side. *May as well start making a white man's horse out of him.* In the saddle he flew and, keeping the horse's head high up, nodded for Cally to open the gate as the paint danced on his toes.

She swung it back and Cochise came out on his toes. "You be careful, Phil Guthrey. I need you. He still looks like he may go to flying."

"Aw, he's just full of energy. I'll be back when I can, but especially on Saturday."

"I will be here."

He let the horse out. Cochise single-footed at first, and once free from the bit on the road, Guthrey let him out. With his face in the wind created by Cochise running, Guthrey headed for town. What a powerful horse, a little headstrong, but Guthrey enjoyed managing him.

Before he reached the village, Guthrey had Cochise down to a walk and went by his deputy's house. Ike Sweeney was still on the porch, and his wife had brought out coffee by the time Guthrey had his horse hitched securely.

Guthrey thanked her, took the cup, and sat on the wooden chair. "Everything all right in town?"

"It is, sir."

"Where is my brother-in-law, Dan, denned up at?"

"Oh, go down Mesquite Street to the foot of the hill. That place is on the right. You can't miss it. An adobe shack with a brush stick corral out front. You'll see it."

He looked around to be certain they were alone. "Who is she?"

The older man frowned. "She worked up in the big house before he moved her down there."

"Did anyone complain?"

"Naw. Oh, some church ladies told my wife I should make her move on, but nothing serious."

"Well, keep your eye out for the redheaded murderer. And, Ike, don't you try to take him by yourself. The man is a rabid killer."

"I get any word or see him, you'll know about it."

"I damn sure don't want to have to take care of your wife. Love her, but I want you here to take care of her."

"I'm careful enough."

"Stay that way. I'm going to Tucson to see what I can learn about him."

"They brought them army prisoners through here in a jail wagon. They were chained in that iron barred wagon. Hot as hell and lots of tough uniform guards riding with them."

"I heard about it."

"Good luck and you be safe. Folks sure like having law and order."

After Guthrey left, he rode over the hill to the shack Sweeney had told him about. He sat on his big horse at the front door. Wrapped in a robe held shut with her hand and unkempt hair hanging in her face, a girl came to the door and squinted against the sunlight.

"Who are you?" she mumbled.

"Tell Dan to get out here."

"Who is it, Effie?" Dan called out.

175

"Some guy and a huge paint horse's standing in my damn doorway."

"Get back," Dan pulled her aside. "What do you want, Guthrey?"

Phil checked Cochise. "I want you sobered up and back on the ranch where you belong. If you're going to live with her, then marry her. If I have to come back here to get you, you will go home belly down over a horse. Am I clear?"

"You aren't any kin to me. You can't order me around."

"Listen, I can bust your ass, but I think you know better than to want me to do that. Get home. Be a man and grow up. You have three days to do that. Noble and the new man need help. If you take yourself back, don't pick on them or your sister or you will answer to me."

"He ain't your father," the girl whined. "He can't make you do nothing."

"If he don't marry you, girl, you be on the next stage out of here."

"You can't —"

"I can by law run undesirable people out of my jurisdiction. So you have my word." He checked his horse again. "Dan, I mean just what I said here. Get your ass in gear."

He didn't wait for an answer. With Cochise reined around, he short loped for town

176

and headed for the county seat. He spoke to Baker briefly. Everything was in hand, so he left for Tucson. He needed to see the sheriff plus the butchers he knew; maybe one of them could give him a hint that would tell him what he needed to do to find this killer. The man might be selling stolen beef, and the butchers there might recognize him from his description.

The stableman in Tucson wanted fifty cents more a day to keep his stallion and grumbled about having him. It was mid-afternoon and the temperature was sweltering in the walled city. Narrow streets and poor sanitation made the small city even less desirable to be in.

Guthrey found Sheriff Ramos in his office, a stuffy place that stunk of cigars. The man welcomed him and showed him a chair. This was their first face-to-face meeting. Carlos Ramos was a man who was big around and not so tall. He wore a tan uniform and had a thick mustache. His oily hair was curly and he spoke with a Mexican accent.

"Nice to meet you at last. Have a seat. What brings you to Tucson on such a hot day?"

"Thanks. I had a bloody murder of a family in my district about a month ago. Then another murder of a huge white man. The man must have worn a size sixteen boot. I think he was involved in the first murder because I have his footprints from the scene."

"As I wired to you earlier, I think Johnny Cord is your dead man."

"You knew him?"

"I had him in and out of my jail. He was a thief and a bully. My deputies hated him. He was hard to arrest when he was drunk."

"And a redheaded man was with him."

"Randy Looman. He was in Yuma twice, and the last time he escaped. I do not know where he was at."

"He was up in Crook County, and some Mexican people saw him but did not know his name. In his thirties, five foot eight, real red hair."

"That's Looman. He was in jail for raping a teenage girl. And they say he's shot some men in the back but there were no witnesses."

"He shot Cord for some reason. A deputy and I dug up the grave."

Ramos shook his head at the notion. "In this heat that's a bad job to have to do."

"A very bad job, but part of it. I have a finely made goatskin glove from the murder scene purportedly made by a woman named

Ramona Garcia."

Ramos shook his head in disbelief. "I don't know her. But people said you were a tough lawman. They did not tell me how determined you are, that you'd dig up a dead man in summer. I am amazed at you."

"Thanks, but it's not me, it's my men. There was no law in Crook County before I took office. A major rancher was forcing people to leave by strong-arm tactics. Forcing people to sell out at ridiculously low prices. Arrested criminals were turned loose. Drunks were wearing badges and forcing people to do their will."

"It's a wonder they didn't shoot you."

"They tried."

"You got a big reward for getting the stage robbers, no?"

"I paid all of that to my men."

"Oh my. What else can I do for you?"

"Need some leads on where I can find this Looman."

"Maybe on the border. I don't have any information to help you or I would send my men down there to arrest him."

"You have any information where on the border he might be hiding?"

"No. But don't go down there by yourself looking around. You won't come back."

"You know of a Mexican outlaw named

Royal Montoya?"

"Yes. What did he do?"

"He stole a rancher's horses in my district and went to Mexico. Four of us tracked them down there into Sonora. They had a big fiesta that night and we stole the horses back plus all of his too."

Ramos broke into laughter. "They told the story different than that. A big mob of supposed American ranchers charged them, shot his men up, and stole their horses."

Guthrey shook his head at the man. "We caught two herder boys, tied them up, and took those ponies for the border. Never fired a shot. Four of us."

Ramos laughed some more. "That is some story."

"They must have set off a couple hundred dollars' worth of fireworks partying while we rode like hell for the border."

"Four men is all you had?"

"Yes, and one is close to eighty years old."

"If I ever have any problems, I will call on you. Sorry I can't help you more."

"I'll find a way." Guthrey shook the man's hand and excused himself.

After his meeting, he rode out to talk to the man who'd rented him the pastureland when he'd brought some steers up to sell there. He found him on his porch in a worn-out chair.

"You need more pasture?"

"No, sir. Not today. I am looking for an outlaw named Looman."

"I never met him personally. He escaped jail in Yuma last I heard. He had a woman at one time named Sheila who still lives in the barrio. If you could find her maybe she would tell you where he hides. She'll want money but she's a cheap *puta*, so it won't cost much and she'd probably share her bed with you besides telling you where he could be."

Guthrey sure didn't need her body, but if she knew anything about Looman, he wanted that information so he could pursue him. Politely he thanked the man and told him that when he needed more pasture he'd sure contact him.

"I could sure use the rent."

He crossed the shallow river and went back to town. Headed for the barrio, he stopped to get more information about this woman Sheila from a few folks along the way. The dirt street was choked with carretas, saddled sleepy burros, and many shopping women. There were cloth shades over the produce stands. A butcher chopped meat off fly-speckled carcasses on a blood-darkened wooden block, his apron badly stained red with blood. He wiped his hands on it and then wrapped a purchase in paper for the woman who paid him in coins.

"I'm looking for woman called Shelia," Guthrey said to him.

"Ah, such a woman, huh?" The big man laughed like he knew her secrets. "If she is the one you look for, senor, she works across the street in the Estria Cantina." He waved a big ham of a hand. "Right over there."

"Thanks." Guthrey put Chochise in the livery, then moved through the traffic on foot and pushed open the once-white batwing doors with the peeling paint.

He let his eyes adjust to the smoky darkness of the interior.

"Come in, senor," said a sleepy-eyed woman with a tray on her hip, looking him up and down. "What can I get you?"

"A beer and ten cents' worth of information." If she wasn't Shelia, he'd soon find out.

"Take a table?"

He motioned to one.

"I'll bring the beer."

"Good." He pushed his hat back and moved to sit down with his back to the wall.

When she returned and delivered his beer, he indicated the chair across from him.

Her dark eyes checked him hard. "You want me?"

She set the tray on the table and adjusted her blouse to better expose the tops of her full breasts.

"What do you know about Looman?" He tossed her a silver dollar.

She deftly caught it and handily deposited it in her cleavage. "He is a mean *bastardo*. Why do you want him?"

He nodded slightly that he'd heard her answer. He pitched another silver dollar to her and she caught it. "Where is he hiding?"

She hesitated to drop it in her hiding place. "I don't know. I hope he is not near here."

"That's yours." He meant for her to have it.

She nodded and let it fall into her bank. "Where can I find him?"

"Beyond the law who wants him."

"He was in the Arizona Territory a few weeks ago."

"I know that. I was afraid for my life until I learned he went back there."

"Why? Did he come up here?"

She turned up her white palms. "I never learned. But I heard —"

Something made her stop. He glanced at

183

the two vaqueros who had come in dressed in dust-floured leather. He could tell their presence bothered her.

"Do they know him?"

"No." She lowered her voice. "They are more trouble is all."

"What're their names?"

"Morales brothers. The one with the scar is Thomas, his brother is Fred."

"What do they do?"

"Murder. Beat up whores. Strong-arm and rob innocent people in the barrio."

"I can see they're nice guys. Where is Looman?"

"I think Nogales."

"Big place. Where is he at down there?"

"Probably in the district of the whores."

"Will those men pick on you when I leave?"

She shook her head. "You paid me money. Do you expect —"

He shook his head. "If you hear anything about Looman, wire me at Soda Springs. Sheriff Guthrey."

"Oh, you're the guy in the newspaper who ran off the old sheriff." She laughed out loud.

With a nod for her, he rose. The scar-faced man followed his moves, then turned back to say something to his brother. Guthrey went on out the swinging doors. He made his way up the crowded street to collect his softly nickering paint horse from the livery and then, careful that he wasn't being followed, he rode on south.

TWELVE

The King's Road to Mexico followed the Santa Cruz River. Many small farms were joined to the stream for water. These places had been started years ago by the Catholic Church, but by this time belonged to landowners. Mostly Hispanic people inhabited the area.

Guthrey met two local ranchers in a small hotel and cantina in Tubac for supper. The waiters recommended a local wine for him to try while he feasted on his fine fire-roasted steak. They served what he called fried squaw bread along with locally raised vegetables browned in a skillet.

Over supper he spoke to the two men, both large ranchers in that area. One of the men was Javier Batista and the other Hernando Silvia. They complained to him about the lack of rain, which worried anyone with livestock. They were also concerned about the rustlers coming up the valley and rushing stolen animals into Mexico.

They laughed at Guthrey's story of recovering the stolen horses in Mexico and congratulated him on his return of the man's horses.

"We need more men like you in the law."

Silvia, the smaller man, agreed and said, "Congress should have bought all of the northern part of Mexico in that last treaty. The Mexicans can't use it because of the Apaches, and it would be ours and be over a hundred miles south of the current line."

"Too many Catholics lived down there," his friend said warily. "They didn't understand how much they lost in copper and gold resources they could have developed."

"All I know is we need more help on these border jumpers, both for the sake of Mexico and the U.S." Guthrey cut some more bites off his flame-touched steak. "I'm looking for a killer named Looman. He has red hair and is a fugitive who escaped from Yuma."

"I know of that scum. He robbed a friend of mine on the highway and then beat him up. There is a private reward for him of five hundred dollars."

"I want him for murdering a family in my district."

"But you have no power in this district."

"I am just a citizen interested in justice

187

when I ride out of Crook County. This man escaped the territorial prison and obviously has robbed and murdered others. Boundaries and districts should not be a barrier to let the lawless run free."

Both men nodded. Batista spoke. "I agree, senor. I appreciate your service to your fellow man."

"I am not here for any glory. I am here to preserve the law as a citizen. Looman is a wanted fugitive. I want him apprehended and to stand trial for his crimes."

Silvia agreed. "You ever need a horse or help, we can lend you some, just call on us. We appreciate your concern and determination."

His friend agreed and they ate on, and the discussion changed to crossing the native cattle with British breed bulls. That argument was endless and at last, his meal completed, Guthrey thanked the two for such an enjoyable evening and went to his room to sleep. In bed all he could think about was not having his wife to hold, but he finally fell sound asleep.

Up before dawn, in the cool air Guthrey saddled his horse at the livery. A man named José who worked there asked him if he knew where Looman was at.

"No, do you?" Guthrey listened closely.

"I heard Senor Silvia say that you were looking for him."

"I am. What can you tell me about where he's hiding?"

"There is a woman who lives near the Kitchen Ranch who is his concubine. Her name is Lucia Contreras, and he may be there. He sired several kids with her."

"Where is her place from the Kitchen Ranch?" He felt that famous place he'd heard about would be easy to locate and to recognize. That should lead him to her operation.

"There is a wagon road turns east up Rivera Creek and her place is on the left past the Kitchen Ranch." The man waved his dark hand to the east. "She has some small crops and a garden plus an adobe jacal."

"Will I see any markings or anything?"

"She has lots of goats."

"Lots of goats, huh?"

He turned up his palms. "*Sí, muchas cabras.* I can't recall if the first or second place is hers."

Guthrey paid him a half dollar. *"Gracias, amigo."*

The man beamed. "You are a very generous man, senor."

He nodded and led his anxious paint horse across the dusty street to the hitch rail in back of the hotel. The woman in the kitchen had promised she would have his breakfast ready when he had his horse saddled. He washed his hands on the porch at the dry sink, dried them on a towel, and went inside. His food was set out and she sat in a chair across from his plate.

"May I join you, senor?"

"Certainly. You have no business yet?"

"Only you." She smiled.

He tasted the coffee and considered the woman to be in her thirties, perhaps. Her hair had some gray in it but that only added to her attractiveness. He'd seen her at first in the near-dark kitchen earlier when he made a request for some breakfast. Obviously Mexican, she smiled when he spoke to her and she said, "No problem."

She about chuckled as he started to eat. "I'm not the cook here, senor."

"Oh, I thought — sorry." He set down his fork and sat upright.

"My cook was not here yet and I was looking for her." She laughed some more. "Then this handsome man came in and asked me if I'd cook him some breakfast so he could ride on. Why, of course. He must be in a rush to leave here and this would be my

190

chance to meet him."

Guthrey removed his hat, half stood up, and offered her his hand. "Guthrey is my name."

She shook it. "Ida Bartlett. I own the inn."

"Mrs. Bartlett?"

"Yes, I am a widow. My husband died in a mine accident a few years ago. And you are married?"

"Yes, for two months or so, maybe more — early June was the date."

"It's a shame. I have a ranch and a mine, and when I heard about you being here, I thought my savior had come at last to manage my operations."

"No. I'm the sheriff up in Crook County and very happy with my job and my lovely wife, Cally. You need a man to run things for you?"

"I'd like to find one. He could even be married." She smiled. "I have some men that are loyal to me, but they are not managers. I need someone who thinks about things and sees things that need to be done."

"If I see someone like that, I'll send him to you."

"Thank you, sir. You are a sheriff now?"

"Newly elected."

"Oh yes, it was in the Tucson paper. You rounded up several criminals and even the ex-sheriff." She raised her eyebrows like he had accomplished a big deal.

"Things were really bad up there. No law anywhere."

"And you are here today?"

"Looking for a murderer as a private citizen."

"May I ask his name?'

"Looman."

A shocked look came to her smooth face as if she were alarmed. "Be very careful, *mi amigo.* He's killed many good men."

"I have heard that. Do you know where he is hiding?"

She quickly shook her head.

Busy eating the rich food she fixed, he looked up. "You're a very good cook. I am surprised you don't have many men after you."

"Not the men I want. They only want my money. They are lazy. They drink too much. They shout too much. I am so damn fussy I can't take a one of them."

"Now, ain't that the truth. I met some nice ladies needed husbands, but I found things they did that upset me, so I never got married for a long time. My sister said I was too fussy too."

She laughed. "Find me such a man."

"I will look."

"No. You have in mind to find this killer. You are being nice to a lady, but you have no time to go and look for a man for me. But I forgive you."

"What do I owe you for this breakfast?"

"Hmm," she snorted. "I have fed a new friend and sent him off to war. I don't want your money."

"I thought I had found the cook in the dark kitchen this morning." He laughed.

"You are a devil, Guthrey. Stop by again and see me."

"Someday I will. Thanks, Mrs. Bartlett." He put on his hat and headed for the front door. Outside in the cool shadows of a dawn that was hiding behind the tall mountain in the east, he unhitched the horse, took the stirrup, and then swung aboard. He checked the horse with the bridle bit, then he saluted her, standing in the doorway, and rode on.

Cottonwood leaves the size of silver dollars fluttered overhead and birds chirped in the sanctuary of the trees. Along the road bold ravens fed on horse apples for the grain they contained, and the topknot quail scurried off in the weeds. Guthrey heard a cow bawl for her calf and some mules honked in the distance. Already some rigs were on the road and passed him going north. He headed for the border as the heat began to rise up from the hard road surface and into his hat-shaded face.

He located the Kitchen Ranch by speaking in Spanish to a man walking along the highway. Then he cut off on the road the liveryman told him about and went past the ranch until he heard the goats. Not much happening. He wanted to try to scope it out from a distance, and then he spotted a nearby hill. He took a farm path and his horse stepped over a rushing small ditch, carrying him to the base of the hill. In the willows, he hobbled Cochise, then took the field glasses and climbed up the backside of the hill with a canteen.

This day would require lots of patience on his part. Guthrey felt confident he'd found a reliable spot to spy on Looman and one Lucia Contreras. The place had lots of vegetation and goats. He saw some children playing with the kids and some stock dogs. A young woman caught a couple of chickens in a cloud of dust and feathers, obviously intending the fowl for slaughter — was company coming?

Butchering of poultry usually meant there would be visitors to feed and special ones to be around the table. The hours passed and two men rode into her place, but they were hard to make out, though Guthrey could see one was a Mexican boy who led their horses around to a corral. Though not very old, maybe ten or twelve years, he unsaddled the horses, currycombed them, and fed them green corn and stalks from the garden. The children had been herded outside too. The oldest ones cared for the younger ones in the yard. No sign of the woman or the man. All Guthrey wanted was to see him and verify that his wanted man was there. What those two grown-ups did to each other, he didn't care about — just so Looman would be there when the sun came up and he was ready to arrest him.

He spotted the man's red hair when he came outside to empty his bladder. It was Looman, all right. Satisfied on that matter, Guthrey collapsed his brass telescope. Having had enough of that for the day, he climbed off the hill and found the paint stallion, unhobbled him, and rode on into Nogales. He put his horse in a livery. He told the stableman to grain him and went to where they said there were some clean rooms to sleep in.

The streets were quiet on the U.S. side. After he secured a room for the night at the inn, he ate supper from a street vendor. Sitting on his haunches, eating his wrapped meal, he noticed several hipshot horses standing at a hitch rail across the open border in Mexico in front of a cantina. Must be payday for some vaqueros and they were celebrating in that place. Guthrey didn't need any celebrating after he finished his meal. Returning to the inn, he found the ten-cent bed and the blanket the clerk handed him. Tired, and anxious to get up early to go to Lucia's place and arrest the killer, he soon went to sleep. His revolver was near his hand under the covers just in case. . . .

Before dawn Guthrey found a woman cooking in the town's street. She made him a large flour tortilla, filled it with meat, beans, chili, and a sauce for a dime. He gave her two dimes and then went for his horse. The hostler saddled Cochise for Guthrey. They talked softly about the need for the monsoons to start, the cool air sweeping out the canyon that formed the sides that Nogales huddled in. The rich, spicy contents of the burrito tasted good to him.

He swung into the saddle, thanked the man, and tossed him a quarter for his troubles.

"Anytime you come back, senor, look for me. My name is Agnos."

"I will, Agnos. Thanks."

The air was cool in the predawn. Guthrey, wondering how this day would turn out, checked his anxious horse, who also acted like he understood things were going to happen soon.

Noticing a stranger in the yard, the goats stampeded away in a panic away when Guthrey got beyond the gate of Lucia Contreras's house. Then, filled with curiosity, they came back to check him out. None of the dogs even barked, and once he had the horse hitched securely, he checked around. He went across the ground to the adobe jacal, hoping the goats wouldn't follow him too soon.

He made the house and the goats had begun bleating. Six-gun in his hand, Guthrey went to the green, peeling-paint door and jammed it wide open with his boot.

"Don't go for a gun!" Guthrey shouted. But he saw the figure diving for a holster and he shot in that direction. The man screamed.

The woman yelled, "You've killed him!"

"Don't move or you're next." Breathing loudly through his nose, Guthrey stepped around the bed in the thick gun smoke. Two children on pallets were crying. He jerked the woman away from the outlaw to stop her from getting a gun and tossed her aside on the bed. She shouted, cussed in Spanish, and charged him on all fours.

Guthrey gave her a rap on the head with his gun barrel, and she went facedown on the rumpled blankets. Guthrey never liked to hit a woman, but she wasn't taking his orders. He caught Looman by the collar of his underwear suit and dragged him outside, the outlaw screaming that he was shot and dying.

Guthrey had to handcuff him, then go back in to get Looman's gun. The woman might recover and try to use it. Looman was lying facedown in the dirt with the cuffs on his wrists, crying, "I'm shot. I'm shot. You're killing me."

"I'll do worse than that." Guthrey straightened in the midst of all the curious goats that were jumping all over each other trying to back away.

Looman's left arm was bleeding and there was a tear in the sleeve, but Guthrey couldn't see any other wounds on his dust-floured union suit. That outlaw ought to be grateful to be alive, but his kind considered freedom their only salvation.

"Stay put," he ordered and, holding the six-gun in his fist, he went back inside. The woman was holding her head.

"Don't hit me again," she screamed and

crawfished away from him with blood on her forehead and hand.

"Don't never threaten me again, lady. I don't hit women unless they try me."

The spent gunpowder left a powerful sulfur smoke that hung in the air when he finally located Looman's gun belt. Guthrey holstered his own gun and then put the prisoner's in the sheath, latched the buckle, and slung it over his shoulder. A half dozen dark eyes followed his every move. Nothing else in there worth ten cents — only a fecal smell mixed with the sharp haze. He went back outside. Dressed in white clothing, the Mexican slave boy stood there looking at his handcuffed boss, wide-eyed and afraid, ready to run.

"Saddle your horses, and get ready to ride." Guthrey spoke in Spanish. "We're going to Tucson. One mistake and I'll shoot you. You savvy?"

"Oh, *sí,* senor."

"What is your name?"

"Raphael."

"Is she your mother?"

"No. But I will work for you."

"Good, Raphael. You behave, I won't cuff you."

"I will, senor."

"My name's Guthrey."

"*Sí*, sen— I mean, *sí*, Guthrey."

He watched the woman and her kids, all in a huddle, come outside from her jacal, coughing hard. They stopped and stared at him.

"Put his clothes and things in a blanket. Tie them up. He's going back in his underwear."

"What about his wound?" she asked.

"He should of worried about that when he tried to get the gun. Now get it all loaded. We're leaving here shortly."

She made a face. "He may bleed to death."

"I doubt it. Get his things. I'll find a doc along the way."

The boy was back with their two horses. Guthrey checked their saddlebags for knives and guns — none of the above. The woman brought him a blanket full of stuff, which he tied onto the boy's saddle horn. He told the youth to fashion a lead from the saddle horn of Looman's horse to his and then he put a halter on the boy's bay horse. Guthrey locked the second pair of cuffs on the horn, jerked up the moaning killer, and loaded him backward up on the saddle. With one cuff on the horn, he latched the second one on the outlaw's hands behind his back. No way he could run off riding that way.

"I'll fall off," Looman screamed, facing

the rear of his mount.

"Better hope you don't. It might break both your arms. I don't want to have to look at your sorry face all the way back up to Tucson."

The woman had a Mexican cussing fit and spat at him, all at a safe distance. At the gate, Guthrey unhitched his horse and mounted up. In the saddle and holding the lead to Looman's horse, he led them out the gate. The boy followed his boss.

When they were down the way a bit, the woman discovered her nannies were leaving out of the gate as well and began screaming for them to come back. Waving her arms, she drove them back through her gate and inside her yard. More of her screams and cuss words followed him. Prodding their mounts into a trot with the boy and prisoner bringing up the rear, Guthrey turned up the King's Road and set out for Tubac.

THIRTEEN

The whole journey, Looman was moaning that he was dying from his wound, and Guthrey was hoping that he would. It would save the county a hanging. But there was no chance of him being so lucky. He'd find a doctor in Tubac and get him seen to.

How many friends did the killer have that might try to get him freed? It was a good question. Guthrey knew little about the criminal element at the border and how close Looman was to them. His helper, Raphael, so far acted simple enough and did what he was told, but he still needed to be watched for what he might try. Looman locked up in jail would mean the boy would be out of a job and that could be tough for him. Slaves like him were fed and given money at times to keep them. They also were savagely beaten on occasion to keep them in line and to enforce their slavery.

Abe Lincoln might have turned all of the

slaves loose in the United States, but Mexico overlooked such status in their homeland and various stages of slavery still existed below the border. No one enforced the slavery freedom law in the territory except U.S. marshals and their deputies. The boy's chances of even being recognized as a slave wouldn't matter much to them.

Past midnight, they reached the inn in Tubac and, unloading the prisoners, made enough noise to bring Ida Bartlett down and outside holding a candle lamp.

"So you caught him. I have never seen this man before."

"He's not much to look at. We had a hassle early this morning and he went for his gun. He was shot in his arm. Is there a doctor available to look at him?"

"Dr. Santos would do that," she said.

"Where at?" He searched around in the starlight.

Ida turned to the girl who'd been standing aside in the shadows. "Macita, thanks for being up. Go get the doctor. Tell him a man has been shot."

The girl ran off with a quick, "*Sí,* senora."

"Bring him inside."

"No, he's filthy and ain't had a bath in six months. Can we move a table out here to lay him on?"

She shrugged. "We will have to hold up lights for the doctor."

"It's not a big wound," Guthrey said, not concerned. "Raphael, go help her bring a table out," he said in Spanish to the boy. The youth moved fast at his order.

"What about me, half-dead on this gawdamn horse?" Looman asked. "Ain't one of you sonsabitches worried about me?"

"I'll get you down in a few minutes. Quit cussing. This nice lady is trying to get you medically looked after and she don't need to hear your profanity. So shut your mouth."

He didn't smart back. Two of her men arrived to help move the table outside. Ida fixed some more lamps and her men put up a rope to string them on. She introduced them as Franco and Sandal. Franco was in charge and he shook Guthrey's hand. "So good to meet you, Sheriff. This man is one of the most feared men on the border, and you captured him alone?"

"See, I was a Texas Ranger before I came to the Arizona Territory, and down there, for one outlaw, they only send one Ranger."

The two men laughed.

"You ever come to arrest me, you say, 'I'm Sheriff Guthrey,' and I will come out peacefully." Franco laughed again and so did his cohort. "That's all you will have to say."

"Help me get him off his horse. Easy on his left arm. That's the one I shot this morning." With his keys, he unlocked the first set of cuffs from the saddle horn, then they lowered Looman to the ground, but his legs collapsed under him.

"Hey, hombre, you couldn't run away if you wanted to," Franco told him with his body suspended between the two of them. The outlaw, on his feet at last, shot up.

"You sonsabitch—"

But Guthrey backhanded him to shut his mouth.

With a fistful of Looman's underwear in his hand, Guthrey drew his face up. "I told you if you started swearing I'd cut it off. You know what I mean now?"

In their grasp again, hanging between the two men, Looman nodded.

"Put him on his stomach on the table. I'll unlock his hands. But if he tries anything, moving in any way, you can gut-shoot him. He don't deserve anything more."

"We understand," Franco said. None too gently they threw him on his belly across the table.

Guthrey stepped in and unlocked the left cuff, then fastened the end of the second pair to the table leg. Looman wasn't going anywhere. Ida came out of the house with three beers on a tray for the men.

"Doesn't take long for you three to get things done." She laughed openly, looking at the outlaw and shaking her head. "How many men has he killed? Does anyone know?"

"Five or six, maybe more," Franco said. "Who knows?"

"He murdered an entire family in my district. A cruel, mean way for them to die."

"Why didn't anyone stop him?"

"He escaped from Yuma prison. I have no idea when. We had no law in Crook Country before I took office two months ago. Besides, I had no idea he was in my area or I'd have had people watch for him. I probably would have imagined he was down in Mexico with his compadres. He slipped in and murdered that family."

"Did they have money?"

"No, they were poor, but they had a daughter of thirteen or fourteen that he and his companion raped and then smothered to death with a pillow. Sorry, that's a bad story to have to tell to anyone."

"If I'd known that, I'd never have asked the doc to come." Ida turned away, her shoulders shaking.

"I'm sorry, ma'am. He's not worth much, but I have to uphold the law, and that requires I protect him and make him go to trial for his crimes."

"Did you —"

"Yes, I was at a dance with my wife when a lady reported the murders. I borrowed a horse and rode up there with another man to look at the murder scene. Not a nice sight —"

"I can imagine. The doctor is here."

A short man with a medical bag came in the lighted front area. "Good evening. Where is this wounded man?"

"On the table. If you need to cut his arm off, we'll hold him down." Guthrey held out his hand toward the facedown outlaw. "It's his left arm."

The doctor shed his suit coat. Ida took it and folded it over her arm. He took scissors and split the stained sleeve of Looman's underwear.

Looman screamed when the doctor lifted the limb to examine it.

"This all the damage?" he asked Guthrey.

"He made a break in the dark after I warned him not to. I shot him."

The doctor nodded. "I can bathe it with a disinfectant and then sew it up. If it turns gangrenous it will have to be amputated."

"I understand."

"Doc, give me some pain medicine. It

hurts bad. It's killing my brain. Doc, please —"

"Shut up," Guthrey said. "Sew him up."

"What did he do?" Doc asked as he washed his hands in a bowl of water the girl brought to him. Careful-like he dried them on a towel, then handed it back to her.

"Murdered a man, his wife, then used their teenage daughter and smothered her to death with a pillow."

Doc dropped his head and shook it. "That sounds horrific."

"The death scene was bad."

"I'm glad you were there and not me."

"Yes, sir. Sew him up. I need some sleep. He ain't worth wasting a minute of it."

"Franco and my men can guard him. Go inside to the second room upstairs and get some sleep. It will be taken care of," Ida said.

Guthrey hesitated. "I want him alive in the morning."

"I understand." She pushed him with both hands.

He laughed. "Gag him if he raises too much hell."

"We can handle him, senor." Franco folded his arms over his chest.

Guthrey nodded and removed his hat. "Wake me early. I want him in the Tucson jail by tomorrow night."

"Go to bed." She gave a toss of her head. "Thanks to all of you."

Guthrey retired. Looman was in his custody and in another day he'd throw him in the Pima County jail. Then he'd ride on home — he missed his sweet wife. But they'd be together in a couple more days. Boots off, he sat on his butt on the bed. It had been a long day, but a good one for his role as sheriff — he shed his britches and soon fell asleep. *Cally, I'm coming home.*

FOURTEEN

The morning held a cool breath. The quail were whit-wooing in the chaparral when Ida woke Guthrey by knocking on the door. "You said early. Breakfast is ready downstairs."

"I'm coming. Thanks." He pulled on his britches.

"Your prisoner is still alive."

"Good." With effort, he pulled on his boots and strapped on his gun belt, then his hat. His mouth was dry and he hoped the coffee was as good as the last time. On the open porch he looked at the sky over the towering mountains to the east. No clouds, and the heat would rise. It was August in the southern part of the Arizona Territory.

He washed his hands and face at the bowl outside the door to the dining room. Before he reached home his whiskers would bristle. He dried his face and hands, then entered the dining room, smelling the aroma of food. Ida steered him to a table already set. "Have a seat. Franco has your stallion saddled and the other horses are ready. We fed the two prisoners already."

"I must have a big bill run up here."

She swept her dress and skirts under her and sat down across from him. "Will your county reimburse you?"

"I suppose they will."

"I will send the bill to them."

"How much?"

"Oh, twenty-five dollars."

"If they won't pay that, I will send you the money."

She shook her head like she was speaking to a small boy. "I won't accept it."

"Thanks. I appreciate all you've done for me. People like you will make this a great state someday."

"I hope so. And you are a good example of real law enforcement. I am honored you chose us to help you."

"Thanks." He busied himself eating.

"Do you expect anyone to try to stop you from delivering him to the Tucson sheriff?"

"No, ma'am."

"Franco said he would like to ride with you just in case someone tries."

Guthrey tore a piece of bread off the loaf on the table. "I'd be honored if he did that.

Can you spare him?"

"Sure. He is a brave man."

"I saw that last night. Sure, I'd be proud to have him along. But I doubt Looman has enough friends anywhere to come and rescue him."

She laughed. "That might be so. I'll tell him you would like him to go along."

"Ida," he said softly. "Thanks, you are a generous lady."

She sucked on an eyetooth for a moment, then nodded. "I am very impressed by your dedication to your job — and your wife."

"Tell Franco I am coming."

"Ride easy, hombre." She went to tell her man.

In a short time, Guthrey and Franco had Looman handcuffed to the saddle horn. The boy, Raphael, was on his horse and Guthrey told him if he didn't try to escape, he could ride his horse without a lead. The youth quickly promised not to do anything. They set out for Tucson with a wave for Ida and her crew.

Looman, his left arm bandaged, clung to the horn with his good arm when Cochise began to trot and his horse kept pace. The road north for Guthrey and company followed a silver stream that rushed north to the Gila. In places there was even shade to ride under the towering gnarled cotton-woods. A nice relief from the surging sun's rays.

Midday they stopped at a community store and ate lunch fixed by a vendor under some ancient trees. Guthrey knew the trip would be a long one, close to fifty miles, but Franco was a cheerful man to ride with and they shared some tales about their lives.

Guthrey told him about being a Ranger. Franco had some good stories about his life growing up in Tubac. Like what Ida's husband, Howard, had been like.

"He was a good man, really like a father to me. No one walked over him. I was with him when he caught three men stealing his horses. They won't ever steal anymore."

"The rope law was once all people had in Arizona," Guthrey agreed with him, riding beside the man.

"No one ever stole another horse from Howard Bartlett."

Guthrey stood in the stirrups and looked over their back trail to be certain no one was trying to catch them. Satisfied that nothing was coming, he poked Cochise with a spur to trot faster and Looman moaned.

Franco knew the way to the Tucson jail even coming through the dark streets after midnight. The prisoner was delivered to the yawning guard. The man recognized Looman when he came inside the main room.

"How did you catch him?" the man asked.

"He was staying with a woman. I simply woke him up."

"He's listed as a killer." The guard frowned, looking at a wanted poster,

"He will be tried in Crook County for three people he killed. My deputies will be back here after him in a few days. He's a wanted felon so you can hold him that long."

"Why is his arm bandaged?"

"He tried to reach for a gun."

"That was stupid. Unlock the handcuffs. I've got a good cell for him. He won't get out of here. Send your men to come get him."

"Tell Sheriff Ramos thanks."

They took the boy and the horses to a livery. They told him to eat some jerky and sleep. They'd be back in the morning for the horses to return to their homes.

Franco knew a woman in town who'd cook them food and give them a place to sleep. Her name was Rosa and she quickly threw a meal together along with some red wine to go with it. She was a middle-aged woman and acted very interested in their business in Tucson.

"The sheriff arrested this man down by the Kitchen Ranch and brought him to Ida's inn," Franco told her. "He knew her and we helped him, then I asked to ride up here so he wasn't troubled by any of the killer's friends."

"Did anyone try you two?"

Franco shook his head. "But we were ready."

Guthrey agreed.

"You should be a big hero. He was an escaped prisoner from Yuma and no one knew where he was hiding at. You found him."

"I'm just happy he's in jail. That's enough for me."

"I savvy, senor. May God bless you for your hard work. There are beds in the room over there. Should I wake either of you?"

"Yes, my wife is wondering where I am by now. A few hours is enough sleep," Guthrey said.

"Let me sleep." Franco laughed. "I am going to take another day off since I am here."

"Thanks for all your hard work." Guthrey rose and shook his hand.

"Anytime. Anytime, *mi amigo.*"

Guthrey found the bed and soon was asleep. The red wine had settled him some. But the time spent in slumber felt like no time at all to him when Rosa shook him awake. "It is about dawn, senor."

"*Gracias.* I will be up in a minute."

"I have some food cooked for you."

He dressed and went out in the candlelit room. She showed him his place at the table. Her food was spicy and fresh tasting. He left her a dollar and she protested about him paying her, but in the end she kept the silver cartwheel.

All their horses were saddled when he reached the stables. Guthrey told the man to put Franco's mount back and that he'd be after it later. He paid the liveryman all the charges on all of them. Then Guthrey asked the boy if he had eaten.

He nodded.

"Get on your horse; you can lead Looman's. The county can sell it for the bills he will cause them."

Guthrey decided Raphael didn't understand a word of what he had told him in English. In the saddle he shook his head at his dilemma about what to do with the teenager. Take him home, he guessed. They left in a hard trot eastward.

By dark he was back in Soda Springs and the deputies were there to welcome him.

"The Tucson sheriff notified us by telegraph that you'd put Looman in the jail there. We figured you were coming home," Baker said. "Your wife is down at your shack. We told her you'd be here tonight and she came to town to meet you."

"We need to send two men to bring Looman back. Raphael here was his slave. Give him a bed in a cell. He is a scared young man who doesn't savvy much English. Assure him he is not a prisoner. We will find a place for him. He can testify for us in court."

"We'll look after him," Zamora said.

"You look caved in," Baker said. "We can take care of your horses."

"Cochise can go in the corral down there. If you can care for the other two, I'll be fine."

"Looman's been on the run since he broke out of Yuma. How did you find him?" Baker asked.

"I started south from Tucson, talking to people until a man told me about some goat lady Looman had gotten pregnant several times. I found her place and caught him

217

when he dropped in to see her."

Baker shook his head. "The Rangers taught you well. One outlaw, one Ranger, huh?"

They all laughed, including Guthrey.

"Good night, boys."

Baker held up his hand to stop him. "Oh, that Walter Pierson is trying to run off ranchers. We have three reports on what he told them."

"Anyone do anything about him?" Guthrey looked them over for an answer.

"No. We knew you'd be back and would want to handle it."

"I will. He hurt anyone?"

"No. All words so far."

"We need to find more than words to do much about him. I'll think on it some."

"Go see your wife," Baker said and turned Guthrey toward the jail door. "She's waiting for you."

"Thanks. We can handle Pierson when I get rested if we get some real firm details or evidence."

"Get real rested," Baker said. "You've earned one."

Guthrey mounted Cochise and turned him downhill toward the shack. Stars flecked the sky as his weary horse moseyed down the road. He knew his paint horse was ready to rest too. At the corral, he dropped heavily from the saddle and went to loosening the latigo straps to his girths. Then he pulled the saddle off his back and set it on the ground atop the horn.

Cally's arms encircled his waist. "You made it back."

Wide-awake in her presence, he twisted around and squeezed her to his body. "Gods, girl, I have missed you. You all right?"

"I'm fine. I must say, I've been worried about you. The telegram said you'd captured that killer and he was in jail. We all guessed you were all right."

"I'm sorry. I was so anxious to get back I forgot about the telegraph. You don't have a telegraph key at the house, so I was riding home quick as I could."

"Oh, I knew you'd come back."

"I am so dirty," he protested as she hugged him close again.

"I filled a barrel of water and I can help you get in it, but what you really need is a shower setup here."

He laughed. "I just bought this place to sleep overnight here."

"Well, it needs some facilities, I can see that."

"Cally Guthrey, you're sure something."

As they left the corral, he asked, "Did Dan come home?"

She nodded. "Oh, he's so pouty, I came in here to meet you."

"What about the woman?"

"He said you ran her off."

"I told him to marry her or she could leave the county."

"She left."

"No big loss. He'll get over it."

She hugged him as they approached the barrel set out behind the house under the stars. "I hope so. I have a chair out here to hang your gun belt and clothes on. There are fresh clothes in the house for you to wear tomorrow."

He undressed, shaking his head. "Darling, I have been so lonesome for you, night after night. This is sure sweet."

"I knew you'd need a bath, so I set this up. I hope it is still warm enough to sit in."

Once in the barrel he found the water was cold, but he squatted down inside to his chin and sighed. "It ain't warm, but it damn sure feels good."

She scrubbed hard on his back with her long-handled brush and they went to work slipping off the dirt he had collected. She leaned over and kissed him. "Glad you're home."

"Me too." He came out of the tub shedding water.

"I swept a path to the back door, if we can find it, so you don't get needles in your soles."

"I'll let you lead me." He slung the gun belt over his shoulder and carried his boots by the ears.

She put on his hat and carried his clothes in a ball. "I want to fix this house up. We have the money. Can I?"

"Sure, darling. Whatever you think."

"You spoil me, Phil."

"No, I'm just pleased to have you. You have hot water in there?"

"Sure. I can shave you."

"Good. I need it."

"Hey, I'd take a whisker burn to get you in bed. Now, aren't I bad?"

"No, just the wonderful woman I married." They went in through the back door. Her plan had worked; no needles or goatheads in his soles.

After he ate some cold biscuits with butter and prickly pear jelly, she shaved him, then they slipped off to the fresh sheets on the bed and enjoyed each other until they fell asleep.

FIFTEEN

Dawn came and the wedded lovers shifted under the sheets. He was wrapped around and kissing her. "Good to be back."

"More than that. I miss you something powerful when you're gone."

"I'd hoped to be back by Saturday to take you to the dance."

"I knew you were chasing down outlaws. I'm so glad you were not shot or hurt."

"That big rancher reared up while I was gone. Three families reported that he threatened them."

She rose on her elbows. "What's his name?"

"Walter Pierson. I may have to look him up."

"What did he do to the people?"

"I'm going to read the reports today. My main men keep good records. Then I'll go and question the ranchers he threatened, and when I learn something, I'll question

Pierson. I have to nip this in the bud."

"We better get dressed."

He agreed and swung his legs out of the bed. "Times I wonder why I took this job."

"No. That's why you did take it — to end the injustice, and you've done well at it."

He smiled. "I simply never had a wife before either and I love her."

"I'm proud to be your wife."

"Good thing. You sure have an upside-down life with me."

"No, no, I love it."

"All right. But most women would complain about it."

She was dressing quickly on the far side of the bed. "You didn't marry most women."

He laughed. "Obviously I didn't. I'll go feed the horse."

"I'll start breakfast. Yesterday I bought some things to eat."

"I saw them. I'll be back."

He strapped on his holster and took his hat off the hanger on the wall. Once Guthrey was outside in the cool morning, Cochise nickered at him. But the person seated on the ground was roused by the noise and scrambled to his feet. He was young — early twenties — and wore a cheap black suit floured in dust.

"Sheriff Guthrey?"

"Yes, what can I do for you?"

He swallowed hard and tried to pat down his unruly black hair with his palms. "You are a hard man to catch. My name is Albert Gooding. I am a —"

"You're a reporter, right?"

"Ah, yes sir. I have been covering your takeover of the law here for the *New York Mirror.*"

"And?"

"I'd like to interview you about your experiences in this process."

"Not much to it. I deputized several ranchers, and the morning we had the authority to enforce the law, we rounded up all the criminals in Crook County."

"They said you brought in several Texas Rangers to help you."

"Sure. Some of the folks helped me came from Texas."

"Who were they?"

"Ask them."

"But they went back to Texas. I need the answers from you, sir."

Guthrey poured out some corn into a smooth wood trough for the stallion. The big horse was pawing the dirt, impatient to eat. Guthrey reached over and patted his head while the stallion crushed the kernels in his molars. This young man and his questions were making Guthrey anxious. Next he fed Cally's buckboard team, pouring corn in their trough too.

How could he turn the reporter off?

"I'm powerful busy right now. Could we do this at another time?"

"I've been here nearly two months and this is the first time I even caught you. I need to send in a story on you or I'll lose my job and be left penniless out here."

"I really don't have time."

"I won't take long. I promise."

Cally came to the door. "Bring your friend in. I have plenty of breakfast." Then she set up the washbowls on the porch.

"She's feeding you. Come on."

"Oh, thanks. I didn't come to beg a meal."

"She invited you, and she's a mighty good cook. Come along."

"She's your wife?"

"Yes, she's my wife. Why?"

"Nothing. She just looked young."

"Don't tell her that." Guthrey chuckled.

"Oh, I won't insult her."

"Thanks."

They washed up on the porch and dried their hands. Albert tried again to pat down his hair without success, and Guthrey let him go in first.

"Cally, this a big New York reporter, Albert Gooding."

"Nice to meet you, sir. Have a seat. There's more pancakes coming."

"Thank you, ma'am. It sure smells good."

"Just pancakes and homemade syrup. Do you drink coffee, sir?"

"My family call me Al, ma'am. Yes, I'd love some."

"Albert has to have a story about my job as sheriff or he'll get fired."

"Oh, what does he need?"

"A story about me and what I do as sheriff, he says."

"My husband is a little stiff about his accomplishments. You know he was a Texas Ranger captain before he came to Arizona to find a new future for himself and, I must say, a wife — me."

"Yes, ma'am. He's very proud of you."

She blushed. "Thank you. Phillip Guthrey rescued my younger brother, Dan Bridges, from being gunned down in the community of Steward's Crossing at the hands of hired gunmen. Then he came home with Dan and said he'd look at the situation that most of us were facing under the threat of a powerful rancher. My father had been shot twice in the back. There was no inquest held nor did any lawmen come to see about it."

Albert was busy scribbling down notes.

"What did Sheriff Guthrey do?"

"He started to investigate the crime and eventually solved it. That man will hang next week."

"How did you find out who the killer was?"

"I asked a banker if anyone wanted to buy the Bridges Ranch. He told me about a man who acted very interested, I followed that up, and he confessed."

"Amazing."

She went on to tell the man about the lazy sheriff and the nonenforcement of the law that allowed a powerful rancher to pursue running off the small ranchers.

In the end, Albert shook his head. "Pure amazing. I am grateful; this report will save my neck. Thank you very much."

"Now eat your breakfast," Cally said, pointing at his plate. They all three laughed.

After he finished, Albert politely thanked them, excused himself, and left hurriedly.

With him gone, Guthrey winked at her. "He first thought you were my daughter."

"Oh, Phil, he didn't say that." Standing over him, she smothered his face to hers. "That's terrible."

"No, he didn't. I am a baby stealer. But I love you."

"Oh my. You are a devil. What will I do

with you?"

"Put up with me." They both laughed.

Later he went to his office and read the three reports on threats by night riders. The incidents involved masked riders with torches. Their numbers ran from six to eight masked men. The attack comprised threatening men milling around and firing pistols off in the air, telling the ranchers to leave the country or face death by being burned out.

He knew only one of the ranchers who had been threatened. Mark Peters and his wife, Olive, were one of the three families threatened by the masked raiders. The party came to their place after midnight. Mark reported that he was concerned they'd burn him out, waving their pitch torches around. Deputy Baker said he had nothing to prove they'd been there. Nor did Mark recognize any of the riders in the group. They wore flour-sack masks and no hats. He saw no brands on the horses either.

Guthrey decided to ride out and speak to Mark and Olive. Such raids were a renewal of the past range war and he had no intention of allowing it to happen again. But he'd have to work swiftly to stop it. He called Baker over.

"There's no one place they started these raids. Peters lives over on the west end of the Dragoons. This Davis family lives close to the Pima County line, and the other, the Cody family, lives up close to north line near San Carlos. No one saw these men gathering?"

"No, sir. They must have drifted in and then formed a gang to raid them," Baker said. "I stopped at every small store and community to see if any strangers had stopped on that day or had ridden by in a group. I learned nothing."

"You did good. Last time we knew the enemy and where to start. This time we may be dealing with a smarter man in charge."

"Walter Pierson?" Baker asked.

"Whoever it is who runs that big ranch, I suppose. Who else wants these small ranchers off the range? I am going to go see the Peterses and learn what they think. Then we'll ride out to talk to Pierson the next day. I'll get a few deputies to go with me and a search warrant from the judge."

"What will we look for?" Baker asked.

Guthrey said, "Masks, among other things."

Baker nodded. "That should point a finger at someone, huh?"

"Exactly. I had some men prosecuted in

the last range war that I arrested because they had flour sack masks in their saddle-bags after a raid."

"Will Pierson threaten us?"

"He better not."

Baker nodded.

Guthrey thanked his man and went back to the small jacal to meet his wife.

"Learn much?" she asked.

"One of the ranchers threatened was Mark Peters over at the base of the Dragoons. I'm going over there to speak to him and I will likely be back here late."

"Should I go home?"

"No. Tomorrow I am getting a search warrant to inspect the big ranch run by Walter Pierson."

"By yourself?"

"No, I'll take some deputies with me."

"Good." She looked relieved by his answer. "I have some beans hot."

He looked over the interior of the hut. "Sounds great. But you're working too hard on cleaning up this dust bowl."

"Oh, I'm fine. We did decide to remodel it for our use?" She indicated the hovel.

"Yes, we have a need for a place over here."

"Well, your daughter is getting ready to do that." She broke into laughter and hugged him.

"I'm glad she's doing it. Except we have a sow's ear to work with. Let's keep this and just build a house next to it. We have two acres here."

"Can I find a contractor while you're gone?"

"Sure. I trust you."

"Good. I won't build it until you're back. We need a windmill too."

"I agree. That pumping water gets old."

"And a tank and shower."

"Go, girl."

She hugged him. "Your beans will get cold."

"Yes, ma'am. Like I said, I may not be back until late tonight."

"I sleep light when you're gone. Take your time."

"Don't run off with any reporter."

"Oh, Phil, he doesn't mean anything to me."

"Darling, I know that. I'm simply being funny."

After lunch he rode out for the Peters place on Cochise. When he struck the road, the big horse, who was well rested, charged off eastward in the midday heat. He passed through Steward's Crossing and took the road southwest to the Mormon settlement, then east to the Peters place at the base of the red mountains.

"Hello, sheriff," Olive said, coming out on the porch.

"Evening. Where is Mark?"

"I expected him to be back by now. He was going to check on his water holes today. Get down, he'll be here in a short while. I have some supper. We can eat."

He stepped down and loosened the latigoes, then hitched Cochise to the rack.

"My, he's a loud-colored horse. He looks powerful."

"He is all that. How are things going?"

"Fine, except for those night riders. That scared me half to death. The rest is going fine."

Guthrey washed up on the porch. "That's why I rode out here."

She handed him a towel. "Mark's usually back by this time."

"It'll be dark in thirty minutes. I really need to get back to town tonight. Where was he checking the water holes?"

"We have three windmills on the foot of the mountains. I don't think he rode into the mountains to check on the springs."

"Draw me a crude map. I'll go see if I can find him."

"You need to eat."

"I can always eat. Make me a map."

"You may fall off into a canyon in the dark." Her concerned face shone in the sunset's bloody light.

"I'll try to locate him."

She rushed inside and drew a map on a piece of paper. "This is the south windmill. Take the right-hand trail down there. The rest are on a path that goes around the base of the mountains. You think you can find them?"

"I'll try. Thanks, Olive. Don't cry; he'll be all right. I'll find him or he'll come on in himself."

She sniffed. "He's a damn good man. He never questioned my past. I hope you're right. I really love him."

"I understand, Olive. You two have a great life here."

"Be careful, Phil. I don't want you hurt either."

In the dimming twilight Guthrey set out on the obvious trail as the desert slipped into darkness. The giant saguaro cactus stood about like giant cross-shaped silhouettes. He watched for the cholla cactus, which had a light aura he could see in the dimming light. Surviving in the desert took a tough individual. These ranchers earned their livings in a dry world.

A small owl flew off at Guthrey's approach. Some cow out in the chaparral bawled for her calf in a hoarse call that sounded magnified by the crickets' night music. The clop of Cochise's shoes clanked on some rock outcroppings as he pushed out of dry gulches. In places, the strong creosote smell from the greasewood scrubs filled his nose.

A horse nickered and Guthrey stood in the stirrups. The creak of a windmill on the night wind made him stare hard for the tower. Then he saw the windmill, and a horse nearby raised his head, obviously ground tied by training not to run off.

Where was Mark? His horse was there — Guthrey dismounted and hitched Cochise to the hitch rail near the corral.

"Mark. Mark? Where are you?"

He checked the horse, then lit a match to look for blood. Lit another on the far side and saw nothing wrong. The girth was out like Mark had loosened it to give the horse some relief. Guthrey went around the windmill and, in shock, he stared at two boots swinging at eye level. Mark Peters had been hung by the neck, having been pulled up by a rope on the mill's cross timbers.

Oh damn. Guthrey's stomach revolted and he puked. Then he did it again. His hand found the wooden leg of the mill to steady himself. His eyes wet with tears, he saw a note pinned on Mark's chest.

In the starlight he scrambled up the mill to get to where he saw the rope was tied off on a crossbeam. His jackknife out, he cut the rope and let the body fall. No way to catch him, but Mark would never know a thing. Guthrey closed his large knife and climbed down.

On the ground he straightened Mark out on his back. With a match's light he read the note pinned on his chest.

We tole you to leaf
The Committee

They could not even spell. Guthrey closed his eyes. What a bitter turn of events. How many others would they kill? Mark was only the first and, damn, they hung him in a suffocating, painful act by pulling him up still alive to dangle until he died. *Oh God, what will I tell Olive?*

Numb to the bone, he cinched up Mark's horse, strained to load his corpse on the saddle, and at last tied him down. He staggered over to Cochise, leading the horse bearing the body. This would be a long ride back. A damn long ride back to the ranch house.

Sixteen

Guthrey dismounted heavy on his boots in the dark yard of the Peters ranch house.

"Oh dear God, he's dead." Her sharp "No!" hurt his ears.

Forced to step in front of her, Guthrey stopped her flight to get to her husband. "Olive, I'm sorry. They lynched him. There was nothing I could do; he was dead when I found him."

"Oh, Phil, what will I do?" Her tears came in a flood under the starlight. "But why? He never hurt a soul."

"The note pinned on him said he did not leave."

"Leave? This is his land. Why did he have to leave it? Those bastards! Oh, Phil, you must find them."

He agreed. "Get a lamp. We need to hitch up and get to Soda Springs. They may be killing more ranchers right now."

"Oh." Her hands covered her distraught

wet face. "I never thought about any more being murdered. Will they do that?"

"I fear they might. Get the lamp so I can see to hook the team up. We need to hurry."

"I will. I will." She raised her hem and ran for the house. He started for the corral to catch the horses. He'd need the light to harness them. But time was important and until he had some of his men at those others ranches he wouldn't sleep.

Olive brought the candle lamp and held it up while Guthrey took the first set of harnesses off the corral to toss on the horse. Quickly he settled it, and once the straps were in place, he did the other one. Then, holding the bridles, he backed the horses up to the buckboard tongue. The team was soon hooked up and he led them around in front.

With Olive standing beside the buckboard, sobbing, he nudged her onto the spring seat, apologizing all the way. "If I'd expected any trouble, I'd have come out here sooner. I was down on the border arresting the man who killed that family a month ago."

"I know, Phil. Mark was such a trusting man. I bet he didn't know those men's intentions when they rode up."

"I'd bet the same thing."

"Did you see anything down there to lead

you to his killers?"

"No, it was dark and I had no light."

He reined the horses around, and they set out for Soda Springs under the stars. Olive was crying again, this time on his shoulder. The loss of her husband had her deeply shaken and he could understand that. But why would they lynch him? To show they meant business? If Pierson and his bunch were behind his murder, they'd damn sure pay for it.

When Guthrey got back he'd send a couple of good men out to the scene of the crime and have them search for clues. Criminals always made mistakes, and somehow he had to find that evidence. But he also had to stop the killing. He reined in the team going around a corner, then made them trot hard. Folks would damn sure be riled up over Mark's murder, and they had a right to be.

His arm around Olive's shoulders as they went down the straight stretch, he tried to comfort her, but she was too upset. Cally could help her. He'd leave Olive with his wife. Women shored up other women better than men did.

They were out on the main road and headed for Steward's Crossing. It would be another hour to daylight. The team was doing all it could to get them there.

The sun had not cleared the Chiricahuas when he reined up at the jacal's front door. Cally came rushing out, wide eyed, and about ran into him. "What's wrong?"

"They lynched Mark Peters yesterday and his wife, Olive, is here with me. I want you to tend to her while I take his body to the funeral home. There's more that I can't explain right now but I fear there may be more deaths."

"Oh, heavens. Help her down. Olive, I am so sorry. We can talk inside."

He physically lifted the woman off the buckboard and put her on the ground. "Olive, my wife, Cally." With a gentle push he sent her toward the open doorway under his wife's protection. "I'll be back."

"We'll be fine," Cally assured him and he drove on to the courthouse. He reined up the horses going up the rise and spoke to a young Mexican boy named Roso.

"Roso, you run up and tell Deputy Baker and Deputy Zamora that I need to meet them at the jail right away."

"Sí, senor, I can find them."

Guthrey tossed him a dime; the boy caught it in both hands and smiled. Then, barefoot, he tore out.

A young man named Cripps woke up to Guthrey's pounding on the back door of the Combs Funeral Home.

"Sheriff, what can I do for you?"

"I have a murdered man in the buckboard. I will need a report on his death for a court hearing. Your boss will understand."

Dressed in a nightshirt, the boy asked, "Who is he and who killed him?"

"Mark Peters. Lived on his ranch over east, and I don't know who killed him."

"My heavens, I know him. He was a blacksmith too. He fixed my father's things. He was no gunman or horse thief. Why did they kill him?"

"I don't rightly know. Grab his feet, I have him by the chest. Let's get him inside. I have lots to do."

"Yes, sir."

They toted him inside and put him on a marble table.

"Thanks. I'll check on him later," Guthrey said and hurried out to head for the jail. He set the team down at the front door and hurried inside. The night shift jailer Randolph was sipping coffee when Guthrey reached the office.

"What's wrong?" the man asked.

"They — someone lynched Mark Peters on one of his own windmills."

241

"Holy shit. Who did that?"

"I don't know, Randolph. I've sent for Baker and Zamora. What worries me the most is there may be more killings going on right now at other ranches. This may only be the first spark of things to happen."

"Damn, who's doing that?"

"I assure you, if I knew who did it, I'd have already arrested them."

"Oh, I know. But no one's seen anything?"

Guthrey shook his head. "No witnesses."

"What kin I do for you?"

"Send word to the Bridges Ranch for Noble and Dan to come here and help."

Randolph set down his cup. "You watch things here. I know a boy who can ride up there and get them."

"That sounds swell."

Randolph flopped his weather-beaten hat on his head and rushed off. On the verge of exhaustion, Guthrey dropped into the swivel desk chair. He'd need some sleep before he rode anywhere else. When his two men got here, they could go guard one of those other ranches that might be next. His deputies, who he expected to arrive shortly, would know someone else to send to the other place. His jailer in charge could mind the office. He'd be spread thin but they'd make it.

The memory of seeing Mark's boots at eye level about made him vomit again. These killers had to be hard to do such a cruel thing. Strangling a man to death by pulling him up in a noose. Guthrey's body shuddered in the chair. No way could he imagine what went through their minds when they did that. He had to stop them before they struck again.

"What's wrong?" Baker asked, rushing into the office. "The boy said you needed us right away."

"Someone murdered Mark Peters yesterday." He took out the paper and spread it on the desk. "Here's the note they pinned on his chest."

"Why, they can't even spell. They back shoot him?"

"No, they lynched him by pulling him up the side of a windmill while he was strangling in a noose. It was gruesome."

Baker made a sick face. "Why?"

" 'Cause he didn't leave like they ordered him to. That's the word they mean, not leaf on a tree like they spelled it. My concern now is we need to guard the other two ranchers they threatened before they kill them. I hope we can in time. I sent for Noble and Dan — they can watch one of the families."

"I can get two more men from here in town to take care of the Davis folks on the south, I'm certain."

"Good; you handle that. Noble and Dan can go to the Codys when they get here. That will leave Zamora here to hold down the fort. I want you and me to go back to that scene on the Peters Ranch in the daylight and look for clues."

"I'll go locate those two men and be back ready to ride over there. What about his wife?"

"She's with Cally right now."

"Good deal."

Zamora arrived and Guthrey explained the situation again. When he finished telling him the whole story, Zamora said he and Baker would go and search the murder site and that Guthrey needed to get some rest.

Guthrey didn't argue.

"And we will put up Mrs. Peters's team. You go to bed. You're a sleepwalking man and out of it."

Guthrey took a pencil and, on the back of an obsolete wanted poster, drew them a map to the windmill. The deputy said they could find it. He thanked them, satisfied things were going to be being handled, and then he headed for their place in town. When he got there, after he waved off eating anything, Cally led him around to the hammock in the lacy shade. He took off his boots, hat, and gun belt and crawled in, grateful for the chance to close his dry eyes.

Cally kissed him. "I already thanked God that you were all right. That poor woman Olive is really shaken by all this."

He nodded. "That's why I brought her here. So am I."

Then he slept.

Two hours later, Dan and Noble arrived. Cally had explained about Peters's death. They wanted to know what they could do.

Half-groggy, Guthrey tried to clear his foggy mind. "The Cody family over on Pearl Creek is one of the ranches threatened. You two be sure this doesn't happen to them. Noble, their ranch is near the Pima County line. You know the place?"

"I do. Go back to sleep. We can watch them."

Dan nodded in agreement and Guthrey went back to sleep. He finally woke up in the heat of the afternoon and threw his legs over the side of the hammock, scrubbing his face with his hands. Cally told him that Dan and Noble had already ridden for the Cody's Ranch to watch it.

"I have some food for you," she said from

the doorway, poised to feed him.

Still numb, he nodded. He couldn't recall the last time he'd eaten, and his stomach was grinding at his spine. Food might be the thing to quiet all that growling.

On a tray she brought him some burritos wrapped in flour tortillas, a bowl of red salsa, and a large tin can filled with sun tea. He sipped the drink first and nodded his approval.

Cally sat on the ladder-back chair that he'd hung his gun belt and hat on and smiled at him. "Our two should be over at that ranch by now. Baker came by and told me he sent two men out to guard the Davis family. Baker and Zamora have gone to study the mur— I mean, the spot where they hung him."

"Good, we have those places covered. They may not try anything again, but I'm worried these killers have a plan to upset all the ranchers enough to run more off than the last guy ever did, though I have no count of all of them."

"Are you all right?" Olive asked from the doorway.

"I'm fine. You and Cally need to go make arrangements with the funeral director, I suppose today. I am going to bathe and have a shave, then go to my office and try to figure out a way to stop these vicious men."

Biting her lower lip, Olive agreed with the plan.

"We can do that while you clean up," Cally said to Olive as he finished his lunch.

"I sure appreciate all she's done for me," Olive told him.

"She's a wonderful woman. She'll help you. My men have gone back to look for evidence. We will catch them."

"There's water in the barrel," Cally said. "I hope it warmed up for you."

He laughed. "It may be a short bath."

Cally said, "We're off to the funeral home. Let's go, Olive, and get that over with."

After his bath and shave, Guthrey put on the clean clothes Cally had laid out and went to the office. The big jailer, Cam Nichols, was there. At Guthrey's arrival, the jailer stood up and shook his hand.

"Bad deal about Mark Peters. He was a helluva nice guy. What will his wife, Olive, do?"

"I don't know, Cam. She's really upset and has no plans I know about."

The man closed his mouth and nodded like he was deep in thought before he spoke again. "I'd sure like to have her for my wife if she gets over losing him. Reckon I'd have a chance? My size scares most women away. You have a small wife; what do you think?"

"I think you could succeed in the future. Maybe dress up for the funeral and afterward offer your assistance. If she accepts you being helpful, she might consider you."

"I don't own a suit, but I do have a nice white shirt and a tie. Would that do?"

He considered the man's size. Not many stores had ready-made clothes that large. "I bet you'd need one made to fit you. Sure, dress nice and be helpful. She may see the whole Cam Nichols like I do. A dependable, great guy."

"Damn, boss man, you'd make a fighting chicken think he was a duck and could swim."

They both laughed. "I imagine the funeral will be tomorrow. Her team is here. I'll get it set up for you to take her from my place to the funeral home. We can get the jail watched tomorrow."

"You'd do that for me?"

"I sure would. Best of luck."

"Wow, that's sure nice of you. I won't disappoint you or her."

"Cam, I know that, but a week from tomorrow we have a hanging to attend to. So don't run off until that's over."

"Run off?"

"Life's short out here. Folks have done those kinds of things quickly. I'd honeymoon up on Mount Graham. It's cool up there. Cally can borrow a cabin for you to use."

With a smile, Guthrey nodded at Cam's shocked face. "I mean that too."

"Holy cow, boss man, you gave me the jitters. But I will politely try to do my best."

"You ever been married?"

"My wife, Manda, died five years ago. It's been a long time. I miss her. Always will. But I'd sure be proud if what you say could happen does."

"You have my best wishes for it to succeed."

"You mind if I go see about some things? My swamper can handle this place."

"No, go ahead. I'll be here."

"Thanks a lot."

Leaning back in the chair, Guthrey nodded to himself. *They'd make a good pair.* He went through the wanted posters that were fresh. Not a face showed up he'd seen lately. The Combs's funeral director's aide, a young man, brought him all of Peters's things. There was a pocket watch that still ran. A short pencil, a log book in a leather cover that no doubt had all the information about his cattle in it and probably his expenses and debts listed. Twenty dollars in folding money and gold coins plus a medal from the Civil War.

He would deliver them to Olive. What else? He hoped his men could find something around the windmill to point a finger at someone. None of the men he'd assigned to look after the two ranches had had time to get there yet. He could only hope there weren't any more murders.

Thayer and his wife, Nell, came by to see what they could do for Olive and him. On a trip into Steward's Crossing they got the word, and the news was spreading fast. He sent them to Cally, figuring the women were back by that time.

By nightfall several ranchers had ridden in to offer him their help. He told them to be aware and go in pairs to work cattle away from the ranch house. On the desk he made a list of those who'd checked in.

Baker and Zamora returned with little information or evidence. The night man named Pat McCaney came in, and the deputies and Guthrey left to go home. Guthrey felt disappointed but he'd done all he could — no news of any more killings was good news. But these men had struck once, and they'd do it again. He walked down the hard caliche hill in his high boot heels, deeply engrossed in his own thoughts.

"I think Olive's better," Cam said, meeting him halfway. "I told her I'd pick her up and do anything she needed done. She accepted my offer. The funeral is at ten A.M."

"Good. Very thoughtful of you." They shared a nod in the twilight and both went on.

Cally met him with a hug. "That man you sent to help her, Cam Nichols, is sure a nice man. Big as a bear, but polite and kind. He really helped us today."

"Good. He's fine man."

"He's getting a second seat put on the buckboard for the funeral tomorrow. It's at ten. Can you come?"

"Certainly."

"Come on. I have food cooked, and they've brought more dishes than the three of us can ever eat."

"I bet so. Lots of folks came by the office and offered their help today. We will find the killers."

"Did your men find anything?"

"No. Nothing to find but tracks."

"I understand. We must be quiet. She's finally sleeping."

He agreed.

After the meal, with the sun down, the two of them slept in the hammock in the backyard.

In the morning, Guthrey dressed for the funeral and had breakfast with both of them. Their conversation at the table over the meal was polite. Olive mentioned Cam and thanked Phil for providing such a nice man. He nodded and then went to the office.

Cam was at the desk when he came in. "Have you read his tally book?"

"No, why?"

"I was wondering about his herd numbers but that's not important. Read what he wrote."

Guthrey read the page written in pencil.

Three men rode up. One was Mex. Clark, Freeman, and a Box K horse brand —

Then the writing ended. That was the last thing written in the book.

"This is the last thing he wrote," Guthrey said. Shocked by what Cam had discovered, he slumped in the chair. "He wrote the names of his killers in here. Lord, this is powerful. Don't tell a soul about this. After the funeral I'll talk to my men and we'll start to unfold this information. By damn, Cam, you found a deep secret that survived his murder. Have a good day with Olive

252

today. It will be a tough one, but you being there will help her. We'll get these killers."

He filed the tally book in a drawer in the open safe. He didn't need anything or anyone to get it. *Thank you, lord. You have saved me.*

SEVENTEEN

The preacher's voice carried over the strong, hot wind. Women's full dresses and hats were close to being swept away in the oven like blasts that struck the hill where the dirt was piled beside the grave and the pine coffin that would deliver Mark Peters to the hereafter.

Guthrey stood beside Cally and Cam loomed next to the veiled widow Peters. The oration was too long, the stinging winds punishment for the sinners. Guthrey grew weary standing beside his wife, on his feet through the entire service, until finally the last amen silenced the oration.

Word was passed that lunch would be served after the funeral at the Methodist Church, and friends went by Olive to give her their sympathies. Cam was there to help her and added what needed to be said in response to the folks trying to express their concerns to her. In his bright white shirt and a short black tie, the gentle giant looked like a guardian beside her on the scene.

Folks began to disperse and most headed for the meal at the church grounds, Guthrey and Cally among them. Lots of people were in town and most were very upset about Peters's murder. Guthrey asked several men he trusted to find some time to help him get the men responsible for doing it. He was sure the note in Mark's tally book would lead him to the killers — but it would not be easy to sort out. He obviously knew them well enough he wrote their names down before they rode up to him.

These men had not been seen by anyone so far as he could tell when they made the three raids. There were more than three men involved in those raids. They all occurred within a few days, but then had they concealed themselves. Eight men, their horses, and a housekeeping outfit all had to be concealed somewhere. That place might be something someone had seen recently. He and his men needed to find this thread to their presence when they were all close in the county for those first raids. Three men came back from God knew where to lynch Mark. They could have been concealed, but likely someone saw them come and go. He needed those witnesses for the trial when he caught these men. They must not have had masks on when they confronted Mark — but he was suspicious enough to have written down their names and a brand.

His main deputies were back when he reached the office late that afternoon. Guards were supposed to be in place at the other two ranches the night riders had threatened, and there were no reports of any other attacks. The door was closed to the jail and the hall.

"I have something for you to see. I want no word about it told to anyone. In Mark's tally book, Cam found a note. Last thing Mark wrote in it was this." He handed Baker the leather-covered book, open to the names.

"Mex, Clark, and Freeman and a Box K branded horse. I don't know who this fits but it must be the three that lynched him." Baker handed it to Zamora.

"One thing I say, he knew them on sight."

"Who uses a Box K brand on their horses?" Zamora asked.

They shook their heads and turned up their hands — none of them knew, Guthrey decided. He spoke up, "I can wire Preskit and find out from the state brand inspector. It may not be registered in Arizona, but they can find out if any other states use it. We have a small clue. Thank God that Mark left us this tally book."

Baker removed his hat and scratched his head. "Zamora and I looked hard at those signs. I think they swept some away. We have no idea where they rode off to after they left the windmill."

Guthrey nodded that he understood. "Let's keep this to ourselves. I think we have enough things to go on. Now we need to find out where they stayed. We also need an Apache tracker who can read tracks. They say they can track a titmouse over a rock."

"There are some good ones. We used one over at Socorro."

"I wonder if San Carlos would lend us one."

"You met them and bought Cochise from there. You know them."

"There's a wire up to there. They report runaways on it and the message is sent through Tucson," Zamora said.

"I'll wire them tomorrow."

"If not, General Crook at Fort Bowie might loan us a couple of his scouts."

"Good. We need a tracker first, I guess. Thanks, men."

"I'll test the water tomorrow. Cam is off for a few days to help Mrs. Peters, so we all might need to keep an eye on the jail."

"He did a damn good job out there today," Baker said. "Who's on the execution party that's coming up?"

"Cam said he'd be back for that. The three of us, unless either of you want to be excused?"

"We work for you," Baker said.

Zamora quickly agreed.

"Thanks. I'm going home to my wife. You two do the same."

Guthrey checked around. The night jailer said he was fine, and so Guthrey walked back to the jacal. A light was on and Cally rushed to hug him when he arrived.

"Been a long day?" she asked, sweeping his hat off as he kissed her.

"A real long one. I'll wash my hands after I feed —"

"Wash up. I already fed the team and the big one. Your man took Olive home to her ranch and I have beef roast fixed and some cold biscuits. What happens next?"

"You can't say a word about this. In his tally book, Mark left three IDs and one horse brand we think fit the killers."

"Really? How wonderful. Your man Cam was sure a big help for Olive. He's a very sincere man, isn't he?"

"He said his wife died five years ago and

now he is very interested in Olive. No better time to meet her than now, when she really needs someone. He's polite and smart."

"I hate to bring it up, but next week is the execution?"

"I have it marked on my calendar. Yes."

"I'm not vengeful, but that day is important to me. I'm not certain I can stand it, but I feel strongly it is my duty to be there for Dad."

He nodded. "I understand. It has been long time coming. The man I captured had no remorse about killing your father. He may have regrets on the scaffold, but I don't expect him to apologize. He shot your father thinking it would give him a chance to buy your place and thus have the gold source."

Wrapping her arms around him, she muttered into his vest, "What would have happened if you hadn't come here?"

"You'd not have a dusty lawman to hug."

She looked up and the tears sparkled in her eyes. "Oh, Phil, much more than that."

"I want to eat, clean up, and share your bed."

"I can hardly wait." Then as if realizing her remark sounded bold, she put her hand to her mouth and winked at him.

"You are a real rascal. Good, let's eat."

After supper he took a bath in the barrel and she shaved him. They blew out the lamps and went to bed. Two honeymooners in their own bed at last; damn, he loved having her for a wife.

An execution and a murder to solve all would be hard work. Somewhere there was an answer — he must find that link.

In two days a telegram came with the information that a horse with the Box K brand belonging to a Lonnie Sikes in Silver City, New Mexico Territory, had been stolen a few months earlier. No doubt the animal could have been sold to someone — maybe, maybe not? There was no answer there. Silver City, Guthrey thought, must be two hundred miles away from Soda Springs. North a good ways from Lordsburg and the site of lots of mines and smelters, he'd learned while riding over from Arizona. Mines and smelting were not anything he wanted to do so he never went up there to investigate the industry.

Still, they had a clue from Mark's notes worth hanging on to. Guthrey's wire to San Carlos, sent the day of the funeral, hadn't been answered. So he dismissed the notion of finding an Apache scout from over there. Besides, he had no trail for the scout to sniff out. Days counted down slowly. He was on office duty while the deputies searched for the way the killers went or where they might have stayed. Even the "cow counters" were looking for something.

A man dressed in Mexican cotton clothing and a straw sombrero came in on Wednesday and softly asked, with an Indian accent, where the sheriff could be found.

"Howdy, what can I do for you, sir?" Guthrey rose from behind the desk.

The man, holding his hat in one hand, handed him a letter with his other. "This tells all that."

Dear Sheriff Guthrey,
We met when you came through San Carlos after those stage robbers. I have sent you Vancenta Carlos. He was kidnapped by Apaches as a boy in Mexico and lived with them ever since. He knows all the Apache ways about tracking and finding men. He wishes to join his own people since the Apache woman he was married to died recently. I told him you needed him and so I have sent him over to offer his services. He was always a good man here and very helpful to the agency. I hope you have work

for him.

Respectfully,
Subagent Woodrow Styles

Guthrey looked up at the stone-faced man. "Have a chair. Can I call you Vance?"

The man nodded and pulled a folding chair closer to the desk. "That would be fine."

"I want to hire you as a deputy. I need a man who can track. He said you know how."

"I do."

"Find a room. I can pay you twenty-five a month. You will have to ride in posses and help us keep order. Maybe buy some gringo clothes. We can do that with a storekeeper. I want you to be sure that you really want this job."

"Oh, I do. My wife is dead. All San Carlos does is remind me that she is dead. I can speak Spanish, Apache, some Yavapai, and English."

"That sounds good. Tomorrow we must execute a man for murder. You saw the scaffold outside?"

"Yes."

"I may get you a packhorse and send you out searching. How would that be?"

"I can do that. What do you want me to find?"

"A horse with a Box K brand on his shoulders."

"Who rides him?"

"One of the men who killed a rancher a week ago."

"I can do that if he is still here."

"Let's go to the store. Your white outfit is too bright for a deputy to wear."

"I can go as an Apache warrior."

Guthrey shook his head. "No. Someone might probably shoot you."

Vance agreed with the possibility. Guthrey grabbed his hat. "Let's go."

On the way to the store, Guthrey said, "I want you to go to the crime scene and try to find where the killers were camped from there. That will be hard, I know, but they lynched a man with a hangman's noose by hauling him up on a windmill."

"That was bad. Why?"

" 'Cause he would not leave, the note said. A group had threatened him with torches and masks a few days before — but he didn't leave, so they came back and hung him."

"I see why you are upset."

"We'll get you dressed and then you can go search that country over there looking for something and a Box K branded horse."

■ ■ ■ ■

Execution day faced him. His condemned prisoner, Burroughs, had been visited in his cell for long spells by the Methodist minister Lester McClain, praying for his soul. Cam came back for two days. A lot more somber than before but he never mentioned Olive except to say that she was settling some at last.

The process on that day of carrying out the sentence had begun long before sunrise. The time set by the judge was eight A.M. Guthrey asked his part-time deputies to report for duty at dawn to keep an eye on the large number of people already gathered there who were determined not to miss the spectacle. People were camped out all around Soda Springs, the smoke of their campfires strong on the wind.

Dan had come in from the Cody Ranch the night before and promised to bring Cally in the buckboard. Things had been quiet out at the ranch that he and Noble guarded. Guthrey was relieved. His new man Vance had ridden out dressed like a gringo with a loaded packhorse to look for the raiders' hideout.

Armed with shotguns, his main deputies

walked the prisoner, who was dressed in black, to the scaffold. Sheriff Guthrey stood on the platform. The carpenters had done a good job on its construction. The sound of gritty soles on the steps resounded as the prisoner and his jailer, Cam, started up the stairs.

Then, in a small pocket, the assembled crowd began to sing, "Nearer, my God, to thee . . ." People struggled to their feet and the hymn's words grew louder, until, when James Burroughs was standing beside Guthrey, the entire hillside was singing. There was no emotion visible on the prisoner's face.

Reverend McClain cleared his throat and in a loud voice asked for everyone to pray. "Our dear Heavenly Father." His words were clear and directed at all those assembled, but the final prayer went on and on asking for forgiveness, for blessings for everyone there.

Guthrey read aloud the judge's order for James Burroughs to be executed for the murder of Harold Bridges. "Found guilty by a jury of his peers, this man should be hung by his neck until dead."

Burroughs stood, securely bound by ropes that Cam had made certain were tight around his legs and arms, with his hands behind his back.

"Do you have anything to say?" Guthrey asked the prisoner.

Burroughs shook his head.

Guthrey announced, "The convicted man has nothing to say."

Several in the crowd booed him but quickly hushed.

Guthrey put the noose around Burroughs's neck and tightened it behind his left ear, then put the mask over his head. The drop Burroughs faced should snap his neck when his body reached the end of it — otherwise he would strangle. Applying the rope, Guthrey silently prayed the drop did the job.

Guthrey pulled the lever he'd tested a dozen times with a sandbag at Burroughs's weight that was used for practice. The rush of the man's form went through the open hole and the rope creaked when his weight hit the end. The crack of his neck was loud enough Guthrey heard it, and he turned to his men. "It's over. Let's go down."

They silently nodded.

Doc used his stethoscope to listen to the man's heart while he lay in the wagon that had been backed under the scaffold in preparation to receive his body. Doc took the instrument out of his ear and said, "The man is dead."

The ropes were untied. Next the noose was removed, and Cam coiled up the rope as the jail's property. Then the body was covered by the two helpers from the funeral parlor.

Burroughs's corpse, accompanied by the reverend, lay in the coffin that was now nailed shut by the two men. They hauled him out for the grave already dug. The matter of Cally and Dan's father's death was over — Guthrey hoped his wife and brother-in-law would have some finality on this day.

"Some guy wanted to buy the rope," Cam said with a scowl.

"No. Store it at the office and we will burn it later. They'd only want to cut it in pieces and sell it at carnivals."

"I told him hell no."

"Good. I need to check on my wife. I'll be back in short while."

"I'm going back to the Peters Ranch and look after Olive," Cam said.

"I understand. Tell her we all share her loss."

"I will. Thank you." Cam went for his big horse.

Guthrey walked downhill to his house as the dispersing crowd left the center of town. Several people spoke to him but he just waved. He was in no mood to talk about Burroughs or the man's intention in killing Bridges. At the doorway, Cally rushed to hug him, and it was obvious she had been crying.

Dan stood up from a kitchen chair and nodded. "It went well."

"Yes, thank God."

"I'm going back to the Cody Ranch and help Noble. We haven't seen anyone who looked threatening, but after Mark's murder, who knows."

"This is secret. I telegraphed the agent at San Carlos for a tracker. He sent me a Mexican man, Vance, who had lived among the Apaches most of his life. His Apache wife recently died and he wanted to leave the agency. They said he's a good tracker. He's searching for a Box K branded horse and where these men have holed up. I gave him a badge to keep out of sight unless he needed it. He has a packhorse and supplies. Those men had to have a base and he might find it."

"That was smart. They simply popped up. No one in that country saw them come or go. Noble and I have checked with about everyone up there. The old man thinks they rode smoke."

"I agree, Dan, which is why I hired Vance.

He may find how they did it."

"Noble will sure approve of your plans. I'll go back, and we're keeping our eyes open."

"We'll get things to normal someday," Guthrey said. "One of us needs to check on our man at the Bridges Ranch. Cally may soon want to go back home, but I'll handle it. You get back with Noble — nothing may happen but we can't take a chance."

"I agree. If you learn anything let us know."

"I will, Dan."

"Bad day for you?" Cally asked, holding his hand.

"Yes, but a part of the job I accepted."

"I was up there with you spiritually, at least, and I felt every pain in your heart. Thought about Dad, who loved this dry land and worked to water it. How proud he must be up there of us able to carry on his dream."

"Yes, Cally, we are fighting to keep it, and winning."

She hugged him and sobbed. The day must have been a killer for her, bringing all those memories back. He squeezed her tightly. It was too much for anyone with a heart, and Cally had a soft one. She'd hidden it behind a façade the day he first arrived on their ranch. Who would want an old Texas Ranger on their place anyway? She said openly that she could not afford him. Lots of sand had blown by them since then. It damn sure wasn't water save for the shallow river.

He was proud he'd stayed and even more so for his lovely wife — someday law and order would prevail in this stickery land of cactus.

"I guess I'll go home in the morning," Cally said, wiping away the tears with a handkerchief. "Things have settled down some. We really should, seriously, consider building a house here. You will only get more involved in this job in the future."

"I thought we decided and that you would do that?" he asked.

She wrinkled her nose. "No, that's a husband's job. I will furnish it."

"There is a man builds houses here. His name is Dresscoe. I think he does a fine job. Stay another day and we can look at his work."

"If you think I need to be here, I'll stay. Now sit down and eat lunch. I have some sun tea. It isn't hot but it may not be cool either. Sorry."

"Sure. You join me. Dan's already gone back. I simply need to sit here and let the day go on."

"You don't drink. I noticed that a long time back when you first came here. Men offer you liquor and you turn them down. I am proud that you don't drink, Phil. Most men on days like this would throw a drunk."

"I saw that the getting drunk business didn't solve much. I just don't care for it. Haven't for years. A few times in my youth I considered it, but I didn't like anything that took my thinking and regard for others away. So sometimes I have a beer but that's all."

"Don't change. You know, Olive said — well, she told me she had a crush on you years ago when you were in the Rangers."

"Olive and I met several years ago. I didn't really let on I knew her from before until one day I came by their place and she thanked me for keeping my secret about her. She ran off back then to a wilder life. I don't know how, but she finally reached her senses when she met a man who had a freight business, married him, went back to church, and had a good life until he died of a heart attack. A few years later she married Mark, also a widower. She's a good Christian lady today."

"I took what she said as nice to know, not as a scandal, and you know the Lord for-

271

gives us for those past sins."

"Amen." He chuckled and picked with his fork at the enchiladas she had fixed for him. "I sent Cam, who is a widower, to care for her. He's a kind man. I didn't want to be — well, involved, even as a friend, that close to her. I don't need Olive — I have you — but I can resist things better at this distance."

"Thanks, big man. I appreciate your honesty."

"No problem." He began eating his meal, feeling good it was all out.

"Dan acts more normal when he's working for you than he does working on the ranch, right? What can we do?"

"Did you ask him what he wants to do?"

"No. I simply figured the ranch is half his. What else could he do?" She turned up her hands, seated across from him. "That might be what he needs. Someone to ask him what he wants?"

"Do that someday when you two are alone."

"My, my, we seem so serious today. Maybe we need some time — in bed today?"

"I agree."

They both laughed.

The next morning Guthrey met his deputies. Cam was still out at the Peters Ranch.

No one said a word. The jail was empty. Guthrey sent Baker to check on the other two men at the Davis Ranch. His men all knew about Vance and no one had seen him either so he must be looking hard in the chaparral for any signs of the killers. Poor man had so little to go on, Guthrey about felt sorry for sending him out there.

Midmorning, Guthrey went to locate Dresscoe. He found the man, in his forties, amid a mountain of coffins of turpentine-smelling wood stacked around in his shop.

They introduced themselves to each other and shook hands.

He showed Guthrey to some new wooden benches to sit on.

"I want to build a house on my property under the hill. There are two acres there and a decent well. And I need a windmill, holding tank, and the rest. Probably even move the corrals in back."

"I have one thing to say. If you want a good house to last here you need all redwood in the foundation and lower part. There are ferocious termites here that will eat your house up in four years. They won't eat redwood."

"How expensive is it?"

"More so than pine lumber cut locally. But we can get some."

"Can you come to my house for supper? Bring your plans."

"Sure. I will be there at six?"

"Fine. My wife is here today and I want her approval as well."

"I understand. See you then."

He went back to the house and told Cally that Dresscoe was a nice man who'd be there for supper.

"What will I fix him?"

"Food, of course."

"Oh, Phil, you are no help at all."

That evening after her fine meal, they settled with their builder on a plain bungalow with stairs to the attic as a place for guests to sleep and four windows to ventilate it. The corrals would be rebuilt in back of the old and new structures, plus a windmill and shower area were included. Dresscoe promised to save them all he could but thought the entire plan would approach fifteen thousand dollars.

"We can afford that," she said.

"Fine."

The three shook hands. Dresscoe hurried off to his own house to get the project going.

The two hugged each other inside the jacal.

"Well, you will have the nicest house in

town someday," he teased.

"I already have the best husband."

"That is in doubt," he teased some more. She was sure enough heady company for him.

Excited about her house plans, Cally decided to stay in Soda Springs for a bit. Things were quiet enough in town that Guthrey rode out to the ranch two days later and checked with his man Guermo. Midday he rode up on Cochise and Deloris ran out to greet him.

"Good day, senor. Get down. I can make some coffee and serve you some of my sopaipillas. Guermo is out checking cattle today. The screwworms are bad this year."

Guthrey dropped off his horse and loosened the cinch. "I'm glad you two are here. Have any troubles?"

"No, everyone who came by has been very helpful. Is your wife okay? I miss her."

"She is going to build a house in town so we can be closer. I imagine she will be back here soon. I hope you're comfortable in the house while we're both gone. You have plenty of supplies?"

"Oh, sí. We have enough of everything. She likes to be with you, like I do my man."

He agreed and went inside after Deloris.

The little children drew back at the sight of him and he wished he had brought hard candy for them.

"Is the baby fine?"

"He is very healthy."

"That's swell. You're certain that Guermo doesn't need anything?"

"No, senor. He is so pleased to be a vaquero again he comes home singing every night."

"I know the feeling," He nodded, amused. The man probably was pleased to be back in the saddle after squatting at that empty ranch and trying to get by for so long.

"Dan and Noble will be back in a week or two. But I'm glad he's happy."

"You don't know how nice it makes me feel. He is never sharp, never angry. I will try to be sure he always gets to stay in the saddle."

"I understand." He sipped her rich coffee and approved of it.

Obviously things were in good shape at the ranch. The boys could help catch things up in a few days if Guermo was behind. But the situation looked to be in good hands. Since Guthrey had promised Cally he'd be back, he rode over to Soda Springs after thanking Deloris and eating some of her honey drizzled sopaipillas. My, how delicious they were.

Back at his place near sundown, he put up his stallion and Cally met him coming in.

"Is it all dried up?" she asked.

"It's dry and I saw a few cows and calves. They're finding things to eat. And Guermo is treating several cattle for screwworms each day, but says he's keeping up. He is so happy, Deloris says he sings coming in each night on his horse."

"Really?"

"I don't blame him. He likes the role, and after the near starvation they had squatting on that deserted ranch, your place is heaven."

She smiled. "You did good hiring those two."

"Yes. Has my new deputy been here today?" He wondered where the man was at.

"No, did you expect him to come by?"

"I guess he'll come in when he needs us."

"Come." She took his hand. "Your meal is in the oven."

"More clouds today. No rain again."

"If I could wring some out I would."

He hugged her shoulder. "I bet you would."

Eighteen

When Guthrey woke up before dawn, he went outside to relieve his bladder. He discovered the silhouettes of two horses hitched to his corral and someone rolled up in a blanket on the ground.

He squatted down and the man woke up.

"Senor Guthrey. I found some things you might want to see."

"You found them?"

"I think they stayed at this place I found."

"Good. I'll get my wife up and after breakfast we can ride out there."

"*Sí,* but they are not there now. I think they may come back. They left some things. I think they rode from Peters's windmill to this place."

"Sounds great, Vance. I'll be ready to ride up there right after breakfast."

His man stood up and folded his blanket. "You will see."

"Cally, we have company —"

"I know. I'm dressed. I'll make you two breakfast. It's nice to meet you, Vance," she said to him.

"It is nice to meet you as well, senora."

"He's found something and thinks it's their hiding place." Guthrey finished dressing and soon found his chair.

"I have ridden many miles. I have seen many things. But I think you will agree this is their hideout."

"Have they been there lately?"

"No one was there while I was in there. Their trail goes to Tombstone. I think they may stay down there most of the time."

"Good. Why're you so sure that they are the same ones?"

"I found two more nooses made up there."

Cally sucked in her breath. "Oh my God."

Guthrey agreed with her. "Two more nooses?"

Vance nodded. "That is why I am so sure these are the men that lynched the rancher." He turned his palms up at both of them.

"How did you ever find this place?"

"I found some tracks near the windmill. At a distance from where they must have waited in the brush cover for some time for him to come out there."

"I'm not complaining, but my men lost their tracks leaving there."

"They carefully swept those tracks, I think, but to the south is where they stayed and, I think, they hid to watch for him to come check on his mill. Maybe for as long as two days."

"Determined, huh?"

"I have some coffee. You drink coffee, Vance?"

"Sure. Thanks for having me in your house."

"You can come anytime. In my house, you're his man and we are family."

The man nodded but he still looked uncertain.

"Listen, what she says is the truth."

"Since my wife died, I have had no family. I am very grateful for your invitation."

She waved the pancake turner around. "Don't ever worry. You've got a big family with all of us."

"Vance, I'm amazed at what you found, but the fact that they had two more nooses worries the fire out of me. Those others are still being guarded, but I had about thought those men had left the country."

"No, they have a packhorse grazing around there and all their things are in that cabin."

"That packhorse have a brand?"

"It is not the Box K brand you mentioned.

He has an E K on his shoulder."

"Nice work. We might ride to Tombstone and check the liveries first. If they are staying there we could find out, if that pony is in the stables."

"I didn't go there. I was afraid I might make the killers nervous and they'd run."

"You have spent all your life as an Apache and you talk straight English for a man that's been there that long."

"A preacher from the Dutch Reformed Church and his wife raised me. They were assigned to that reservation. So I lived in his house and we learned Apache together and I learned English. He corrected me a lot. Then I married Yellow Flower after her corn ceremony. She was a very lovely woman."

"I imagine so."

"I had proved myself as an Apache warrior. Some complained about me taking her as my bride, but no one challenged me. They knew I could fight." He looked away. Obviously he'd reached into his heart talking about his life. Guthrey understood.

After the meal, they rode to the office and Guthrey told Zamora their plans.

In a whisper he told Zamora, "This hideout he found still has two more nooses inside it."

"Holy Mary, do you think they have plans to hang the others they scared as well?"

"It looks that way. Baker should check on both places today and tell them to keep up their guard. And don't tell them what was found. Simply that we are concerned the killers may still be around here."

"Nice to have you helping us," Zamora said to Vance.

The man nodded. "I like the work."

"We're going back to check this place out."

"Do you think they work for Walter Pierson?"

"I'm not sure. But who else would hire enforcers to run folks off?"

"My thoughts too."

"Who is this Pierson?" Vance asked in the hall.

"He runs the largest ranch in the county. My men hate him. But we don't know he's part of these killers. You can't go accuse someone like him unless you damn sure have the facts and evidence. And when we do, if he is involved, we will run him in with the rest. Till then we'll keep him in mind. But, amigo, we are going get to the bottom of this."

Vance grinned. "*Sí,* we will find out."

■ ■ ■ ■

In no time they were headed southwest toward the Dragoon Mountains. Clouds began to build and Guthrey felt certain they'd cry some rain on someone in the region before sundown.

Robbers Roost, as he called it, was in a tight canyon. Probably the rough shack belonged to a company cutting timber in the area. Lots of logging signs but they were all old. This was a snug log cabin with a good spring feeding a large stone mortar tank and a water supply tank.

A thunderstorm caught them and they took shelter in the cabin.

Guthrey searched for anything he might find and he could learn something from. One was a perfumed letter from Fort Stockton, Texas, no doubt from a whore.

Dear Tim, darling,
There damn sure ain't no work for me here. I'll be coming to Tombstone on the next stage, darling. I'll mail you another letter when I get there so you can find me. I sure miss you, and them running us out of Dodge was a crime. Why, them councilmen that did that, I'd

tossed them in my bed for free I bet a dozen times. Ain't no justice for a lady of the night.

Love You So Much,
Theresa

"You want to read it?" Guthrey handed it to Vance. "One of them is Tim someone — wait." He found the envelope. "Tim Clark. Damn, that matches Peters's notes."

Vance smiled. "When I found those nooses I knew they had stayed here. Now we must find Tim Clark, huh?"

"There were more than three men on the first raids. They could get to the Peters Ranch by sneaking around the mountain and not many would see them go to his place. But they had seven or eight men in total by the reports when they carried the torches and threatened the other ranches."

"I bet you could hire men for that in Tombstone," Vance said.

"I don't doubt it, but I need to prove they did it. If we had the men hired for it, they might talk more than this last three would, especially if I have a murder warrant. And I need lots of information on them to make a case in court."

"Time will tell, huh?"

"You've done good."

Guthrey sat down on a bench at the table. On a piece of paper advertising an auction sale, he began to draw a crude map. "They must have left here and rode to Peters's and threatened him. Easy, no one saw them. Then they must have ridden by back trails to the Cody Ranch. That meant they stayed in the chaparral along the base of the mountains, avoiding being seen, striking at night, and going back into hiding. Then the next night they raided the Davis Ranch; they live this side of Codys', maybe ten miles, and went back in hiding. This made three ranches in a line from east to west and they never crossed the main stage route, though it sounded like they had swarmed the whole area."

"Are we going into Tombstone?" Vance asked.

"I think my appearance there might spook them. Someone would say the sheriff is here. I don't want them spooked. Not yet."

"I can go and learn about the horses they ride. Find out where they stay when they are in Tombstone. Also notice when they leave town if I find them."

"You must be careful. They learn that you're a spy, they'll cut your throat. These men are killers."

"I have no fear of them, but I will watch

closely."

"I'll give you some money to live on, but in a week or ten days report back to me. If things get hot, you get out of there right then."

Vance smiled. "I can do that. I can send you a telegram from Pedro Espinoza — that means things are breaking or going to happen."

"That'll work. Be careful." He gave his man ten dollars in change and folding money.

"I will spend it wisely."

"I know. You've done a great job. I'm counting on you."

"See you then, amigo."

Guthrey rode Cochise back to Soda Springs that afternoon and arrived at the jacal about sundown. Cally quickly joined him and asked about his day while he unsaddled.

"We found the cabin hideout in the Dragoons. The man in Mark's tally book named Clark is Tim Clark. His lady of the night is joining him in Tombstone. We think those three killers are staying in Tombstone and we figure they hired some men from in town there to make the raids. That's their headquarters and we'll investigate some more about it. That's all I can say. I was pleased my new deputy did all this work. Maybe he can find out more about them."

"Good. My sheriff is digging up the facts."

"Oh, it isn't easy." With Cochise loose in the pen, he swept her up in his arms and kissed her."

"Water in the barrel?"

"Sure but it will be cold."

"Anything else happen?"

"Dresscoe found the redwood lumber we need. It will be here in ten days."

"That sounds good."

"I was pleased. Will you be here until this Peters matter is settled?"

"You want to go home?"

She swung on his arm. "Not unless I have you."

"Then we stay awhile longer."

"Fine."

He wondered what else he could do about the murder. Not much until things opened or his man found out enough to make some arrests. It was good to be back in Cally's company; she relaxed him. He needed lots of that.

In the morning he'd get his men's heads together — maybe they could figure out what to do next.

NINETEEN

In the office the next morning, Guthrey, Baker, and Zamora talked about their problems behind closed doors.

"Yes, Vance did a great job of finding that place in a deep canyon. They left a packhorse and all their things. He's going to try to learn if they have horses stabled in Tombstone that match the Box K brand. If we get a telegram from Pedro Espinoza, things are going to break."

His men laughed.

"It is serious though. We speculated they hired some hard cases to make those torchlight raids. All those ranches they raided are in the south part of the country. They never crossed the stage line road and could keep in the chaparral and out of sight. Those three killers who met Peters are lounging around in Tombstone. I didn't go down there, fearing my presence might scare them into running off. Vance is down there checking things out. In a week we'll know lots more."

"Were those nooses there?"

"Yes. We left them so they wouldn't know we had found their camp. Vance's pretty smart for a man raised as an Apache. A minister on the reservation actually raised him and that's why he can read and write but he grew up with Apaches. Was a warrior too and that was how he won the girl who became his wife. Her death ended his Apache days. I was with him and, in regular clothes, he looks like one of us."

Baker shook his head. "We were lucky to get him when you wrote for help."

"Worked out good. Now we need to keep the guards up. I don't think these killers are through. Who they work for I still don't know, but somehow this time I am half convinced they are part of Pierson's men."

"Maybe Vance can find out?"

"Yes, he's not known down there so we may get a break. Keep his name and presence under your hats. We don't know the enemy that did this violent act. They may walk among us."

"I replaced the two men at the Davis Ranch," Baker said. "The other two had work to do."

"Fine. Has anyone checked on Dan and

Noble?"

"They said they were fine, saw them two days ago over at the Cody Ranch," Baker said.

"Thanks. All we can do is wait, watch, and listen."

Several days later, Guthrey left the office to have lunch with his wife. Two men standing in their own wagons were having a cussing match in the middle of the road. He frowned and headed over there.

"Hey, quit cussing out here. There are woman and children all around."

"Who in the hell are you?" demanded a red-faced man seated in the wagon on the right, headed for town.

"I'm the sheriff of Crook County, and you don't stop cussing, I'll arrest you and toss you in jail."

"By God, you don't look tough enough to do that, mister."

"What's your name?"

"None of your damn business. I'll cuss where I want." He had to rein in his sweaty team to keep them in place.

"Hold that team," he said to a big, strapping boy coming to see what the problem was.

"Yes, sir," the boy said, then jumped to it.

The other man, whiskered and wearing overalls, came off his wagon like it was on fire. He charged like a bear at Guthrey. For his trouble, Guthrey gave him three fast fists, and the man stopped in his tracks. With his boots planted, Guthrey swung again and struck him.

The attacker staggered backward two steps and with a roar came at him again. All he got this time were two more fast, hard blows to his face. One fist had bloodied his nose, and he looked wild, slinging blood all over and trying to get at Guthrey.

"Why, you —" He went into a torrent of cuss words that made Guthrey so mad he let go with a haymaker that put the man on his back — silence.

"What's wrong here?" Baker shouted, coming on a hard run from the courthouse.

"Who's he?" Guthrey asked the crowd.

"Henry Ackers," a woman under a sunbonnet said in disgust. "He's drunk like usual."

Guthrey looked around but the other man had driven off. "Who was he arguing with?"

"His neighbor Clyde Fremont."

Guthrey frowned at Baker, who had jerked the man up and disarmed him. "Lock him up and charge him tomorrow, in city court, for disturbing the peace. Young man, take his team to the livery, and he can bail them out and pay you a dollar. Leave your name with the livery man."

"I sure will, sheriff," the youth said. "Did you learn to fight like that as a Ranger?"

Guthrey held his sore hand in the other one. "Yes, that and backyard brawls."

The crowd laughed. With Baker now handling things, Guthrey was going home to soak his hand. It would be sore for days. And he knew just how sore.

"You got in a fistfight?" Cally asked, inspecting his hand at the table.

"Nothing else I could do. He charged me."

"Do you need to see the doctor?"

"Naw, I'll be fine. Sore, but fine."

She hugged him and laughed. "You should stay out of fights. Especially fistfights. I wonder if we should go check on the ranch while you have time?"

"I should go check on Dan and Noble out at the Davis Ranch, I guess. Those two will think I left them."

"Do you think those killers will strike again?"

He shook his head. "I have no way of telling. They could, any day, maybe. Though I am more interested in who hired them. I'm hoping we can find that answer."

"Your man found them."

"He's a pretty smart tracker and I am fortunate to have him."

"Sheriff Guthrey," Baker called out, and Guthrey hurried to the doorway.

"What's happened?"

"Telegram from Pedro whoever that says to meet him at Dragoon Mine."

"That's one Vance sent to me — that was our code. They must be on the move. Get a horse to ride and tell Zamora to watch things here. Get a rifle and some ammo as well. There must be something underfoot down there. We need to ride over there and find out what."

"Are you going with your hand that swollen?" his wife asked.

"I have to go."

"All right, but I'll worry about you anyway."

Baker had headed back for a mount while Guthrey went to saddle his horse. Tossing the saddle on Cochise's back hurt like hell, but he made no sign for Cally to interpret that he was in any pain. He quickly cinched the horse up, fit the bridle on, and tried to tie his bedroll on behind.

Seeing his ineptness with his hand, she elbowed him aside and finished the job on her toes. "There. See what I mean?"

"I will be fine."

"Sure. A one-handed gun shooter. You couldn't hit a barn left-handed I bet."

"It will work out."

"Sure, in a month or six weeks."

He swept her up with his left arm and kissed her good-bye. "I love you, Cally."

"You know I'll worry about you."

"I will be fine."

"Just so you are." She stepped back and he swung into the saddle as a sharp pain ran clear to his shoulder.

With a smile for her, he headed for the office to catch Baker. His .44/40 Winchester was under his right fender skirt and the big paint was single-footing it.

The day's heat was rising and big clouds had gathered in the south. It should rain somewhere before sunset. Baker joined him and they left Soda Springs in a long trot. Guthrey used his left hand to hold the reins and worked his right one to try and maintain some use of it. It felt awkward to him but it was the best he could do. In three hours they reached the Peters Ranch and stopped to talk to Cam, who was busy shoeing a horse.

Olive came down to join them. "Phil, nice of you two to drop by. I can't give up your jailer; he's too good a man for me to lose.

He's been treating stock for screwworms. They are sure bad this year."

"My man at the Bridges Ranch says so too. We need to push on and meet someone. Glad things are going so well."

"Oh, they are," she said and about blushed.

Guthrey nodded and they rode on.

"That's what Cam wanted, wasn't it?" Baker asked with a sly grin.

"Exactly."

"Didn't I hear somewhere that you knew her before?"

"Olive? Oh yes, when I was Ranger back in Texas years ago. She's a nice lady. What Cam wanted."

"Wonder what Vance found."

"By dark he should meet us somewhere down here near that camp where he found the other two ropes. I have no idea what he learned but the man is sharp on finding out things."

"I bet none of us would have found those nooses," Baker said, booting his horse to keep up with Cochise.

"He must have learned more about those killers or he'd never have telegraphed me to meet him."

"You been hearing that thunder?"

"It may rain on us. You got a slicker?"

Baker said, "Yes."

"We might ought to shake them out."

In minutes the dark clouds engulfed them and cold rain ran off their hat brims. Both men smiled at the luxury, and in a short while a rainbow showed up in the direction of Tombstone and the storms moved on. But more rain was coming and the notion they'd get more made Guthrey smile. "Won't hurt a thing."

"No, never look upset at a rain in this country; you may not seen another for six months."

By late afternoon, they were close to the trail that led into the Dragoons. Guthrey saw his man come riding out of a draw to join them.

"What's happening, Vance?"

"Your man Clark is the one rides the Box K horse. He and seven more rode up here yesterday. They are waiting, I think, for someone. I rode into Tombstone late last night to wire you when I figured they'd gone to sleep and weren't making a raid. One of the four with Clark is the Mexican. His name is Alvarez. Soto Alvarez. He's wanted by the law in New Mexico, a woman told me."

"I've never heard of him," Baker said.

"No idea about their plans whatsoever?"

"Only thing I know is they didn't leave the whores and hell-raising because they were tired of it. A couple of them asked Clark how long they had to wait up here."

"No idea?"

"Clark told them until the man came and gave them orders. Then they could earn their money."

"You were that close to them?"

"Sure, I'm an Apache."

Baker shook his head in dismay at the man while taking off his slicker as the heat began to rise. "Do you think they plan another raid?"

"Something. Maybe a stage robbery. But I think they plan a raid somewhere."

"You think they do other things besides lynch ranchers."

"Yes. A few nights ago I saw them stab a gambler to death in the alley and take all his money. They did it right in the alley behind the Oriental Saloon. He was drunk and had won some big pots in a high-stakes game. While he was pissing in the dark back there they went up behind him, cut his throat, got all his money, and were gone."

"The law know anything about it?" Baker asked.

"No, and they could not prove anything either."

"An Apache saw it." Guthrey shook his head, amused.

Vance shook his head warily. "These men are ruthless. They murdered some drunk whore in about the same way. She was mad about something and mouthed off to Clark out loud in a saloon about how he was a cheap bastard. In thirty minutes she was dead on her back in another alley."

"These guys must be real tough. They strangled a man to death with a rope and did that too." Guthrey flexed his sore hand at his side and wondered about such mad dog killers.

"They weren't saddled up yet when I left them," Vance said. "I don't think they will move until dark. We have some time to go eat. I know a woman nearby who can serve us some lamb. Then I can go watch them and come back to warn you when they do leave. They are only a short way away from here."

"Good plan. Food sounds good. Let's do that," Guthrey said, pleased with his man's work.

They rode their horses up a dry wash to where a couple of wickiups stood, the crude brush shelters had a canvas wrap to shed the occasional rain. The winkle-faced old woman who cooked Guthrey's lamb had no teeth and stood barely four foot tall in a filthy layered dress.

Vance spoke to her in Apache, no doubt telling her these were his friends. She smiled. Guthrey and Baker dismounted and nodded to her to be polite. They tied their horses to a mesquite bush and joined Vance, who already sat cross-legged on the ground.

"Her name is Ki-yah. When she begs in town, she tells people she once was one of Chief Cochise's wives. She was a whore, but got too old. Two younger ones live in that other wickiup — she says they are her daughters by the old chief who died. They're whores too and have already gone to town to find some work."

"Why are they doing this?" Guthrey asked him.

"Hey, it is much easier to make some money lying on your back than laboring as a squaw in the Sierra Madres and avoid the Mexican Army with the Bronco Apaches."

Guthrey and Baker both nodded they understood.

Regardless, their way of life had to be tough. The woman served the lamb on some wooden boards used for trays. The smoky mesquite-flavored meat smelled good, and Guthrey's mouth filled with saliva. The mutton, though it had a peculiar lanolin flavor, was delicious and sure beat all to pieces gnawing on jerky. Hot meat greased his lips and made him hungrier for more.

"Very good," Guthrey said to her as she gummed her part. Most squaws would have waited till the men were done before they ate. He'd eaten with Comanche, Kiowa, plus the Plains Apaches as a Ranger; sometimes he wondered whether the meat they served him was dog or buffalo, but usually he was starved to the point that anything made a meal.

Perhaps living off the flesh trade *was* easier than being a squaw.

After the meal, Guthrey paid Ki-yah a half dollar and she wanted to treat him in her wickiup. He declined and the other two snickered because she was plenty eager to fix him up. In the twilight they rode off for where the sleeping Dragoons lay like some giant red body on its side. Vance had a place out of sight in a side canyon. Horses hobbled for the night, they cleaned a spot of twigs and stickers with the sides of their boot soles to spread out their bedrolls on. Vance was convinced, from the tracks he'd checked on, that the gang had not came out from their hideout. Guthrey went to sleep wondering what they planned to do.

TWENTY

Up before dawn, they skipped a fire for coffee, ate jerky, and drank canteen water. Horses resaddled, they mounted up. Vance wanted to check on the outlaws, but after riding a ways around the mountain, he stopped Guthrey and Baker and drew them off into a dry gulch.

"What did you see?" Guthrey asked, knowing something brought on this move. He got out his scope to see what had triggered the man.

"There is a man on horseback coming toward the canyon." Vance took his telescope and dismounted. He climbed the steep bank and, once on top, lengthened the brass tube. Guthrey dismounted and gave Baker his reins. "I want to see him too."

His sore hand didn't help him climb up the slope, but soon he was on the rim standing in a grove of mesquite for cover. Vance handed him the glass. "I don't know him."

"He's dressed pretty fancy for riding out here." On a big sorrel horse, the man in the black suit wore a mustache and looked like a businessman — about forty years old, he had chiseled high cheekbones that would be hard to forget.

"We need a name for him. Better yet, when he rides out, we may arrest him as part of those killers. What do you think, Guthrey?"

"He's either in charge or the go-between."

"Will we arrest the rest of them?"

"I am considering it. I need one more piece of evidence to take them in."

"What could that be?"

"Anything — Burroughs had a watch my wife's father's killer had taken from his body and he let some guy win it in a poker game. That evidence hung him."

Vance shook his head wearily. "I didn't find anything else but those nooses."

"I know. Maybe we let him slip back to where he came from, learn his business, then arrest him. You ever recall seeing him in Tombstone?"

"No. But there are many people in that town." Vance shook his head. He had no answer for that.

"We better wait and see what the killers do next."

Vance nodded. "I hoped we'd get them red-handed."

"We still may do that."

Baker had taken the horses off east to a watering hole a little way over while they watched for the exit of this new man. In an hour Baker was back, and near noon the man exited the canyon.

"His horse has a spade brand on its left shoulder," Vance said, studying him through the glass.

"Good, we can find him later."

"You think they'll ride out sometime today?" Baker asked.

"That or they'll go back to Tombstone," Vance said. "The other day when I snuck up, I heard them say they were so upset about having to stay out here because they didn't bring any whores and whiskey out, and they thought they might go crazy."

Baker bent over laughing. Guthrey shook his head. "Hard to imagine. But these men are hardcase jerks and have no respect for anyone."

When evening drew close, Vance heard horses coming out of the canyon. If this group were going back to Tombstone — or even planning a stage robbery, unlikely as that seemed — they'd be leaving their shelter sometime during the day, not at night. Guthrey knew what they must do: send Baker to Tombstone to wire Zamora and tell him to send forces to both ranches. The threatened ranchers should not be left unguarded. *The killers were going to one of the ranches tonight.*

Baker left slowly, so the killers wouldn't notice a fast rider making dust, and headed for Tombstone. With Baker planning to catch up with them later, Guthrey warned him not to overrun the killers in the dark. Then he and his tracker set out to follow the gang at a safe distance. One thing Guthrey knew: It would be slow and could be a long time getting there. The danger to avoid was running into them stopped somewhere waiting to make the raid.

The night settled in and the animals of the night began their vocal sounds. Coyotes howled, desert owls hooted to mates, and the crickets chirped. Saddle leather creaked and steel horseshoes made muffled strikes on rocks. Bats darted about catching bugs as the twilight evaporated into a star-filled night outlined by the Dragoons' bulk on his right. The big paint horse carried Guthrey forth through the chaparral.

Vance was very intent in listening for the gang they followed. He pulled up and they watched the silhouettes of the riders as they scrambled, in a line, up the rise among the towering saguaros' crosslike outlines. Reined in, Guthrey spoke to Cochise. He didn't need him to squeal at the other horses. Though there were some mustang bands in this region, the killers might be spooked. The horse shifted under him, impatient, but made no sounds.

At last Vance said, "They're over that ridge."

"They could be going to any one of the ranches. This move had to be a plan to reinforce their threats."

"There are eight men out here."

Guthrey nodded and they moved out again to follow the raiders. On the rise, Vance pointed that they had gone left.

"That means they're probably going to either the Cody or Davis Ranch. Good, because Cam has no guards to help him. I simply hope the others have not been lulled to sleep by no activity."

"They may go to the far ranch first, then strike the one closer before they escape," Vance said, riding beside him.

"Be nice to know which they'll try first." Guthrey flexed his stiff hand. The fingers still worked, but not like usual.

They caught sight of the raiders again

trotting across an open stretch. Guthrey stepped up their speed for a distance. A thick smell of creosote floated on the soft night wind as the desert cooled under the stars and their horses kept a steady pace in pursuit. Guthrey hoped that Dan and Noble had been warned before these outlaws struck that ranch. They had done all they could to get word up there, but it all took time.

"We may have to wake the ranch before they strike them. No telling how much warning they'll have. Between getting the telegraph message, then someone waking help and getting to the ranch, it may all take too long."

"No way we could do anything else," Vance said and held out his hand for them to rein up again. "They stopped."

Guthrey nodded. How did his man hear that? "I thought Apaches didn't like to fight at night."

Vance chuckled. "I am an adopted Apache raised by a Dutch Reformed Church preacher on the reservation. I don't believe in witchcraft and superstition. Yes, if I was a full-blood Apache, I would not be out here with you."

"Did you hear them stop?"

"Yes. An Apache will know when you are

moving. They teach children to listen, and when they grow up, they can hear very good." Vance dismounted to empty his bladder.

Guthrey did the same. "Whew, I wish I'd learned how to do that. I can hear good for a white man but I missed their sounds."

"They are talking as though no one can hear them."

"Any clues?" Guthrey whispered.

"No, they are teasing one of their men about an ugly whore he must use."

They both chuckled.

"He just told them to mount up and that they were going to burn down both ranches," Vance said.

Guthrey's heart dropped. *Damn them anyway.* Well, they could plan to meet the outlaws head-on first. He swung up on Cochise and checked him. "We need to stop them."

Vance nodded and rode ahead of him through the head-high brush and out into the more open desert. Guthrey checked the big horse and ducked under the taller mesquite. Lots of clouds of concern spun in his skull. How was his wife? Would Dan and Noble be awake when they swept in? These were the things that he wished he could have made sure about, them being taken care of. All these concerns made his empty stomach growl as he and his horse moved through the silver night after the killers bent on destruction.

For the hundredth time, he dried the palm of his sore hand on the chaps he wore to protect against the spiny cactus. The night wound on further and further. He felt it must be near midnight. Time ticked slowly. Trailing known killers intent on burning out innocent ranchers felt like being a rope walker like the one he saw once in Wichita on a high strung wire. One bad move and he'd fall to the ground. He calculated they were an hour out from the Cody Ranch at this pace.

"They may speed up," he said under his breath to his man. "If they intend to burn both places."

Vance nodded he heard him. He pointed out the line of riders topping another ridge across the desert from them. They weren't especially hurrying.

Guthrey and Vance flushed some surprised quail and they exploded. Horses in check, they halted to see if the riders came back — the sound was loud to both of them. Nothing. They pushed on.

When they reached the basin's height above the Cody Ranch, Guthrey could see the riders were divided. One bunch went left, the other bunch went right. In a few minutes they'd open fire and charge the ranch headquarters with lighted torches. Guthrey slid the rifle out of his scabbard. The shot was way too far away but it might stop them and wake up the ranch.

"I don't know if the ranch has been warned. I need to stop them."

Vance jerked his own rifle out of the scabbard. "I'll try to stop these over here."

The explosion of Guthrey's rifle rang out over the area and echoed back. The blast spooked the outlaws' horses and some broke loose, bucking, as he kept firing and the outlaws sought to hide in the poor lighting.

Then a bevy of flashes signaling gunshots from the ranch toward the killers warmed his heart as he forced more cartridges into the Winchester's chamber.

"They're shooting back down there," Vance said between shots.

"Yes. If the killers want to ride back, they face us."

"Your deputies must have several guns down there."

Guthrey agreed as the shooting continued. "I'm riding down there. You try to cut off anyone who heads back. Be careful."

"I will."

He swung his horse around, rifle in hand, the stallion stomping to be in the melee. They tore off for the faint lights of the ranch house with the shooting about stopped. He soon reached Noble, who kicked some wounded outlaw in the butt, heading him toward the others they'd captured.

"Took 'em long enough to get here," Noble said.

"They came a long ways. We've been tracking them."

"I'm damn sure glad you warned us."

Guthrey shifted hands with his rifle and reached down to shake his old friend's hand. "I made those first shots to warn you."

"We were waiting for them, but thanks."

"Guthrey, where did you find them?" Dan asked, coming with a pistol in his hand that he looked like he could use.

"Hiding in a canyon. I saw the man who, no doubt, is behind all this. We'll get him next."

"Whew, we about gave up on them coming."

"They were moving slow. We've been in the saddle tracking them all night."

"There's fresh coffee at the ranch house. Where is this deputy Vance they told us about?"

"He should be over there. He went to see about the rest of the gang on that side."

"I want to meet him. Come on, we've got all the outlaws."

Guthrey shook hands with several ranchers and people he knew on the way as lanterns lit up the ranch.

Herman Cody shook his hand. "Thanks for sending these two. They've been a great help watching for trouble. We sure appreciate all you've done. Why, had we not been warned, we'd've been asleep when they struck."

"We're glad you're safe. These men needed to be stopped. I want a count of the men we've shot or captured. Before this news leaks out, I want their leader arrested. He's probably in Tombstone. Is Clark alive? He's the leader of this gang and I want him up here to talk to."

"He's been shot, but he's alive," one of the ranchers said. "He's on a blanket down in the draw."

Guthrey put his rifle in the scabbard and handed Cochise's reins to a boy. "He's a stud. Put him by himself. Thanks."

"Is Zamora over at Davis's?" he asked Cody.

"Yes, and they have several other men there too."

"Send them word, but tell them we need to hold this news down."

"I'll go find somebody to do that."

Guthrey found Vance squatted by the outlaw leader in the sandy wash.

"He tell you anything?"

Vance shook his head and then in tense voice said, "I want to carry him up there and put him on a red-ant hill."

"That's a consideration. Clark, you can take a choice: ants or a doctor? You don't get the doctor unless you talk."

"You can't put me on an anthill." Then he broke up coughing.

"Listen, Vance is an Apache. He works for me and I need information. A doctor or an anthill, you choose."

He held up a hand in the lamplight. "All right — what do you want?"

"Name of the man who sent you here?"

He shook his head. "I don't know who you're talking about."

"Yes, you do. He rode into your camp yesterday riding a red horse with a spade brand on him. I want his name."

"Sumbitch, you were watching then?"

"We've been watching you for days. Who is he?"

"Ralph McAllen."

"What's his part of this deal?"

312

"How should I know?"

"He didn't hire you and these others without a reason." Guthrey was about ready to put him on the anthill.

"He's got a part interest in a ranch over here."

"I know which one," Guthrey said. It had to be the place Pierson ran — the old Whitmore Ranch. "He have an office in Tombstone?"

"No. He just stays over there sometimes. He's from El Paso."

Guthrey stood up. He knew enough. "Boys, get a wagon and load him. And load the rest of them for jail." On his boot heels, he started uphill to get his horse.

Baker rode up. "Did they get the word?"

"Yes, thanks to your hard riding. And we have the name of the man who hired them. Ralph McAllen. He owns part of the old Whitmore Ranch and, I guess, wanted to expand it."

"What happens next?"

His hand was bothering him by then. Not catching much sleep and riding in the saddle twenty miles more that tired was not what he saw as a good idea. A few hours' sleep in coach and he'd be more awake to face this guy and maybe his hand would ease up. "I'm going home and then taking a stage to Tombstone. McAllen will be waiting there for news about his ranch-burning plans."

"Two of the outlaws are dead," Dan reported. "Three wounded. Three unscathed. We have all of them in the wagon."

"We need an inquest held on those deaths. None of our people were hurt?"

"No, sir. We were ready for them."

"Dan, you and Noble go home and get some rest. Cally's getting herself a new house built at Soda Springs. She can tell you all about it."

Dan shook his head warily and walked off, and Guthrey looked at Baker. "Good job tonight. You go home and get some rest too. You can get the death inquests done when you wake up. Thanks to you and Vance, they didn't kill anyone here. Tell Zamora that he played the other part."

"You need some rest, Guthrey. We'll get McAllen," Baker said.

"Kinda figure that's my job, and since we have no jurisdiction down there in Tombstone, it makes it even wilder. I better go see if I can do it."

"Hell, boss, we aren't afraid of either that sheriff or the law down there."

"Still, I better handle it — myself."

"One of us could back you."

"Let me handle it. Thanks, all of you."

"Get some rest," Baker said, looking as done in as he must have felt.

Guthrey nodded to him. But he wanted the real man behind Mark Peters's death to stand trial. Being rich didn't exclude him from justice. At that moment, he knew if McAllen slipped out of the territory, he'd fight extradition and hire some high-priced lawyers to buy his way out. He wanted him in the Crook County jail. And, by damn, he would put him there.

TWENTY-ONE

When he rode into the yard of the jacal in Soda Springs at dawn, Cally ran out to greet him. "How are the others?"

He dropped heavy out of the saddle and hugged her. "All of them are unscathed. They're bringing the six prisoners and two dead men to the jail. Dan's in charge of jailing them."

"No one was shot?"

"All my men are all right."

"You look so tired. When did you sleep last?"

Amused, he shook his head. "I need a bath, clean clothes, and then I need to take a stage to Tombstone. There's one more man, McAllen. We found out he is the head guy, and he is still on the loose. I need to go down there to arrest him and this deal is wound up."

"You haven't slept in two days, have you?"

"That's not important."

As they went to the house, she grabbed his hand and opened it. "My heavens, you really bruised it."

"It's better."

"Oh yes. I can see it's more healed. How did you use it?"

"Easily."

They both laughed.

He bathed and a messenger brought word that the stage for Tombstone would arrive in Soda Springs at five o'clock in the afternoon. Cally thanked the lad and turned to her husband. "Now you can sleep some."

Reluctant, he accepted her words and slept until afternoon. She fed him and then they walked to the county building where the stage would stop. Both Zamora and Baker were at the jail.

"The ringleader, Clark, died this afternoon. Dan got him to sign a confession and had it witnessed," Zamora said. "That should end that, huh?"

"I hope McAllen is still in Tombstone when I get there." Guthrey considered the situation. He had his work cut out for him.

"I had the judge sign a warrant for his arrest for you to carry." Baker handed it to him.

"Either of you personally know the Tombstone constable?"

They shook their heads. "Virgil Earp is the one in charge. He's a brother to the law in Wichita, Wyatt, I think."

"Must have been Dodge City. I was already Rangering when they used it for a delivery point for cattle drives."

"Anyway, Johnny Beyhan is the sheriff down there," Zamora said. "But he belongs to old man Clanton and them border outlaws."

Guthrey shook his head. "I'll find Earp when I get down there. And if McAllen hasn't fled, I'll find him."

"Be careful," Zamora said. "He could have some hired protection."

"I'll watch for it."

The stage rolled in before sundown. Guthrey kissed his wife good-bye, climbed in the empty coach, and left in a cloud of dust. He sat back in the seat; he'd be in Tombstone in a few hours. Grateful for the few hours of sleep he'd gained in his own bed, he rocked around in the coach seat and smiled. Riding a stage was never a comfortable ride, being tossed around on every bump. The only thing worse was riding a log wagon with no springs.

Alert and looking around, he stepped down in front of the stage office in Tombstone. He hitched his holster when his boot heels struck the dirt of the street. Tombstone had not yet put in effect its "no gun" law, though it had been threatened by the city council. He spoke to the stage driver who let him out.

"Where is this town's Marshal Earp?"

"Oriental Saloon, down the street on the left, more than likely."

Guthrey thanked him and walked the crowded boardwalk under the porch. Due to the three-shift mining operations, the saloons were busy around the clock. Whores screamed and laughed at a high pitch. Their voices were heard over the tinny pianos and the cussing that rang out in the dark.

Guthrey had no desire to try to keep a place like this straight. Boomtowns were the worst places to have to patrol as a Ranger. Too many quick-triggered individuals got involved in arrests when it was none of their damn business. Instead of facing a lone drunk or crook, the matter soon turned into a public forum in the street. Tough job, and it grew worse when something stirred them up. Guthrey pushed into the smoky interior of the Oriental Saloon and spotted a tall man in the back of the room.

"Marshal Earp?"

The man nodded and in a strong voice

said, "I don't believe I've met you."

"My name is Guthrey. I'm looking for a man who hired a band of killers to run off ranchers."

"You're the sheriff in Crook County. I've heard of you. I understand. Let's go back into the office where we can talk."

Virgil closed the door. "Who are you after?"

"Ralph McAllen."

"I have bad news for you. I think he left for El Paso today. I hate to tell you that, but you can check over at the hotel. I watched him close the past few weeks. I had word he was hiring tough gun hands for some operation he planned. But his purpose was a secret and I couldn't find out what it was."

"His men hung a rancher friend of mine on a windmill up in Crook County. We cut off their next raid with the help of a scout who found their hidden camp in the Dragoons. Three are dead and the other five left are in jail — I really wanted him to join them."

"Unless you go in there as a bounty hunter, you will never get him out of Texas." Virgil shook his head.

"I might. I put in some time with the Rangers."

"That might get you in. But El Paso is a

tough place, Guthrey." Virgil looked at his dusty boot toes. "He's rich and will be hard to prosecute as well."

"I don't care. He paid those men to spook more ranchers and to murder one of them. He can sit in Yuma till he dies, for my money."

"You're the one who had that public move to throw out the old sheriff, aren't you?"

"Yes. There was no law in Crook County."

Virgil took off his hat and shook his head. Amused, he looked hard at Guthrey. "I'd bet a man who got that done could drag that scoundrel McAllen back and jail him in Yuma."

"I intend to."

"Nice to meet you. If I can ever help, you wire me."

"I will, Virgil. I'll go get a room and go home on the morning stage. Thanks. Just damn disappointing he slipped away."

"You drink?"

"No."

Virgil chuckled. "I'd have bought you a drink."

"Maybe some other time. Thanks."

"Yes."

Guthrey found supper in a hole-in-the-wall diner that served Irish beef stew. The narrow room was crowded with miners frosted in dust who were coming off duty. The man next to him spoke with an Irish accent. "What'cha doing in here?"

"Eating."

"Oh, I can see that, but you look like a rich rancher."

He shook his head. "Where do you say I should be eating?"

"Down the street at the lady's restaurant — Nellie Cashman's place."

"I like stew good enough."

"Suit yourself." He went back to slurping it off his spoon.

Guthrey laughed. What was his point? Just rattling off. If Guthrey had been down in a dark, wet mine for a work shift, he'd probably have wanted to eat at that nice café. Lord, he needed a good night's sleep.

After an uneventful morning, he caught the stage for home and arrived about noon. He told his deputies that McAllen had fled Tombstone for El Paso.

"You going down there and find him?" Baker asked.

"Do you know El Paso?"

"Not really, but it's a tough place. Right, Zamora?"

"Oh, that is a bad place."

Guthrey nodded and rose. "Tomorrow I

want to go out to the ranch and tell that superintendent, Pierson, to load his ass up and get gone."

Baker smiled. "Can we do that — legally?"

"Legally, probably not, or I'd arrest him if I had real hard evidence. But if he don't leave, I will promise to include him in the trial of the killers as an accessory. That should make him get out."

"I want to go along," Baker said. "I can get a warrant today from the judge."

"Good. Do that. Zamora, run the office. I'd like Noble to ride along too. That old man knows lots about people. It might get to be serious over there."

"I'll send him word," Zamora said.

"Anything else wrong?"

The two men shook their heads. "Things are slow," Baker said.

"Good. I'm going home, prop my feet up, and eat my wife's food."

"You should do that. You've been running hard," Zamora said. "Your new deputy is tracking down horse thieves today."

"Good; he'll find them. We may need to build on to the jail," Guthrey teased and waved good-bye.

Intent on getting to Cally, he hurried down the grade on his boot heels and crossed behind the corrals. At the doorway, he stopped and smiled at his wife, who was busy taking baked bread out of the oven. Turning to put it on the table, she saw him.

"Oh, you're back." She put the brown loaves down and discarded her cloth hot handle holders to run over and hug him. "I'm so glad to see you."

He kissed her. She told him to stay right there. Then she stuck her head out the door and looked both ways. With that done, she closed the door and put the bar in place. Then she turned around and, with hands on her slim hips, said, "Undress. You are mine."

He toed off his boots, laughing. "Darling, I am always yours."

She was right before him. They were both laughing.

"Damn, I'm glad I married you," he said and kissed her.

The next morning, Noble was there on a fresh horse. He joined them for a breakfast of hot oatmeal with coffee, Cally's fresh bread, butter, and prickly pear jelly. "We have the cattle all treated that had screwworms and they're doing good. You could sell some more big steers. They're in good shape."

"The way they're stacking lumber around

here, we may need to sell a hundred head," Guthrey teased Cally.

"No. We have the money in the bank and we are in no trouble."

Guthrey looked at Noble. "I guess we don't need to sell steers."

"If you men want to sell steers, I'll put it in the bank."

"We need a ranch meeting with Dan present."

Cally agreed.

The men rode off to pick up Baker and then go on to find Walter Pierson at the big ranch. Guthrey had not been on that place since he had run down and arrested the past owner. He wondered how many men they had on the payroll. Outside of some quiet rumors of trouble, Pierson had kept his harassment to strictly verbal, despite his loud charges at the start. Still, a part owner of the outfit had chosen to hire thugs to drive ranchers off the range.

Near noon they rode under the crossbar and up to the house. A large, straight-backed woman came out onto the porch, drying her hands on a tea towel.

"Who are you?"

Guthrey removed his hat. "Good morning, ma'am. My name is Guthrey. I'm the sheriff of Crook County, and I'm here to talk to Walter Pierson."

"He ain't here."

"I don't have your name?"

"Hattie Milgrim."

"Nice to meet you, Hattie. Has Pierson left the country?"

"I have no idea."

"Hiding a fugitive is a crime in this territory."

"Are you saying I am hiding a fugitive?"

"I just told you the law. I have a warrant from the circuit judge to search these premises."

"What in the world for?"

"A man who works for this ranch operation had a rancher murdered. We intend to find the person responsible and have him tried. Do you know a Mr. McAllen?"

"No, but I'm protesting your search of this ranch."

"Sorry. Take a seat on the porch, please. We are going through everything here."

"I suppose you will."

"Baker, take the house. Noble, you look over the grounds. I want any fresh hides that belong to other ranches. I want any evidence we can charge them with."

"Are you telling me I may be arrested?"

"No, ma'am, but we are looking for crimes we can prove."

In a short while, Noble brought two fresh hides that did not bear the ranch's brand. The woman refused to say anything when Guthrey asked her about them.

Later, when Guthrey checked inside with Baker, his deputy had found the books detailing where money was drawn to pay the leader of the raids. The dead man, Clark, was plainly the receiver of a large amount of money. Baker closed out the book. They were taking the records along as evidence.

"Hattie, where are all the hands that work here at? No one has come around since we got here."

"I don't run the cowboys or any hands here."

"Isn't that strange? I mean, no one is here but you?"

"I control the house, that's all."

"Fine, but were they here at all?" he asked her.

"I told you, I only run the house."

"Damn strange, no one is here but you."

Noble came over. "I checked the bunk-house. The workers took most of their things with them."

"I have no idea where they went. They told me nothing."

"Boys, I guess we're a day late," Guthrey

said. "Baker, is there a list of who they paid last?"

"They didn't pay them their last check out of that book."

"Hattie you know more about this than you're telling me."

"I simply run this house."

"You know why they left. Were they afraid of arrest?"

She shook her head. "They told me nothing."

"By damn, you know more than you're letting on, woman," Noble spoke up.

She shook her head.

"Boys, we have what we want and we can make a list of the men and run them down," Guthrey said. They'd be wasting time talking to her any longer. Maybe in court she'd tell the truth. He was having her as a witness on every trial.

Guthrey and his team went to their horses and rode back to Soda Springs. It was near sundown when they finally reached the courthouse. He stopped into the office to talk to Zamora. Baker had come along with Guthrey, but Guthrey had sent Noble on to their jacal in town.

"No one was there but a haughty old woman," Guthrey told him.

"Not one hand?" Zamora looked at the

two like he didn't believe it.

"Not a one. They must have gotten the word. I wish I'd gone there first instead of to Tombstone." The whole day's findings had left him disappointed.

"We did find that they paid the dead man Clark," Baker added. "And Noble found two hides where they'd butchered two animals weren't theirs. Those are the books."

"What next?" Zamora asked them.

"I guess we need to send a telegram to El Paso and see what happens."

"I can do that," Zamora said.

"Maybe add, since no one is in charge, the sheriff may need to gather the stock and sell it at public auction."

Baker laughed. "That should get someone off their asses."

Guthrey agreed, told his crew good night, and headed home.

The whole deal left a lot hanging out. Pierson and the men had fled just like McAllen had done in Tombstone. Gone as if they were smoke, and no word had reached town that he knew about. Guthrey would have another night to sleep with his bride, and the notion appealed to him a lot. Whew, this job had more loose ends to run down than a prairie dog town eradication.

Twenty-Two

The next day near noontime, his tracker, Vance, brought in two horse thieves and six stolen horses.

Guthrey and Baker hurried down to the livery corral to meet him after some kid stuck his head in the office and shouted the news. "Your Injun deputy got two prisoners and a mess of stolen horses down at the livery. You better come quick," he said.

His man stood by the corral with a half dozen men questioning him.

Guthrey joined them and asked him to start over.

"I trailed these men to the New Mexico border." He motioned to the pair of white men in handcuffs seated on the ground. "I arrested them at dawn yesterday and brought them back here."

"You did wonderful, Vance," Guthrey said. "We will try to locate the owners of the animals and will charge these two with horse stealing."

"He arrested us in New Mexico. He can't do that," one of the rustlers grumbled.

Guthrey jerked both to their feet and spoke softly, herding them toward jail. "Can you prove that? No, you can't, and you are going to prison for stealing those horses. Better shut your mouth or I'll see you get two more years on your sentence down there in Yuma."

"That's all, folks," Baker said to the crowd. "The judge will handle them. Everyone get back to work or to minding your own business. The law in Crook County will take care of them."

Guthrey figured, for the moment, they were past the lynching idea festering in the minds of those men who had come to see the culprits brought in. It wouldn't take much to raise a hemp party over horse rustling. His new hire was going to be great at this tracking down business. The thieves would soon realize horse taking was a surefire way for them to get three years in Yuma prison.

"What next, Vance?"

"Oh, a man told me that there were cattle rustlers over in the east."

"What was his name?"

"I don't recall he gave me a name, but I

331

know where he lives. May I go see about it?"

"Sure, check back with the office once a week. We may need you on something else. Do you need to rest?"

He shook his head to dismiss and concern. "When I am busy I forget about my wife."

"I savvy. You did a neat job. Zamora will book them in. Be careful, hombre, and you find too many outlaws, you come get us."

His man smiled. "I will be fine. I am proud to work for you."

"I'm damn glad to have you. Keep your head down."

Vance rode off. When Guthrey went back in the office, he shook his head.

"He's trying to forget his dead wife. He's off checking on some more rustlers."

"He's some guy," Baker said. "No pack-horse anymore; he parked him. He simply lives off the land."

"You think they were across the territory line?" Zamora asked under his breath.

"How can they prove that?" Guthrey laughed. "No, we have us a tough man. Rustlers better watch out."

No news about Pierson or his bunch. Baker had heard some gossip that they all rode like hell to get out of Arizona when McAllen sent them word by a messenger.

A law office in El Paso sent back a telegram that the help situation on the ranch would soon be settled and promised that a new crew would be at the ranch in the next week.

Guthrey nodded. "I may have to see that happen. I'm going back to the house. Today they're laying out the house plans for Cally."

"Must be a big house. You've bought lots of lumber already," Zamora said.

"That's her business and she handles it well. I may ride up to the Bridges Ranch tomorrow and check on things if it's quiet here."

"Go," Baker said. "We don't have a problem we can't handle."

"Good." Guthrey left the office and walked back to the jacal.

"Can we go up and take in the dance day after tomorrow?" Cally asked when he came home.

"I don't know why not."

"First I want you to look at the floor plans. Dresscoe will be here and show you the plans after lunch," she said.

"You know what you want —"

"We are married and we should share in our future plans. It won't hurt to put your opinion on it."

"Yes, Mrs. Guthrey."

She threw her arms around his neck and, on her tiptoes, she kissed him hard. "That's why I married you, big man."

"I always wondered why." They both laughed.

Over lunch they discussed the business with his tracker and the telegram from El Paso.

"Can you solve this McAllen business?"

"I'm going to write the West Texas Ranger office and see who's in charge and what they think about my coming there with a warrant for his arrest. Rangers are kinda clannish when it comes to their own, and since I was one of them — well, they might help me."

"Those other three came to your aid here."

"That was pure friendship why they came. But I believe I can get the same kind of support at El Paso."

"Oh, I knew that it was friendship, but folks here thought the entire Ranger force had come to help you. Those were exciting days. I just knew I'd lose my new husband in some shoot-out going after that many men. But they cut the pie and all of them did their part."

"We were lucky and it went smooth."

They went over the plans with the builder,

Dresscoe, for a couple of hours. Walked the hot yard to check the stakes he had driven in the hard ground as corners. He promised the corral would go up quickly and be well back of the house instead of in the front yard.

A hot wind swept Guthrey's nose full of creosote scents. He suppressed his amusement at Cally's expanded plans for the structure. The floor plans were twice as big as he felt they started with, but it was her dream and they could afford it. He'd never be a dream buster toward his sweet wife. In all his years Rangering, serving in the depressing Civil War, then making those tough cattle drives to Kansas, and finally back at being a Ranger again, he'd never felt this good about his personal life as he had during the nearly three months since they were married.

He closed his eyes, reveling in thoughts of the success and pleasure he had found with her.

"You all right?" Her words jarred him to awareness.

He put his arm around her shoulder and they started for the house. He laughed. "I am as fine as a fiddle, and your new house will be gorgeous."

"Do you really like it? I mean, what it will be?"

"Yes. I was raised in a jacal not much bigger or better than ours here. I've lived in tents and slept on the ground. This will be a nice house for both of us."

"Good. I was worried you'd think I was crazy."

"No way, lady. Build away."

"I worried every night you slept on the ground at the ranch a rattlesnake would crawl up and bite you."

"I never saw one around there."

"Oh, we had them. I was really relieved when you moved into the bunkhouse after that."

"I didn't figure you worried a moment about me back then."

"I sure did, but I never figured we could work past my opening remarks to you for coming."

He chuckled. "I was as lost as you were that day. Don't ever fret over that again."

"What was your first thought when you met me?" she asked.

"Nice young girl who acted like she was Dan's mother."

"Someone had to worry about him. He was so impulsive then."

"Did I hear some thunder?" He peered

out the open door.

"Monsoon rains. We haven't had many this summer."

"No, and we can use a boatload."

When the rain began, they danced around on the dirt floor. Two lovers lost in a cool afternoon that produced a good soaker.

In the morning they drove for the ranch, the buckboard rims splashing many puddles in the cool air, and arrived around lunchtime. Deloris ran out of the ranch house to greet them as her small, bashful children stood back in the doorway.

She and Cally talked while Guthrey put up the team. Then he joined the tour and saw all the things Deloris had growing in her garden.

The woman turned to him. "This is such a wonderful place to grow things. I am so pleased to be here."

He nodded, and when he and his wife were alone, she spoke about the employees he'd hired. "She has done lots of work to grow all that in the heat. You said they were hard workers, but she is an angel."

"She no doubt had learned those skills to survive. They were raising things on that place where I found them. I knew with all your irrigation system they could really show off."

"Squash, tomatoes, and many more plants are doing well. I thought they would die when I left."

He agreed and said, "The ranch house here is pretty small, but it seems like a good size for the Diazes, and I think you and I won't be here much after our house in town is built. Should I build us a place here for when we're away from Soda Springs or find one for us up on the mountain?"

"Can we afford both?"

"Sure. We can do that."

"I may go see the gold crew this afternoon," he said.

"I will stay and help with Deloris's lovely children. One day we will have our own."

"You bet."

He found the men at the mine working. They showed him the vein of rich gold they were following.

"I believe we are finding more as we go down. The vein widens all the time."

"Do you need more equipment?" Guthrey asked.

"In time, maybe. Get much deeper and we will need a pulley system to raise and lower things. Not yet."

"Keep up the good work. I need to get back."

"Hey, this has been fun rather than work. I never saw such a vein of rich gold. As long as it holds out, we'll be fine."

Guthrey thanked him and rode out.

The three men were back at the ranch when Guthrey came in.

Dan was bragging about the rain and Noble about the cattle's good condition, and Guermo was proud to be there. Things sounded fine on the ranch as they made plans to sell more cattle. This time Guthrey instructed Dan on how to talk to the butchers and learn their needs, then for him to rent the pasture if the man had anything to graze, and at last drive them over there.

"I'm excited about doing that," Dan said. "I can handle it."

"I know you can."

With that complete, he went back to the house. Since Guermo and Deloris had fully moved into the ranch house with their family, Cally had a hammock hung outside for her and Guthrey to sleep in that night, and they'd go on to the dance in the morning.

They took a shower after the sun went down and came back to sleep in their swing. The crickets were making a symphony;

coyotes added lyrics and a hoot owl joined them. On his back in the hammock squeezing her hand, Guthrey mused about the one night they dumped themselves out on the ground while busy making love.

"Not tonight," she stated. "But that was funny."

In the morning Cally helped Deloris make breakfast for the crew. Cally had made friends with the children and they would be her friends for life, in his opinion. But he knew how bad she wanted one of her own as well — they were working at it.

They drove over to the schoolhouse, and many were already there by midday. The men sat in the shade and talked about rain, cow prices, and the disappearance of the old Whitmore Ranch's crew.

"Never worry. A lawyer says there will be a new one here shortly," Guthrey said.

"What did you figure out about the undercover boss?"

"He left Tombstone shortly after we caught the raiders."

"Kinda sneaky, wasn't he?" one rancher asked.

"We'd have never tied them to that if they hadn't left two more nooses lying around in their cabin exactly like the one they used to string up Peters. My new deputy, Vance, found those ropes in their camp and knew that was where the killers hid out."

"He's pretty smart."

"But the crew had already fled the ranch when you got there, huh?"

Guthrey nodded. "There was only one haughty woman at that place when we went down there."

"What was she doing?" another asked him.

"Minding the house, near as I could tell." Guthrey shook his head over the situation the ranch might pose in the future.

"What are you doing next?"

"I'd like for them to sell out, but I can't find a way to get that done yet. But I will."

Heads bobbed in agreement around the crowd. "We're banking on you doing that.

"And Vance is doing a great job. He brought back two horse thieves this week and six stolen horses."

"And we have law and order around here."

Guthrey and Cally enjoyed the company of their neighbors as they ate supper, and they danced a lot that evening. He felt better that the crew at the old Whitmore Ranch had moved on. But what and who they'd send to run it left him wondering if the threat of the big ranch against the small ones would ever be over.

Dan had gone to Tucson to set up the steer sale. Cally thought he was being very businesslike about the entire operation.

"I'm glad. He needs to take over the administration of the ranch and expand it." Seated with his back to the schoolhouse bench against the wall, Guthrey crossed his dusty boots, which were stretched out in front of him. Nice to be inside such a cordial place with friends.

"I think he's better. The deputy job did him good, and Noble is no slouch at talking sense to people." She squeezed his right hand and it did not hurt. He needed to mend his ways about getting into fistfights with troublemakers. Maybe he'd learned his lesson.

They parted from their friends about midnight as the dance broke up, and they went to their tent. In the darkness, Guthrey unbuttoned Cally's dress for her and she changed into a nightshirt while he shed his boots and then undressed.

"I never get over the idea that being married would be this nice," she said, lying beside him.

"Neither did I. Guess I was waiting to find you."

She snuggled against him. "I'm sure glad you waited. You don't think I'm spending too much on the new house, do you?"

"I figure you earned it."

"Good. I hate to keep bothering you with my small problems."

He hugged her. "Cally, you are the biggest thing in my life. Don't ever fret about anything to do with me."

"Good." They kissed to settle the matter.

TWENTY-THREE

A lawyer named Shelton Woods showed up the next Friday in the sheriff's office. A rather well-dressed man in a tailored suit and square shoulders about forty stood before Guthrey. He spoke rather loftily. "I am representing the organization that owns the ranch you call the Whitmore. Actually, it belongs to the El Rancho Corporation, and I am their lawyer."

Guthrey sat back in the squeaking chair and appraised him. "Is your client ready to surrender to me?"

"Excuse me? I don't know what you are talking about, sir."

"McAllen. I have a murder warrant for him."

"You can't be serious?"

"Woods, I was there to witness when he rode out of the camp after meeting with his man Tim Clark and planning the last raid. I also have a signed deathbed confession from

Clark implicating McAllen in the murder and the raids."

"That is absurd. Mr. McAllen lives in El Paso. He's never been in this territory."

"Sorry, but Marshal Virgil Earp of Tombstone will testify he was staying in Tombstone at the time and fled back to El Paso to avoid being arrested."

"My client is completely innocent of these charges."

"Then have him come here and stand trial."

"And face these ridiculous trumped-up charges? No, sir, and I will have no more illegal searches of the ranch property."

"Look it up. I had a legal search warrant to find out that your clients had butchered stolen beef and paid the confessed murderer Clark for doing his underhanded work."

"I can see you are entirely misinformed, sir."

"Tell McAllen to get back here and surrender, or some bounty man will shoot him and deliver his chopped-off head to me for the reward we plan to offer for his arrest, dead or alive."

"You can't do that."

"Sorry, but I plan to do that this week. His skull will be here on my desk in less than a month. These bounty men on the border are treacherous."

"I am filing an injunction against you and this county to stop your false persecution of my client."

Guthrey rose and pointed at the door. "Get the hell out of here, before I kick your ass up between your shoulders. Move!"

"I am —"

"Get out of here." He chased the man out into the hall. Woods left the building looking back after him.

"What's that about?" Tommy asked, standing up at the telegraph desk.

"Damn lawyers in here demanding things when they represent murderers make me mad."

"He sure dresses fancy."

"I bet he charged that killer a hundred dollars to come up here and try to talk me out of raising a reward for his man."

"No, that would be too cheap for him."

"Hell, I'm in the wrong business."

"So am I." They both laughed and Guthrey went back to his desk. As soon as the Rangers answered him, he'd go get this killer. All he needed was one more blowhard to come by and threaten him. He'd throw him, gagged, in a cell and keep him there forever. Some people really knew how to make him mad.

Baker took over and Guthrey went to have lunch with his wife. The hard sawing and hammering was loud and he knew she was proud of their progress. Dresscoe had found some expert carpenters from Tombstone who were out of work and the house was taking shape fast. The bare walls were standing and while they ate lunch the men also took a break.

"Happy?" he asked Cally.

"Yes. Are you?" She looked up for his answer.

"I had a lawyer in my office demanding things. I finally ran him off."

"Oh, I'm sorry."

"Not your fault. I will survive. I came home to escape idiots like that."

"Oh my, here I am excited about a new house, and they are driving you crazy."

"Not for long. When I get a letter from the Rangers, I will go get McAllen."

When they finished lunch, he hugged and kissed her and went to go back to the sheriff's office. The workers were back to pounding and sawing. He smiled at the racket. "Your new house is going up."

"Yes."

■ ■ ■ ■

That afternoon, Vance came in with one prisoner. The prisoner looked to be a teenager and had three stolen horses in his possession.

"I think he was going to meet a man and sell them. But someone must have warned him off. So I arrested the one and brought him in."

"Whose son is he?" Guthrey asked with a frown.

"Some woman who works at Fort Grant. She is not married. He has no father that claims him. He's been on his own most of his life."

"What is your name?" he asked the youth.

"Buck Smith."

Guthrey doubted that was his name but he didn't mention it. "Buck Smith, have you any idea what happens to horse thieves?"

"No."

"No, sir, is what you say to an adult."

" 'No, sir.' "

"I am going to send you down to Yuma for a week to see how tough that place is. Then, when you come back, you will be under my thumb and do hard labor every day for two years. If you don't like that, I'll have a trial and you can stay in Yuma for five years or until you die."

"I don't want to die — sir."

"I don't blame you but you only get one chance not to be in prison."

"I think I understand, sir."

"Stand up straight. You can stay in an empty cell for now. I'll handle the rest. But if you run off, you will be caught and put in prison for a full term."

The boy shook his head — hard.

"Go back and sit in an empty cell. I'll tell you more about your new life later."

The boy went to the back of the jail and into a cell and closed the door.

Satisfied, Guthrey went back to his desk to talk more to his deputy.

"Nice job, Vance. What's next?"

"I heard that Mexican outlaw who stole the horses you got back is coming up here again."

"Royal Montoya?"

"Yes. He's been bragging down in Mexico that this time he will kill everyone and take their horses."

"Keep listening. He may try that."

"Another thing I learned was about two men who are staying at a place south of here. They are up to no good."

"Who's that?"

"Thomas and Fred Morales are their names. Two tough guys from the border. There are some *putas* there and a few other crooks, but these men are tough and I am certain up to no good."

"I know them. When I went after Looman I ran across them in a saloon near Nogales. What are their plans? Do you think they will do something?"

"I don't know what, but they aren't there for a rest stop."

"Have you been in their camp?"

"Yes, they don't know my job yet. Maybe we should raid it?"

Guthrey, deep in thought about the matter, shook his head. "We have no evidence to hold them for trial."

"So we must wait for them to try to do something?" Vance looked perplexed by the situation.

"I'm afraid so. But keep up the good work. If we can change that boy's mind about crime, we may make him worth something."

Vance agreed and smiled. "I sure like this job."

"Be careful. They learn you represent the law, your life maybe in danger."

"I understand."

"By the way, where is this place you mentioned?"

"South. It recently had a fire that must have burned the ramada. It once was a ranch, I think."

"I know the place. I burned it. Do they have tents?"

"Yes. Tents and shades made of canvas. It is a tramp town to me."

"Watch your back. When Noble and I left, I burned that squaw shade so trash wouldn't use it anymore."

"It didn't matter to them; they camped there anyway. I will see about them."

Before Vance left town, Guthrey made sure he had his pay, though it didn't matter too much to Vance. He was happy being busy.

There was no mail and it would be weeks before he got a letter back from Austin.

Guthrey left the office and headed downhill. The hammers still rang and the sawing continued but he could see the fresh-cut rafters in the sky like a comb. Cally's house was taking shape.

A familiar-looking buckboard was parked in the yard. He soon saw the large-framed Cam standing with Olive and Cally as she pointed out what would be on the upper part.

"Hey, how are you two doing?" Guthrey asked.

"We come by for some advice. Mark hasn't been buried for very long. Would folks look bad at us if we got married? Olive and I want to be together and I said we should get married."

"If she agrees, who gives a damn about the rest?"

"I sure agree, but how long is decent?"

"Tomorrow sounds all right to me."

Olive nodded. "I guess you're right. Cam, I'll marry you."

"Great! You've made me the proudest man in the world. I knew Guthrey would know what we should do. Miss Cally, you married a great man."

"I think so too."

So plans were made and the wedding date set. A large number of women agreed to sew Olive a wedding dress and get Cam a suit coat. They'd be married in three weeks at the schoolhouse and honeymoon on Mount Graham in their friends' cabin.

That night, Cally whispered in his ear when they were in bed, "Part of why those two are so excited, do you know why?"

"I don't have any idea."

She made certain no one was in the dark room. Then she whispered, "Don't tell anyone. They're going to have a baby."

"Has she ever had one before?"

"No, and his wife and four children died in the epidemic."

Guthrey chuckled. "They'll have fun raising one."

"Maybe they'll have more in the future."

"You're right. Strange though about her being married before and not having any."

"Well I'm not myself — yet."

"Don't worry about it. It'll happen."

"I hope so."

"When you are great big, you may regret it."

They laughed and kissed.

TWENTY-FOUR

Vance came into Guthrey's office on Tuesday morning.

"I learned their plan."

"Whose?" Guthrey frowned at him.

"The two brothers. Thomas and Fred Morales."

"What are they planning?"

"To rob the store in Steward's Crossing."

"Old man Hayes's Mercantile?"

"Yes."

"But he's doesn't look that rich to me." Guthrey pointed for Vance to pull up a chair.

"They say he has thousands of dollars in his safe."

"He might, but I better get Sweeney some backup. I'll have Dan and Noble keep an eye on the store. You want to be there?"

Vance nodded.

"When will they try to rob him do you think?"

Vance shrugged. "Fred told a Mexican

woman named Rosa that they would be very rich when they rode for Mexico with all of Hayes's money."

"You're a great detective, *mi amigo.* I am going up there to warn Sweeney, plus send word for Dan and Noble to join me. Between five of us, we should be able to stop them."

"I better go there and watch the store until you come."

"Yes. We will be coming." Guthrey called for the new jailer, Sam Green. "Watch the desk and the jail. Send word to Zamora to come in. I need to go up to Steward's Crossing. We have trouble up there."

"No problem. I'll send a boy to get him."

"That's good, Sam."

Guthrey set out for his house and the big horse. No telling when they'd try to hold the robbery. The hammers and sawing were loud from the crew working on the house. They were shingling the roof that morning.

"I have to go to Steward's Crossing," he said to Cally as he stood in the doorway, then hurried on to saddle Cochise.

He was cinching his horse when Cally arrived by the corral. "What's wrong?"

"Some border bandits plan to rob Mr. Hayes. Someone said he had thousands of dollars in his safe."

She shook her head. "I don't think he has lots of money. He is frugal but there isn't that much business in his store."

"These bandits must think his safe is full of money."

"I've been in his office in the past and the safe was open. I didn't see any money in it."

He dropped the stirrup and laughed. "They still think they will be rich robbing him."

"He is a nice old man who extended credit to my father when we had no money."

"I thought so, but these crooks think it's there."

"Be careful." She stood on her toes and kissed him.

He pulled her close to kiss her, and Cochise gave him a shove with his head. Taking a few steps with her in his arms, he laughed. "He's ready to go."

"Yes," she agreed, amused, and clapped his shoulder. "I'll be here."

He made the trip quickly and sent a boy to the ranch to have Noble and Dan come in and help him. Sweeney was on his porch when Guthrey arrived at his house.

"What's wrong, boss?" he asked, standing up.

Guthrey hitched his horse and crossed the yard, not anxious for anyone to hear and become upset about the robbery attempt.

In a low voice, he said, "Some Mexican border bandits are planning to hold up Hayes's store."

"Who?"

"They are the Morales brothers. Tough hombres."

"Pretty hard up, ain't they? Why, that old man don't have that much money."

"I have no idea. They think he has a safe full of money."

"No way. What do we need to do?"

"I have Noble and Dan coming, and my new deputy, Vance, should be here already. We'll set up an around-the-clock guard."

Sweeney rubbed his whisker-bristled mouth. "Sounds strange, them thinking that old man had any large amount in that safe."

"Why don't you go down there and quietly tell him what might be coming. I don't want him or his employees to panic. When Dan comes, I may make him an extra clerk to work in the store."

"That would be smart."

"The Morales brothers know me, but not Dan and Noble. They may know you, no

357

doubt they've checked on this store. They are at that old ranch where I burned down the squaw shade."

"I heard there were some whores and tramps down there. But I didn't figure they were any threat."

"These two came up here looking for someone to rob. They talked a little too much and Vance picked it up."

Sweeney nodded. "I'll go warn the old man. And get it set up for Dan to go to work there."

"Good. Tell him don't panic. We'll stop them. I'll put Cochise in the livery and leave him saddled, just in case."

Sweeney agreed and set out for the store.

After he stabled Cochise, Guthrey ate a burrito he bought from an old woman vendor with a small grill. He stepped back in the shadows and faced the storefront of Hayes's Mercantile, where women under sunbonnets went in and out the front door. Children trailed along, and that worried him. He wanted no one hurt, but if he ran them off, he might alert the outlaws. More than that, he wanted this over.

The man inside the saddle repair shop came out and offered him a crate to sit on.

"I know you must be watching for something. Sit on this crate, sheriff. My name's

Rob. I voted for you."

Guthrey smiled. "Thanks. We're watching out for a robbery try on Mr. Hayes."

"Oh."

"I don't want any panic. I can't arrest them for mouthing off about a plan of robbery. But when they try, I can slam them in the hoosegow."

"Tough outlaws?"

"Very tough. I'm going to whittle out here and keep watch in case they try."

"I got a double-barrel shotgun if you need it."

"Thanks, Rob."

"You need a drink, I have some cool water."

"I'll be fine."

Noble and Dan rode in and he waved them around back of the saddle repair shop. He quickly explained how he wanted Dan working in the mercantile and Noble to be loafing around there since the outlaws didn't know either one.

The plan was set as the day's heat rose. Sweeney came by and leaned on a porch post and, not looking at Guthrey, said, "Everyone is in place. Any idea when they plan to do this?"

"No. My new deputy, Vance, is somewhere around here. He's in cowboy clothes but he was a Mexican kidnapped by the Apaches. He's a good tracker and a tough new lawman. Don't shoot him. The Morales brothers were dressed like vaqueros when I saw them last."

"I see. Guess this is all we can do?"

"We have it covered. Now we must wait."

"I'll go back to my porch, which is the best lookout for anyone coming or going."

"Yes."

They didn't come that day. Hayes closed up the store about seven and everyone but Vance parted with Guthrey. Vance said, "I'll be back in the morning."

"Be careful," Guthrey said.

Guthrey, Dan, and Noble went back to the ranch, and after Deloris fed them, they slept in the bunkhouse. She had breakfast ready before sunup. Guthrey and the other two had their horses saddled before they went to eat.

Guermo greeted them and Deloris had plenty of food fixed. Her hot coffee was rich and the pancakes fluffy with her sweet homemade syrup.

"Your food's sure good," Guthrey bragged on her.

She blushed. "The senora, she teach me."

"She did a good job," Noble said. They all

laughed.

Back in town, the men all took their places. In a short while, Vance rode up. "They are coming," he whispered, passing Guthrey, and then he rode behind the store. Noble, hanging around, and Dan in the store, would be warned.

Guthrey stepped inside the saddle repair shop, and at the sight of him, Rob picked up his shotgun.

"Not yet."

"They're coming?"

"Yes, but we need to be quiet."

"I understand."

Guthrey checked across the street from the saddle repair shop's front window. Not much customer traffic — good. That made less chance of an innocent bystander getting hurt or shot.

The two outlaws rode up, looking all around, eagle-eyed. They dismounted and one stayed by the hitched horses. Guthrey didn't know which brother was Fred and which Thomas — he remembered that Thomas had a scar on his face, but he couldn't see the scar. One brother started for the front door, a six-gun in his hand.

"Give me that shotgun. There might be shooting."

Handing over the scattergun, Rob said,

"Both barrels are loaded."

Guthrey opened the shop door and shouted a warning to the brother who'd started for the store's front doors. "Drop your gun!"

The man whirled and started to shoot at him. Bad mistake. Guthrey's blast knocked him into the paned glass door. He crashed through the right-hand one, struck hard by the blast. Both of the brothers' horses broke their reins and bolted. They fled bucking down the street.

Noble had wounded the brother that had been holding the horses.

Guthrey put down the shotgun and raced over.

Stepping out of the cloud of black powder smoke, Dan, with his six-gun in one hand, shoved an obviously wounded outlaw outside with his other hand.

"Dadgum, let's get away of here. I can't breathe in all this smoke," Noble grumbled, looking hard at the ruined door and stepping over the prone outlaw.

Vance followed with the bald-headed Hayes in his new fresh apron.

"Your men did a helluva job," Hayes said, shaking his head, dismayed by it all. "They probably would have killed me when they found out how little money I've got."

They all laughed.

"Thank Vance. He did all the scouting work," Guthrey said, shaking hands around the circle of men. "Thank Rob for his shotgun. I was afraid to shoot a pistol and miss, but his twelve-gauge worked fine."

"That one in the doorway might not live to get to Yuma," Noble said.

"He might not," Hayes said. "Don't worry about that door. I'm alive and still got fifty cents in the safe."

"You all did a great job," Guthrey said. "Plenty of folks down here in the street now. Dan, you and Noble get a wagon and take them to Soda Springs. Doc can look at them there. It seems the horses have been caught. They will be county property. I'll tell the crowd what happened. Where are you going, Vance?"

"To check on Montoya." He waved and started out the back way.

Guthrey gave him a nod. "Be careful."

"I will be."

Guthrey, standing on the porch in front of the crowd gathered there, held up his hands for silence before he began. "Folks, two dumb Mexican bandits, the Morales brothers, tried to hold up Mr. Hayes this morning. Thanks to a warning, we cut them off. None of my men were shot. Those two are both wounded and will face long prison time for trying to rob him."

The crowd applauded.

"You can all go home now. Mr. Hayes is fine and is open for business as usual, except for the front door. Use the one on the left."

He drew a laugh from them and shook hands with several who thanked him. Then he went to the livery and tightened his horse's cinch. He and Cochise were going home. He was ready to be back with Cally.

He short loped Cochise all the way. One more bad situation over. He bet those hard-eyed brothers had no idea what had hit them in Steward's Crossing.

TWENTY-FIVE

Two weeks went flying by with little happening but progress on the new structure. Cally's house was fast being closed in. Dresscoe had studied the prevailing summer winds and assured her that they would sweep through her house all summer long.

"They may blow everything over, but it was a good way to design one."

Guthrey agreed. "He's done a great job for you so far. I'm proud."

"So am I. How is Deloris getting along?"

"Well, she fed us good."

"Dan and Noble have not complained either. Can I make a watering system and a garden here?"

"It is your house, my dear. I can live in it, but you decide what to do with it. As much as you enjoy a garden, you better add it to your plans."

"Noble witched me a new well. He had a forked peach branch to witch for it and found it in back where I need water for a garden here."

He chuckled. "Another well — another windmill?"

She nodded. "He also has a windmill spotted no one is using."

"Better buy it."

She hugged him. "You are wonderful, you know that?"

"No. I am laughing at my very busy wife."

"Speaking of busy. Olive's dress is made and Cam has a new suit for this Saturday night's wedding." She dropped her head and shook it as if something was too much. "She's so tickled she's pregnant, she's about to bust."

"She waited a long time."

She put a finger to his mouth. "I may be finished waiting too."

"Good."

"Don't tell anyone — yet."

"I won't, but it would be nice."

"Oh, a new house for my firstborn. Yes, Phil Guthrey, with you thrown in I'd be the luckiest girl in the world."

"I may ride down and evict those squatters down south tomorrow."

"Is that the trash that those brothers stayed with?"

"Yes."

"Just be careful."

He hugged her tight. "I will."

In the morning he took Dan and Noble with him to the squatters' place. There were lots of them in the camp. Some of the women walked around bare breasted and it never bothered them. Many of the ragged army curled their lips at the three lawmen when they went past them to the center of the camp near the low cooking fires where the smoke swirled around close to the ground.

"Listen up, folks!" Guthrey shouted, sitting on his spotted horse and looking over the tough ragtag squatters. "This is not public land. This is private land and you can't stay here any longer."

They booed him.

He paid no heed to them. "You have forty-eight hours to leave or you will be jailed for trespassing."

"That's bullshit, lawman."

Guthrey reined around Cochise and gave the man who'd spoken a hard look. "Wait forty-eight hours and you'll see what I mean."

Then he spun the paint horse around. "You've been warned." He rode over to join his two deputies. "See anyone wanted?"

"Who'd want this bunch?" Dan asked.

367

They laughed and went on. There must have been thirty of them there. If they left this place they'd simply move somewhere else. Guthrey could hope, maybe, out of his territory. But such gatherings made a hang-out for real bandits like the Morales brothers. They needed to be gone.

Guthrey and his two men checked by the Bridges Ranch to see if Guermo needed anything. A four-mule team hauling a loaded ore wagon came down from up at their mine.

The big red-faced driver, Asa Birk, sat on the seat and reined up his mules, then spoke to Guthrey. "Howdy, sheriff."

"Howdy, Asa. Heading for the stamp mill below Tombstone?" Guthrey asked.

"Yeah. I take a load a week down there for you all. Leave an empty wagon and take a loaded one out. Takes me two days to get back here and two to get down there to the mill without any breakdowns, so I don't get much done but haul ore for your operation. Sure is high-grade stuff. Most small mines peter out fast. This one sure ain't."

"We don't want it to," Noble said. Everyone laughed.

Asa clucked to his team and went on his way.

Deloris told them Guermo was fine and

all was well. She offered them some food. Guthrey said no, thanked her, and they all headed back for Soda Springs. By late afternoon, Cally met him at the corral.

"Doc told your deputies today that Fred Morales won't live through the night."

"He made the decision when he tried to rob Mr. Hayes. He sure hung on long enough with those serious injuries."

"I know. Just wanted to tell you."

He hugged her. "Asa hauled off another load of rich ore today."

"Good. By the time it gets smelted we may need that money."

"We will?"

"No, I'm just teasing."

"Good."

"I have supper for all of you," she announced.

Dan and Noble nodded.

Dan told them about his plans for the cattle drive and how he had everything lined up: butchers, pasture, and help. They talked about it over the evening meal. He planned to hire three day-hands to help him drive them. Noble never objected; he and Guthrey had talked about how it should be Dan's operation. So they encouraged him and finished their meal.

Guthrey knew his wife was proud of her

brother. Maybe the boy was going to grow up. He hoped so.

"Guthrey, I checked at the courthouse. That place down there we were at today could be a good ranch headquarters. It's deeded land and the record shows some guy in California owns it. What's it worth?"

"Since I burned down the squaw shade, not much."

They laughed.

"Are you interested in a place of your own, Dan?" Cally asked.

"I've been thinking about it," Dan said.

Cally looked at Guthrey for his answer.

"You better ask her. She handles the money," he said with a smile.

"What are you going to offer him?"

"Five hundred dollars."

Noble nodded. "He might take that. Sure ain't making him any money sitting empty."

"You know him?" Guthrey asked.

"Yeah, he was one of those guys left here early when things got hot. But he wouldn't sell it to Whitmore. His name's Coleman."

"That's his name," Dan said. "Euless Coleman."

"Tell him you aren't a part of them and make him an offer."

Dan nodded looking smug. "I'll do that."

"No word from Texas and the McAllen

thing?" Noble asked.

"There was no mail from them today," Cally said. "I went by the office and checked."

"They will answer in time. No doubt they're shorthanded."

"You think more Rangers quit over the scrip payment business?" Dan asked.

"More than likely," Guthrey said. He had no idea, really. Eventually they'd tell him what they could do about the man.

Next morning at dawn, Guthrey found Vance down by the corral sleeping in a blanket on the ground.

"What's happening?" he asked, squatting down beside him.

"Montoya is coming."

"When?"

"He is on his way now. He sent a man named Paschal up here to check things out. Last night Paschal had too much to drink and told me his boss was coming with many men."

"How many?"

"Five or six is what he said."

"Who will he strike?"

"The same ranch he did before. He is still mad about them stealing back their horses and his as well. It is to teach the gringos a lesson."

"I'll have Dan go down there to warn Jim Duval. We'll have a large posse to meet them when they get there."

Vance agreed. "I will ride south and try to scout them coming."

"Eat some breakfast with us first. Cally is up fixing food now. You be careful; I need you."

Vance smiled. "I will. She is a good woman and a good cook."

"I think so. Thanks for coming. You must have been in the saddle all night."

"I am fine."

Things moved fast and in a few hours Guthrey had a posse of ranchers and cowboys ready to start for the Duval Ranch. When they arrived, Dan and Vance were both there waiting with everyone rifle-armed and prepared.

"You found them?" Guthrey asked his man.

"They have a camp down by the Whetstones. I think he wants to raid this ranch at night. His men's horses were not saddled and they were lying around drinking."

He shook Duval's hard calloused hand. "I guess Montoya didn't have enough the first time. We need to put our horses in your pens so they aren't noticeable. String some rope across where we can to take any raiders off their horses that try to drive through. I have told all the posse they need to stay out of sight in case he uses field glasses on us. You heard Vance's report?"

"Yes. I never thought about ropes. Damn good idea."

"We need to be ready for them."

"We will. Gladys has hot beans and corn bread. Get something to eat."

Guthrey nodded. "I'll tell the others to file in and out the back door for food and the rest of the time stay out of sight."

"I want to give them a real welcome," Duval said with a grim nod.

Laughing, Guthrey headed for Gladys's beans and corn bread. "So do I."

The hot day passed slowly. By sundown everyone had a rifle and was ready. Guthrey had been over all the plans of how close the thieves needed to come before a shot was fired. He wanted them down low and hoped his ropes strung up caught some of the raiders.

At twilight, Vance made a circle of the ranch house perimeter and came back to tell Guthrey they were out there on horse-back.

"Seven men."

"I have a dozen rifles loaded. That's two bullets for each man, nearly."

Quietly, he circled the ranch headquarters, checking each man as the crickets started chirping. He paused and told each man to keep low and that they had the bandits severely outnumbered. The round complete, lights were put out in the house, and he heard horses approaching.

They sure had a big surprise coming. Then the raiders charged, shouting and whipping their horses, firing guns wildly. They reached the edge of the open space in which they turned rigs around when Guthrey yelled, "Fire!"

The barrage of bullets caught horses and riders in a tough cross fire. Those that missed being shot were snatched off their horses by the ropes, and posse men jumped on them in the night's darkness and pinned them down.

A curtain of gun smoke slowly drifted away on the night wind. Lanterns were lit and Guthrey dispatched a few wounded horses with his .45, while his crew gathered prisoners.

"Over here," Vance called to Guthrey. "I

think he's dead. This is Montoya."

The big man's blank eyes stared at the stars for eternity. He had a bandolier strapped across him loaded with rifle cartridges. Wounds in the chest and the side of his head had bled a lot. He wore a walrus mustache and a grim look — the bandit was dead.

"I sure wish it had been my bullet killed him," Duval said.

"It probably was," Guthrey said. "This matter is over, thank God. None of our men are hurt?"

Duval shook his head. "Only the raiders. Your rope deal worked great at knocking them off their horses. I'd never thought of it."

"Jim, sometimes in this business you need to level things. Ropes strung like that will do that for you. Tell my deputy Vance thanks or we'd never have had this much luck."

"I will."

"Good. I heard your wife say she had fresh coffee made. Let's go have a cup."

Dan reported later, "There are two dead, two wounded, and the other three just beat up after getting clotheslined off their horses."

"All we need now are some fireworks to

celebrate," Guthrey said, reminding them about Mexico. They laughed.

Twenty-Six

Guthrey was busy filling out his monthly expenses on his jail with Baker and Zamora.

"I've decided none of us are accountants or smart enough to do this. After lunch, I'll ask Cally if she'll go over these figures. It's damn expensive running a jail and operating a sheriff's office. No wonder they didn't do it before."

"The county board complains every month they don't have the money to pay it," Zamora said.

Guthrey nodded. "But they find ways every time to pay. They don't want our job; they only want us to do it cheaper."

His men agreed.

"I am going to Cam and Olive's wedding tonight. So let it ride till next week," Guthrey said.

"I'm willing. We would like to go but figure we might need to be here," Baker said.

"Tell him to have good luck from both of us," Zamora added.

"I will. They look real happy."

He left the office, and when he got home, he saw the team was already hitched. He decided he better get moving.

"Who harnessed the team?"

"Noble. I asked him to. We have a long drive if we are going to be there."

"Yes, ma'am. Monday you need to look at our expenses."

"Fine. I can drive. You can eat your lunch on the way."

"What about my clothes?"

"You look fine to me. We will both be dusty by the time we get there anyway."

"You are in a hurry." He picked up the large burrito and motioned to the doorway. "Okay, I'll eat on the way."

The ride proved dusty enough and, with the heat, long enough. But they arrived on time. Guthrey carried Cally's covered food inside the schoolhouse for her and she brushed her hair, standing beside the wagon.

"Well, we made it," he said.

"Thanks, I thought you'd forgotten about today, you were so late."

"Guess I tucked it away in my mind is all."

"No wonder. You've had enough happen

378

lately for three sheriffs."

"I still would like McAllen up in my jail."

"That will be a big order."

"I haven't given up yet."

"You'll get him. It all takes time and you are an impatient person."

"Am I impatient with you?"

"No."

"Good. The rest don't matter."

"Oh, my impatient man, I love you."

"It's a good thing you do. Go see about the bride. I can see Cam's ready out back."

The wedding went smoothly. After Guthrey had kissed the bride, she whispered, "It's been a long time since the last time you did that. Thanks for Cam, I love him."

The newlyweds were off for a night at a secret hideout and on Sunday going to Mount Graham for a honeymoon.

"*Vaya con Dios,* Olive."

"Same to you, Ranger."

"I'm not a Ranger anymore."

She mildly shook her head. "Once a Ranger, always one."

He had to think on that one as they parted. Old flames he thought were extinguished flared up. He felt no need for her as a woman in his life, but he'd never really taken time to consider her words about *once*

No answer to the letter he sent to Ranger headquarters and more than a month had dragged by. Maybe he should write the marshal of El Paso or the police chief and see if McAllen was around there. No telling. Mail took time and even got lost or spilled beside the road after stage robberies.

At last he received a letter from Austin and Colonel Steve Arrens.

Dear Sheriff Guthrey,
I received your letter and have pursued with my office in El Paso the notion that this person, Alfred Jones McAllen, was in the area. My El Paso office reports that he now resides in Mexico on a large hacienda he owns down there. He does not frequent north of the Rio Grande, according to my men that are on that scene.

I think you will find the authorities down there unwilling to help you apprehend him, since he is such a prominent businessman. I am sorry to be so long in answering you, but correspondence between Austin and El Paso is very slow too.

May I wish you good fortune in apprehending him. If I or my men can help you further, contact either office for assistance.

Respectfully,
Colonel Steve Arrens

"What can we do?" Zamora asked that afternoon when Guthrey met with him and Teddy Baker.

"I'm thinking of asking Vance to go with me and try to bring him out of Mexico."

"Whew. Risky business," Baker said. "I bet he has plenty of bodyguards down there."

Guthrey nodded. "But he needs to be on trial."

"You better scrap that idea," Zamora said. "Going into Mexico is way too risky."

"Once in Mexico, there was a really bad outlaw who'd committed murder in Texas and we knew he was hiding down in the Sierra Madres. The Mexican *federales* let three of us in and we went down there, found him, and brought him out to Texas to hang for the murders. Mexico City complained to Washington, D.C., that we had invaded their land to get him illegally, but by then he was already on his way to the gallows."

"But he wasn't rich like this man."

"Rich or not, McAllen needs to be arrested and tried for murdering Mark Peters. That's my job here, to enforce the law."

"It's a different world down there," Zamora said.

"I know that. I'm going to talk to Vance when he comes in. We'll see."

"Zamora is right, he knows Mexico," Baker added.

"I know you two want me alive, and so do I. I'll investigate it some more."

He left the two shaking their heads and went downhill to have lunch with his wife amid the smell of sawdust and shavings. The men were making great progress on her new house and she grew more excited over it by the day.

Dan and three hired cowboys were already driving the steers to Tucson and he should be close to turning them in at the pasture he'd rented. The price was thirteen cents a pound, and that was a good one. And the two- and three-year-old steers were still fat.

The sky in the south looked like rain was moving in again. A big bank of thunderheads were moving his way. They'd cool the day off some if and when they dropped their moisture. It was already October and they hadn't had such a bad season.

Noble was there for the noon meal and

then was heading for the home ranch. Over the meal, he told them about witching for some wells on the place Dan wanted to buy.

"You know, they missed a big vein of water on that place when they drilled that well where the windmill sets. A hundred yards away there's a helluva stream under the ground."

"Did you tell Dan yet?"

"No, but I will when he comes back. Might even be artesian water. That would really make that place worth something."

"Just so that the seller don't know about it. Were the squatters all gone?"

"Oh yeah. No one was there."

"Good. Dan wrote that guy a letter making him an offer," Cally said, putting their lunch on the table. Rice, gravy, fried ham, and biscuits.

Guthrey put a brown-topped biscuit on his plate, opened it, and buttered it. He took a big bite and smiled. "Now, that is fine eating."

The other two laughed.

"I do love your biscuits."

Her hand on his arm, Cally laughed. "I thought you liked them more than me when you first came here."

"I camped with three Rangers and none of us could ever get them like that."

"Well, ain't that funny. Four Rangers could figure out crimes and criminals and not one could make a biscuit worth a damn."

"I'm not lying. None of us could ever get it right."

Cally laughed. "I'm sure glad I got it right."

Guthrey, Vance, and Noble climbed into the stagecoach headed for Lordsburg with tickets for El Paso. Cally was waving from the boardwalk. Their saddles, rifles, and war bags had been loaded in the back under the tied down tarp.

Guthrey prepared himself for being stiff from the stagecoach ride when he got off in El Paso three days hence. He hated such a trip, with all the rocking and swaying while hanging on to the straps. The food would be sorry at the way stations and the outhouse facilities at the stage stops always stunk and buzzed with flies. Sleep would be impossible.

He rubbed his itching upper lip with the side of his hand. Though clean shaven now, he knew before this was over he'd need a bath. Worse than he'd needed one when he'd first ridden into Steward's Crossing and interrupted the shootout between Dan and those gunmen that had been unfolding in the street. Hours later that fateful day he met his future wife, Cally, and took a shower. He'd be glad to see her again when he returned from this quest to bring back the man who set up Mark Peters's murder.

After experiencing miles and miles of dust churned up by the horses' hooves and the coach's swaying, Guthrey closed his thoughts down and tried to sleep. That was impossible. The three men finally finished the torturous trip and stepped down in El Paso holding their backs and shaking their heads.

Guthrey told the two, "We'll get a bed. Too hot in the daytime to sleep."

Both men agreed. He had the stage station man hold their saddles, war bags, and guns. They slept in a hotel room on rumpled mattresses and were up at sunup. They took breakfast in a café, and the food was mouthwatering. When Guthrey looked up at his pleased men, he knew he'd struck gold choosing this place to eat. The coffee tasted rich and smooth. No words were necessary.

They went by the Texas Ranger regional headquarters and spoke to Captain Jason Hawks, who was in charge. He remembered Guthrey and they had a nice visit, but all he knew about McAllen was they thought he was living on a hacienda in Mexico.

Vance had gone to check out the Hispanic end of things in the barrio. Noble went to price suitable horses at some liveries for their transportation to go look for McAllen. They met in a cantina in late afternoon.

"We may be lucky," Vance said. "McAllen has a favorite *puta* here and a man told me he slips into El Paso to meet with her quite often."

"Who is she?"

"Donna Lopez."

"You know where she works?"

"He bought her a house. She has some children they say are his."

"Hard to find?"

"No, but it has bars and an iron fence."

"Kinda unusual, isn't it?"

"Oh yes, but it is like a bank, I think." Vance shook his head.

"We can figure that out. How often does he come up here? Did your man say?"

"He wasn't certain. Thinks he tries to change so no one can count on catching him there."

"Keep listening. I may go back to talk to Hawks about that. He had no knowledge of McAllen coming here. It must be a real secret."

Vance agreed.

"Sounds better to me than riding our asses off going down in Mexico to get him," Noble said.

"I won't argue, but we can't wait forever for him to come up here."

"Aw, young as he is, he should have the urge to find her pretty often."

Guthrey and Vance laughed.

"I'll check out this Donna Lopez with Hawks too."

Noble nodded and said, "Maybe I need to check things out too. He don't know me either."

"Don't alert anyone. This could be a good deal to get him on this side of the border."

Two days of detective work moved on to three. Hawks knew nothing about Lopez's relationship with McAllen, but he had contacts too. Things began to leak out about their meetings. Hawks assigned Ranger Tod Enlowe to assist them. He looked like a typical freckle-faced cowboy. Guthrey and Noble interviewed some known snitches, but their information was not valuable enough. They rented a third-floor room on the opposite side of the street from the *puta*'s house, and Noble kept track of the traffic to Lopez's place.

Vance came in the back way late that night

and spoke to both of them. "Christy, my contact, said tonight that McAllen's main man, Don Carlos, was here in El Paso tonight. He may be making sure it is safe for his boss to come over."

"Noble said only vendors — Wait, there are horses in the street."

Noble was watching from the dark window when Guthrey joined him.

"I think our man just rode up," Noble said.

They watched someone under a cape dismount. There were three armed men on excited horses armed with rifles. The person under the cape rushed to the door and hugged a woman in the lit doorway. They kissed wildly, then he turned and spoke in Spanish, "It is all clear. Come get me at dawn."

"Heeyah," came the chorus, and the riders rushed off into the darkness.

Guthrey nodded good riddance. "Noble, go get our Ranger Enlowe. Tell him the chicken is in the coop. Vance, you think we can come in the back way?"

Noble sounded displeased. "It will take over an hour to get him here."

"We have the time. They won't be back for him until dawn."

Noble hustled over. "I'll get him. You two

be careful while I am gone."

Vance nodded. "I may need to kill those two big dogs of hers."

"If you can do it without any ruckus, fine."

"Poison is quiet."

Guthrey didn't know the details, but he agreed with his man. Vance went off to solve the dog problem and Guthrey watched the lit windows of the house. Nothing else. Once, he heard a dog bark, but it wasn't from her place. The same lamps were on by the time Noble returned with the Ranger.

"You sure he's in there?" Enlowe asked, looking at the house.

"We all three saw him delivered," Guthrey told the man.

"Where is Vance?"

"Making the dogs be quiet," Guthrey said. "When he gets through, him and Noble can guard the back side. You and I can crash down the front door."

"Sounds good to me. Will he be tough?"

"I guess, with a murder charge hanging over him. He probably will try to deny us his arrest."

"How in the hell did you three figure all this out?" Enlowe asked.

"We came a long ways to get him."

"What will you do next?'

"Slap cuffs on him and load him on a

stage for Soda Springs so he can't get set loose by some high-priced lawyers hereabouts. Then he would keep his ass in Mexico."

Enlowe laughed. "You got quite a rep from your Ranger days. I've heard lots of stories about you when you were a captain. I'm glad to get to work with you."

They shook hands and Vance returned.

"The dogs are asleep."

"You and Noble hold the back gate. Enlowe and I will come in the front door."

The two nodded and left. Guthrey and the Ranger followed them down the stairs. Soon he and Enlowe crossed the street. With a skeleton key, Guthrey unlocked the front gate, which squeaked loud on the hinges.

Enlowe, six-gun in hand, went up the front steps. They stood aside of the door and he knocked. "Texas law. Open this door."

A woman screamed down the stairs, "The dogs will eat them up!"

No, they won't. He and Enlowe both stomped the door at the same time. The latch broke and it flew open.

A shot was fired at them from the upper balcony and both men returned fire. A man, half-dressed, fell off the rail in a thick haze of gun smoke and crashed onto the table on his back.

"Oh my God, you've killed him!" the woman screamed, coming down the stairs in a nightgown.

Guthrey didn't care if the fool was dead. No way to win a shootout with Rangers, even if one of them was a former Ranger. His fate was sealed when he decided to fight his way out.

Enlowe wrenched the gun from McAllen's limp hand. But even in the eye-watering smoke, Guthrey knew McAllen had seen his last look on this earth. The case was over.

At the justice of the peace hearing, Guthrey and his men were cleared of any wrongdoing. They shook hands with the captain and Enlowe, then walked two blocks to catch the westbound stage.

In the middle of the night three days later in Steward's Crossing, Cally met them with a buckboard and two horses for the men.

Guthrey gathered her up and kissed her. "Good to see you again, girl." He hugged her face to his.

"Good to see you too, sir. Come next June there's going to be three of us."

"Best damn news I ever heard." He swung her around. "The very best. Hey, guys, we're having a baby."

"Here?" Noble asked.

"Lord, no. Next May, and you are all invited to his christening."

Noble squeezed his whiskers. "What if it's a girl?"

"Then I'll have to think of another name."

"You dang sure will. Damn, missy, it don't seem right, but I'll be pleased when you have one."

"See you two in a couple of days. Me and Cally are going up on Mount Graham for a couple of days and cool things off."

The two laughed at him. He loaded Cally on the spring seat and they headed for the cabin. Hadn't thought much about it in a while but he didn't miss being a Ranger anymore.